Vina Jackson is the pseudonym for two established writers working together for the first time. One a successful author, the other a published writer who is also a city professional working in the Square Mile.

Get to know more about Vina Jackson at www. vinajackson.com and on Facebook, or follow her on Twitter @VinaJackson1.

Also by Vina Jackson

Eighty Days Yellow
Eighty Days Blue
Eighty Days Red
Eighty Days Amber
Eighty Days White

Eighty Days
White

Vina Jackson

An Orion paperback

First published in Great Britain in 2013
by Orion Books Ltd,
Orion House, 5 Upper St Martin's Lane,
London WC2H 9EA

An Hachette UK company

1 3 5 7 9 10 8 6 4 2

A CIP catalogue record for this book
is available from the British Library.

ISBN (Paperback) 978 1 4091 2909 7
ISBN (Ebook) 978 1 4091 2910 3

Typeset at The Spartan Press Ltd,
Lymington, Hants

Printed in Great Britain by Clays Ltd, St Ives plc

The Orion Publishing Group's policy is to use papers that
are natural, renewable and recyclable products and
made from wood grown in sustainable forests. The logging
and manufacturing processes are expected to conform to
the environmental regulations of the country of origin.

www.orionbooks.co.uk

Eighty Days
White

I

The Girl with the Teardrop Tattoo

Had I known about its meaning, I might not have gone ahead with the tattoo. But by the time I was made aware of its significance, it was too late and I'd already become known to friends and strangers as the girl with the teardrop tattoo.

I had dreamed of getting one for years. Somehow it was one of those things – like getting a job and maybe one day falling in love – that I felt would be an inevitable part of my future. It was simply a matter of waiting for time to pass until the preordained day arrived. I felt more certain about the tattoo than I did about finding a job when I finished university, or even falling in love.

So when Neil finally disappeared and Liana and I found ourselves alone outside the weathered door that nestled inconspicuously amongst a bevy of retail stores, vintage boutiques and cafes, it seemed obvious to me that the time had finally come. On the pavement outside the door stood a simple white sign, which read 'Tattoo Parlour' in large black italics.

I had lingered here before, had even worked up the courage to push the door open a few times, but I had never been inside. I had often dreamed of walking in, flicking through books of drawings, confidently selecting the one that would suit me best, lying back in the chair and having it done. But I always backed out at the last moment, believing that someone like me, the living, breathing picture of a good girl, would be laughed out of the shop by the pierced and tattooed cool kids that I imagined ran the place.

'Come on then,' Liana said, brushing past me and stepping inside. She had always been the wild one of the two of us, and did not seem to carry even a shadow of the self-doubt that possessed me like a disapproving second skin, no matter how hard I tried to shed it.

The door led to a flight of steep, rough, concrete steps, painted red, now chipped, with a metal handrail up the left-hand side that had the thick heaviness of something that might have been salvaged from a plumbing supplies warehouse. I took hold of the rail gingerly, as though it was the lifeline that might carry me away from the person that I was and towards the person that I wanted to be, and followed Liana up the stairs.

At the top was a studio, its walls painted a deep red and covered in photographs of tattooed limbs, sketches and posters of old heavy-metal and rock bands. I was heartened to see a battered print of Jimmy Page and Robert Plant with guitars in hand. Whoever had decorated the place had taste.

The tattooist ignored us entirely when we entered, until we had been standing in front of him at the front desk for a few minutes. Liana coughed and eventually he introduced himself. His name was Jonah, and he hailed from New Zealand, but had owned the studio in Brighton for fifteen years, or so he told Liana who was attempting to charm him with a stream of chatter.

Jonah was bald and dressed almost entirely in leather, besides a thick metal belt that jangled when he stood up. Both of his arms were covered in tattoos from his knuckles to his shoulders which bulged out from his vest.

'You girls been drinking?' he asked, peering at us with a suspicious eye.

'Oh, God no,' Liana replied. 'Just a glass for courage. We've been planning this for years.'

'You got ID?' he continued.

I could hear the muffled sound of an old-fashioned kettle whistling through a door to the side. It swung open, and another man appeared. He was much younger, probably in his early twenties, and could have been Jonah's son. They had the same mouth. Lips like Mick Jagger's, so full that I couldn't decide whether the feature was handsome or not. Either way, it gave them both the sort of sleazy look that Liana seemed to love and which made me nervous. He leaned against the doorframe and began to roll a smoke, staring at Liana as he ran his tongue along the cigarette paper.

'Come on, Jo,' he said. 'These two look like sensible girls. Don't be a mean bastard. If they've got the money, they get the tat.'

Liana cast him an appreciative smile.

Jonah snorted. 'No ID, no ink. I don't have time to deal with pissed-off parents.

'You know what you want?' he added, barely glancing at our student cards as we handed them over for inspection.

We were both over eighteen, and had been born only a month apart – her on the 21st May and me on the same day in June. A pair of Geminis, on the opposite ends of the cusp, a fact that Liana's hippyish mother believed was the explanation for our friendship.

'Yes. We're both getting the same.'

Jonah raised his eyebrows as if to suggest that this fact was another obvious sign of our idiocy.

Liana immediately volunteered to go first, winking at me as she slipped behind the curtain that separated the inking equipment from the rest of the studio. Her long skirt swayed around her calves as she moved, flashing her slim ankles. She was so naturally thin that she was closer to bony, and she dressed in loose-fitting, bohemian style, wearing the sort of clothes that Neil said reminded him of his grandmother's curtains, but she moved with the sort of swagger that made her attractive in a way that far outshone the sum of her parts.

Her form was clearly not lost on the cigarette-rolling man, who did not make the slightest effort to hide his appreciation of her backside as she sashayed across the room.

'I'm Nick,' he said, still staring at the space that Liana had just inhabited, as if I didn't exist at all.

'Lily,' I replied, under my breath.

'Pretty name,' he said in a bored voice.

I ignored him.

I hated my name. To me it was further proof of my status as a good little rich girl. Pure, boring and practically virginal. If I had to have an old-fashioned English name, I wished my parents had at least picked one I could shorten into something that sounded off-hand and rakish, like Jo or Jac.

Nick lit his cigarette and blew smoke into the air and I

held my breath, refusing to give him the satisfaction of making me cough.

We didn't speak a single word to each other until Liana was finished, and I hurried behind the curtain as she exited it, keen to get the experience over with in case I changed my mind.

'Let's see it, then,' I heard him say to her as I left the room. She giggled in reply, and I imagined her lifting her skirts far higher than necessary and extending her leg to display her bare skin, and Nick responding with a gentle caress.

'Same for you, then?' Jonah asked without looking at me. He was bent over a tray of metal instruments, preparing a new needle.

'No.'

'No?' He looked up and met my eyes. A hint of a smile played across his thick lips. 'Thought you said the two of you had been planning this for years.'

'I want something different.' I was suddenly sick to the teeth of doing what other people wanted. Even Liana, as much as I loved her.

'You sure about that?' he asked, as I told him what I had in mind. The idea had come to me only moments earlier, as I took a final glance at the posters on the walls before heading through the curtain.

'Positive,' I replied.

'Fine.'

He motioned to the chair alongside him and I climbed up into it. I briefly considered asking him for a painkiller, or anaesthetic, like the kind you get at the dentist. But I guessed that Jonah would sneer at the idea even if he was able to provide such a thing, and besides, I didn't wish to appear weak, undecided or to miss a single moment of the experience. The tattoo was going to be so small, I reckoned, that it would be no more than a mosquito bite, surely, sharp and annoying.

I was wrong.

I almost screamed when the needle pierced my skin and I gripped the handles of the chair in which I was sitting tightly as the ring of pain radiated outwards, numbing my cheek and then my jaw until even the nerve endings in my fingers buzzed and jerked as if I was a frog on a dissecting table who's been jolted with electricity in front of a snickering classroom. My imagination was already running wild.

I closed my eyes.

Just as the pain was beginning to ebb or, at any rate, I was getting used to it, the second bite of the buzzing needle hit me. I drew a sharp breath as the hidden smells of the parlour assaulted my senses: indistinct chemicals, the dry odour of all the invisible dust suspended in the air, the manly fragrance of Jonah leaning over me, his old leather vest, the stale whiff of ancient cigarette smoke mixing with fresh, and even Liana's bargain perfume, though she was still waiting in the other room, behind the multicoloured curtain, nursing her ankle and her new tattoo and no doubt flirting with Nick.

The muted sound of Jonah's apparatus slowly faded as my mind finally began to process what was happening, segregating the sensation, isolating the pain until it felt as if it was part of another dimension, miles away, nothing to do with me any longer.

'How's it going, darling?' Liana cried out.

I snapped back, returning abruptly to the realm of reality and mumbled, 'OK . . . I think.'

Jonah took a step back and looked down at his work.

'Almost done,' he said. 'Just have to fill it in.'

'Black, please, not blue. I just don't want it to be blue.'

'Yeah, so you said . . .'

Out of the corner of my eye, I saw him pick up another needle, and carefully slot it into his instrument. I took a deep breath as once again his heavy hand lowered itself to just below my left eye, an inch or so outside my perimeter of vision.

This time, the pain was not as sharp. Fuzzy, even soothing. Almost pleasant.

I'd always enjoyed visits to both the doctor and the dentist, and this was surprisingly similar. I found the sensation of relaxing in the chair and having an expert loom over me soothing somehow, and I took a strange sort of comfort in the spartan surrounds of the room, the cold shine of the sterilized equipment and the movements of Jonah, so precise and methodical. The touch of his gloved fingers was as gentle as an insect alighting on my cheek.

Besides the initial shock and burn, it wasn't as awful as I had expected. I basked in the glow as Jonah busied himself, his eyes just inches away from mine, every pore in his ruddy cheeks magnified under my close gaze, his features deformed as in a fairground mirror, a cartoon caricature, this stranger who was marking me for ever.

'I'm just going out to pick up some more cigarettes, OK?' Liana shouted out, followed by the sound of parlour's doorbell ringing.

'Won't be long now,' Jonah said, carefully wiping a tissue

around the area he had just marked. Cleaning up. The pungent smell of chemical disinfectant rushed towards my nose as he did so, strong and overpowering.

Now the pain was just a distant memory, a blurry warmth serenading my still slightly drunken senses. But I felt more sober than ever. I'd done it! I had a tattoo.

A wave of apprehension swept across my mind as I thought of what my parents would say. Then again, I knew this was exactly why I'd had it done, why on the spur of the moment I'd proposed to Liana that we both have tattoos there and then as we walked down the North Lanes after an afternoon of celebrating the end of term.

I was fed up of being Lily from the Home Counties, the dutiful daughter, the boring one. I wanted to stand out, to be different. To do something no one would have expected from me for once.

'Here we are,' Jonah said, holding out a small mirror in front of me.

I opened my eyes.

It was perfect.

A minuscule teardrop, falling from my left eye, to which it was still connected by a thin black line.

Dark black against my white skin.

Now I no longer looked like Snow White, which is what both my parents and my relatives had always affectionately called me until I was twelve and had rebelled loudly once and for all against the nickname, and they'd never used it to my face again. I hated Disney movies with a vengeance.

'It's beautiful,' I said, as Jonah dabbed some cream over the area and taped a piece of plastic dressing in place under my eye.

'I hope you still feel the same in twenty years,' he answered.

I gathered my things and walked out of the store.

Liana and Nick were both puffing away, standing on the pavement, looking out dreamily towards the seafront.

'Finished,' I said.

She looked up at me.

'*Fuckin' hell!*' she exploded. 'You got him to tattoo your face!' She squeezed her eyes tight to get a closer look. 'What the fuck have you done, Lily?'

'I changed my mind,' I replied. 'Wanted something different.'

Nick grinned his approval and let out a low whistle.

'I knew you were a dark horse,' he added.

'Jeezussss . . .' Liana hissed. 'I thought we'd agreed we'd have the same.' She put her leg forward and pointed at the small, brightly coloured butterfly she now sported on the side of her ankle, visible but distorted through the clear protective bandage.

I smiled.

Maybe tomorrow I would have my hair cut. Become the new 'me' in earnest. It was already jet black by nature, so at least I wouldn't need to dye it.

'You sure are a crazy gal, you know.'

I haven't always been crazy. In fact, if you asked anyone who knew me before I went to university at Sussex, they might well have described me as dull. Middle-class, professional parents, house with garden and pets, room of my own and all that. It was a happy environment to grow up in, despite the cloistered nature of my existence, and somehow it wasn't until I actually left home that I began to question things. Small things at first, then bigger ones. And once the seeds of doubt had been sown in my mind, it all just festered.

When I thought of my mother's life – the long-suffering parent who packed in her career to bring me into the world and then filled her time with nappies, school runs and pulling weeds from our walled garden – a part of me shriveled in fear. Was this all that life was about? I had a few boyfriends, gave away my cherry at seventeen to a nice boy who meant nothing to me but happened to be around to do the deed and so I played along. The sex was OK, though not great, but I had no doubts that one day it would become better. All along I was aware something was missing. Something important. I just didn't know what.

You couldn't even say I was a rebel, because I had no cause. My rebellion had been limited to plastering the walls of my room with posters of classic heavy-metal bands and musicians. Somehow, the fierce images of Alice Cooper and Kiss felt inspiring, though I was aware that even my musical rebellion was a couple of decades out of date, and these days my rock heroes had become ageing and respectable. But mostly I just drifted.

I met Liana on my first day at university. We were sitting at the same table in the student cafeteria, both away from home for the first time and getting our bearings and knowing we didn't fit in yet. We were two outsiders, cut from the same cloth, though her hair was mousy brown where mine was black, and she was taller and thinner than me. Where my parents had both trained as doctors, her father was a patent engineer and her mother had once been an air stewardess.

It wasn't so much the fact that we had the same sort of background that attracted me to her company, but that I saw a wildness in her, a recklessness I aspired to. As if she had broken those unseen chains that were holding us back. We were both studying English Lit and shared several of the same classes, and quickly became inseparable, eventually moving in together a year later into a large flat near Hove that we shared with four others.

Neil was one of them. He was only in his first year and so he came under our wing. We treated him like a younger brother, inoffensive and always present, although Liana once confessed to me that he reminded her of her father, always silently disapproving of her excesses.

It was a Friday afternoon and, together with Liana, Neil and a dozen or so others, our drinking had begun early at the student union bar and quickly moved on to a variety of pubs in town. Liana and I were pacing ourselves – we had a plan to make a whole night of it once we'd lost the others. Neither of us wanted to visit our parents during term time, so, as Liana had put it, we would have the whole weekend to get rid of the hangovers before tutorials and lectures resumed on Monday.

By the time we'd hit the seafront and the Lanes, there were only seven of us left and we wandered in high spirits from bar to bar at a leisurely pace. Liana and I were still relatively sober and amused by the antics of our friends who would be written off in a matter of hours while we still had the whole evening ahead of us.

A few more dropped out after we took a mid-afternoon

pause for fish and chips by the main pier. Further casualties faded from the scene by the time we reached the bar of the Komedia on Gardner Street – Neil was friendly with the staff there and they didn't mind a bunch of rowdy students sitting in a quiet corner and trying to make each round last as long as possible.

Liana was digging around in her ridiculously oversized tote bag in search of money, swearing under her breath as if the act of doing so would conjure new banknotes out of nowhere.

'Damn, damn, damn,' she said. 'I was sure I had some more cash in here somewhere.'

'You always do,' I remarked.

Neil, sitting opposite us, pale and sickly, his tolerance for alcohol still untrained in comparison to ours. His eyes looked glazed and unfocused.

'I don't think I can manage another drink,' he said feebly.

'Spoilsport,' Liana muttered while I just smiled.

'I think I have to go back to the flat,' Neil said, rising hesitantly from his seat, steadying himself with a hand on the table where our empty glasses lay like a deserted landscape after a battle.

Liana now ignored him and looked around.

'Where are the other two?' she asked. 'What's their names? Wally and Dasha?' She'd only just noticed that the science students who'd tagged along with us earlier had now left our midst, and we were the only three left standing. And three was becoming two as Neil prepared to throw in the towel.

'Finally. Just you and me, honey.' Liana winked at me as Neil's silhouette retreated through the door that led onto

Gardner Street. 'We're still in good shape and the night is still young, my darling Lily.'

'Actually, I don't think I can manage a whole night out, even if we could afford it,' I said, watching Liana rummaging through her bag again. The day's activities and the glass of lager that I'd been sipping had begun to take their toll.

A beam lit her face as she extracted two fifty-pound notes.

'I knew it was there. I was sure. My rainy-day money!'

She handed one of the notes to me. 'Pay me back whenever,' she said. 'It's not really my money and, besides, I'm sure I owe you for last time.'

'Fifties!' I exclaimed. 'Since when do you have that sort of cash?'

'Dad sent it to me mid-term. He's obviously feeling guilty about something.'

'Well, don't brandish it around like that.'

'We should put it to a good cause. If not boozing, then at least something worthwhile. What do you think?'

'Haven't got a clue,' I answered. 'Pity Neil left. I'm sure he'd come up with some idea.'

'Oh, yes, I'm sure he would,' Liana said, smiling at me broadly.

'What do you mean?' I asked her.

'Don't act innocent . . . Like you hadn't noticed the way he stares at you all the time?'

I had. But I hadn't given it much thought until now. Neil was nice, decent-looking but . . . unexciting.

'He's just not my type.'

'What is your type? Come on,' Liana quizzed me. 'You'll be single all your life at this rate.'

All those now-distant faces from the bedroom posters came rushing back to me. Men with dark make-up, men in black leather and metal studs, wild men. I had left the heavy-metal posters back home and would have attracted ridicule at the flat had I decorated my room here with them all. I opted for discretion. Noting my closed expression, Lily didn't pursue the subject.

'Damn,' she said, brushing her hair back from her forehead. 'It's hot in here. Even I'm falling asleep. Wanna go for a walk? We're bound to stumble across something to do sooner or later.'

'Suits me,' I agreed.

Night was falling and there was a nip in the air. Most of the jewellery and antique shops in the Lanes were beginning to close and the crowds were thinning.

We were walking aimlessly along, the stark realisation that there was still a whole evening and night ahead dawning on us and we still had nothing to do when we slowed down across from the tattoo parlour.

'Hey!' I said.

'What?'

'Remember how we used to talk about getting matching tattoos?'

It had been shortly after we'd met, and we'd been much drunker than today on that occasion, almost a year ago now, and still high on the exhilaration of being away from home and family and the knowledge we'd found we had so much in common. I only vaguely remembered the conversation but, all of a sudden, the idea appealed to me immensely. There was a touch of the perverse about it; it was just the sort of thing good girls would never do in a month of Sundays.

'Perfect. Let's do it,' Liana said. 'Do you think we've got enough?' She indicated the crumpled note she had stuck into her skirt pocket.

I had no idea what a tattoo cost.

'Well, they'll only be small,' I shrugged, and stepped towards the shop door.

'Oh, Lily, this is going to be so exciting,' Liana giggled.

And now, we'd actually done it.

'So, ladies, what are you two up to next?'

'Another celebratory drink, I suppose?' Liana replied, in good spirits although I knew her ankle must still be burning if the aching on the left side of my face was anything to go by.

'I hate to be the voice of reason,' Nick said, leaning forward and brushing a lock of hair back from Liana's face as though he'd known her for ages. I was beginning to feel like the odd one out, the third wheel all over again, and was tempted to leave the two of them to it and go home to nurse both my jealousy and my new tattoo alone. I worried about Liana though, and what sort of fix she might get herself into next, so I knew that I would be stuck with Nick for as long as Liana let him hang around. 'But it's a bad idea to go out drinking when you've just had an inking,' he continued. 'You need to get it home and wash it. Didn't you listen to the aftercare instructions?'

'Course we did,' Liana replied, taking another drag on her cigarette. 'We're not idiots. But surely one little tipple won't hurt? It's Friday night and we're practically stone-cold sober.'

I remained silent, though I felt like I might well up with tears. I'd been a fool to think that a tattoo would change anything. Different face, but still the same girl with the same life.

'I live just around the corner. I'm done for the day now and Jonah's shutting up shop. You could both come home with me and I'll pour you a glass of something nice. Get some warm water on those tattoos. Make you a coffee. Call you a cab when you need to show your faces to Mummy and Daddy. I don't envy you that,' he added, eyeing the now permanent tear below my eye.

'We don't live at home,' I said abruptly.

'Well then, you are both welcome to stay all night, just to be on the safe side. Wouldn't want you to risk getting an infection in your eye, after all.'

He was laughing at the obviousness of his own pick-up lines, and I resisted an urge to hit him, though I had to admit that the guy was a looker, especially when he smiled and his full lips pulled open to display a row of even white teeth. He was attractive in a dishevelled, uncaring sort of way, the sort of person who would scoff at Neil's daily and seemingly futile trips to the gym, but who still managed to maintain a lean body and bulge in his biceps without any effort at all. He looked as though he hadn't brushed his hair for a week.

'Come on then.' Liana held out an arm to each of us, and we linked together and walked the few streets to Nick's flat on King's Road.

I stood outside the off-licence on the corner and stared at

the sea lapping against the pier as the two of them bought wine and yet more cigarettes. My phone buzzed in my bag.

Are you OK? Want me to come get You?

Neil had managed to sober up enough to check on us and even offer to pick us up and walk us home. He'd probably been fretting since he got in. He was sweet but smothering, just like my parents.

We're fine. Staying with friend. Don't wait up, I replied, in case we didn't end up going home at all and Neil freaked out and called the police.

My tattoo still throbbed, and I had a sudden urge to run down to the pier and throw myself off the side, letting the icy-cold water soothe the sting along with the strange funk that had settled over me and permeated my existence, as if one dunk in the sea could wash away all of my eighteen years to date and leave me refreshed and renewed, like a baptism. I had a sudden premonition that tonight would be the first night of the rest of my life.

Little did I know how true that would prove to be.

'You all right, honey?' Liana's voice interrupted my daydreaming. 'Don't look so sad. I'm sure your parents will get over it. You don't see them very often, so it's not like they're going to have to look at you every day.'

She burst into peals of laughter and took me by the hand, pulling me along behind Nick around the corner and up to the door of his flat.

'Christ,' Liana said when we got inside, walking around the bright expanse of his living room with its large bay window and far-reaching view over the seafront. 'Not such a struggling artist, after all, eh?'

'You can thank my parents for this place. You two aren't the only middle-class rebels in town, believe it or not.'

I warmed to him more after that. His mother was a QC, he told us, and his father a banker. He'd dropped out of his law degree and begun training as an apprentice tattooist with his uncle, Jonah, as a way to get out from under the weight of his parents' expectations.

Liana made herself right at home immediately, nestling into his couch and resting her tattooed ankle on top of an ottoman. I perched uncomfortably alongside her.

Nick handed us each a glass of wine and returned shortly after with a bowl of warm water and a clean cloth. He pulled up a chair in front of Liana and lifted up her skirt, exposing the length of her calf, her bare knee and half of her thigh, although he only needed to gain access to her ankle, which was already uncovered.

I took a gulp of my wine. It was cheap and red and tasted pretty nasty, but I needed the distraction. Anything to ease the discomfort of witnessing Liana and her new man fondling each other.

He ran the pads of his fingers around her ankle bone, circumnavigating each bump as if it were a mini universe until he knocked the protective film that covered her tattoo and she gasped.

'Careful there, buddy,' she said, through gritted teeth.

Her response only seemed to heighten his desire. A flush had spread over his cheeks and though it didn't seem possible for his mouth to become any fuller, his lower lip hung very slightly open as if he'd already begun kissing her, at least in his imagination.

I glanced down at his trousers and immediately turned

away, startled by the size of the obvious bulge at his crotch. Nick seemed to be turned on by Liana's discomfort and I was torn. We should have made a run for it, right then, and I knew that I was the responsible one of the two of us and that, as headstrong as Liana was, she would have come with me if I'd got up and left. She was reckless, but loyal to a fault.

But it didn't seem like my business who Liana flirted with. She wasn't drunk and clearly liked the guy.

'Do you girls smoke?' he asked.

I could tell that he wasn't talking about cigarettes by the way that he rolled the 'o' in his mouth.

Liana grinned at him. 'Why not? More fun than taking an aspirin.'

Nick gave her leg one last stroke and then stood up and rummaged in a nearby cabinet.

'Just enough left for the three of us, I reckon,' he said, tossing a small foil packet and a square of cigarette papers over to Liana. 'You know how to roll?'

She nodded, and carefully dog-eared the sides of the foil open, exposing the flakes of dry green bud within. The smell was sweet, cloying and unmistakable. I had never actually smoked pot before, but I'd often caught a whiff of it on campus.

'Another first time, my sweet, innocent Lily?' she said to me, taking a liberal pinch of green in her fingers and sprinkling it over the paper. I nodded. 'Don't worry, I'll show you how it's done.'

'No need to be smug about it,' I answered. The wine was beginning to go to my head and I was feeling feistier than usual. Liana just laughed.

She lit the smoke and took a long drag, then gestured frantically for me to bring my face closer to hers.

'Not as harsh if you take it from me,' she mouthed, still holding the smoke in. She took hold of my shoulders gently and leaned forward, resting her lips against mine. I realised that she was blowing the smoke into my mouth rather than snogging me just in time to catch her exhalation.

'Hold it,' she gasped, quickly catching a breath as our mouths parted. Her lips were impossibly soft and tasted like wine, and I was surprised to find myself disappointed when she pulled away.

'Ooh, I like that,' said Nick, who had gone in search of more booze and returned just in time to watch our exchange. 'My turn.'

He took the joint from Liana between his thumb and forefinger and sucked the end liberally, then bent down and clasped her chin, raising her face to his. His hand strayed down to her exposed throat and for a moment I panicked and prepared to lunge forward and push his arm away. Her neck seemed so alarmingly fragile clutched in his palm.

But instead of an expression of fright or fear, I watched in shock as she arched her back and lifted her mouth eagerly to meet his. He squeezed her neck tighter, holding her in place firmly as the smoke passed from his mouth to hers. He released her abruptly and as she sank back into the sofa, a look of blissful calm spread across her face.

The image of his hand around her neck and the way that she had responded to it replayed again and again in my mind and I bizarrely began to giggle.

'I think I need the bathroom,' I whispered, when I finally found my voice.

Nick pointed down the hall. 'Second door,' he said, without looking up. His gaze was fixed on Liana. Neither of them had responded to my uncontrolled laughter. It was as if they hadn't noticed that I was there at all, as if they were finally seeing each other for the first time.

I rose unsteadily to my feet, unaware of what I'd just witnessed, and set off down the hall, leaning against the wall to find my way. My head spun as I tried to make sense of what was happening between Liana and Nick and the drug began to take over my senses.

In the mirror my face was red-eyed and distorted by the presence of the tattoo that decorated only one cheek. It was as if I had cut myself in half, and there were now two Lilys: the old, respectable me and the new rock 'n' roll version. I looked like a clown and the bandage itched. I wanted to tear it off and scratch at my skin, but I forced myself to leave it, and just splashed some water on my face and returned to the living room.

Pink Floyd's *Dark Side of the Moon* was drifting through the stereo and the sound affected me so intensely it could have been playing from beneath my skin. I slumped down onto the nearest piece of furniture, a bean bag lying just outside the hall, and relaxed into the soft leather cushion as wave after wave of music washed over me. Even if I had wanted to get up again, I was going to have trouble standing.

It took a few seconds for me to realise that the scene in front of me was real, and not a figment of my imagination come to life.

Nick was now shirtless. His jeans sat low on his hips, exposing the long V of his loin muscles, which were like a marker pointing down to the bulge below. He was cut, though in a lean rather than bulky way, and each time he moved, his sinews rippled like water. The light smattering of hair on his chest blended uniformly into the golden-brown colour of his skin. His hands were covered by a pair of black latex gloves, just like the ones that Jonah had been wearing when he tattooed me.

Liana was totally naked, kneeling on the floor beneath him, with her wrists tied behind her back and secured to rope that was bound around each of her thighs, framing her arse. Her head and knees were both positioned on pillows, protecting her from the hard wooden floor. Considering the way that she had been restrained, the presence of the cushions seemed almost comical, and I thought that I might burst into fits of giggles again.

My mouth was dry and still burned from the inhalation of the smoke. I opened my mouth to speak, but could only manage a croak, which was immediately swallowed up by the music. At first, the vision of Liana tied up like that was simply puzzling, and by the time it occurred to me that Nick might have taken advantage of her, I had caught sight of her face, which clearly painted a different picture.

Her expression was ecstatic, her lips parted and her tongue occasionally darting out to wet her mouth. She was not struggling to get away, not making any effort to resist his advances, but rather kept shuffling backwards and opening her knees apart wider, encouraging him to enter her.

Nick seemed as hypnotised by Liana's bound figure as I was. He stood and stared at her kneeling beneath him for an age, before finally dropping to his knees and testing her wetness with his gloved finger. His first digit slid into her easily and he added another, and another, until only his thumb was visible, resting in the hollow of her arse.

Liana pushed against him, thrusting furiously backward despite the obvious discomfort of the ropes that were cutting into her wrists and thighs. Her sounds of pleasure were clearly audible over the loud music and were much more guttural than a regular moan. She was keening like an animal in a combination of pain and acute arousal, each rising in accordance with the other. The harder Nick pushed his hand inside her, the harder Liana moaned. He was grunting in unison with her, as if trying to orchestrate her responses in time with his own.

He reached his other arm forward and grabbed her long hair, pulling her head back as she screamed.

'What are you?' he cried.

'I'm a slut,' she replied.

'Not quite.'

'I'm your slut,' she corrected.

'That's better. Now, come for me.'

He released her hair and she fell back down onto the cushion as Nick raised his palm into the air and brought it down onto her buttock with a loud spank. His hand then ran down between her legs, and I could tell by the redness that rushed up her cheeks and the sudden change in tempo of her moans that he must finally be playing with her clitoris.

The air in the room felt heavy, and was thick with the scent of sex blended with the slightly chemical smell of the latex gloves. I was intoxicated, not just by the wine, the marijuana and the ache in my still-throbbing tattoo, but also by the vision of my naked friend on all fours not more than a couple of arms' lengths away from me. I could have reached out and touched her, but I didn't. The space between us felt like a chasm, the distance between one possibility and another.

Liana came at last, her final scream the loudest of them all, and as she did so I felt a rush inside me so strong that I thought I might pass out if I didn't come to my own climax. I wanted Nick to abandon her and touch me instead, to bring me to the same strange sort of pleasure that he had brought her, but my mouth felt as though it was made of concrete and my limbs were wooden, unmovable.

He pulled the gloves from his hands with a snap, tossed them away and took Liana into his arms, cradling her against him the way that a parent comforts a sick child. She nestled into his chest in a fetal position as he stroked her hair and her face with a gentleness so absolute that I felt as though I had dreamed the roughness of his earlier behaviour.

They lay there for a long time, and I continued to rest in the bean bag and watch. The intimacy between them was somehow more intense than the sex had been, and after a while I began to feel that my presence was inappropriate. What, I worried, if the spell that seemed to have been cast over the two of them wore off and they saw my voyeurism as unwelcome and unwanted? That I was some kind of pervert? My guilt was ridiculous under the circumstances, I knew, but it was enough to rouse me from my stupor and to my feet.

I glanced at the clock. Hours had passed, though after we smoked the joint each minute had felt timeless. It was close to dawn.

Liana was still curled up in Nick's arms and they were now lying down on the floor with their eyes closed and their heads resting on the cushions that had earlier supported Liana's knees.

I took a blanket that was lying across the back of the sofa and carefully spread it over their bodies. Neither of them stirred.

Then I collected my purse and fled.

I didn't see Liana for ten whole days following that evening. She didn't come back to our flat for the duration, presumably staying with Nick, or maybe she had decided, after all, to pay her parents a visit.

Neither of us tried to contact the other on our phones. Possibly for the same reason: shame at what she had got herself involved in on her part, and a similar reluctance on mine to discuss what I had witnessed and my reactions to it.

I slept most of the next day and never left my room, subsisting on an old tin of biscuits and water from the sink tap, tossing and turning in my bed, clearing the wine and smoke from my system, and trying to rid myself of the images of Liana and Nick and the look on her face as he pleasured her.

I was already trying to formulate what I might say to her next time we saw each other, but none of it made sense and I changed my mind every quarter of an hour or so. Maybe I should just be silent. Pretend I hadn't been there, seen nothing.

I didn't answer the occasional knocks on my door until late afternoon when Neil finally called out my name.

I moaned in response, threw off the covers and tiptoed over to open the door, still in my underwear.

Neil's first reaction was wide-eyed at seeing me so scantily dressed, but that was nothing like the look on his face when he looked up and caught sight of my teardrop tattoo.

I had carefully removed the dressing as soon as I got home, and washed away the mess that had gathered there. It was still red, but the teardrop was clearly visible beneath the light layer of the antiseptic cream that I had dabbed over it as per Jonah's instructions.

Neil opened his mouth wide and just held it there for an eternity as I yawned and stretched in front of him, as if he couldn't call up the right words from his subconscious.

I smiled and mimicked the open O of his fish face. 'Anything you want to say?' I asked him.

He closed is mouth and finally began to express himself.

'What the . . . ?' was all he managed, though his eyes were drawn to the mark on my face, transfixed by it.

'It's a tattoo, Neil. That's all it is.'

He peered, scrunched his face.

'Is it real? Or just temporary?' he asked me.

'It's real. Not a fake. Very real.'

If he'd asked me why, I think I would have just sent him packing, but he didn't. Although I was sure he would do at some later stage.

'When?' He was visibly attempting to figure out how it could have happened to me since he'd left us at the Komedia bar late the previous afternoon.

'Yesterday, not long after you went home,' I informed him calmly. 'Liana also had one done. On her ankle.'

'Her ankle?' The idea of a teardrop on Liana's ankle must have puzzled him.

'A different one,' I helped him out. 'She wanted a butterfly.'

'Oh.' He swallowed hard, his eyes still captivated by the teardrop on my face.

'It's . . . curious,' he said. 'Actually, it suits you, in a strange way. So black, and your skin so pale.'

'Really?'

The fact that he seemed to like my changed appearance threw me – I hadn't expected it from him.

'It doesn't make me look like a clown, or like Alice Cooper, does it?' I had a moment of doubt as I asked him this.

His gaze was unwavering.

'No, not at all,' Neil stated. 'He just had black circles around his eyes, and thin lines, not a teardrop. And, of course, it was just make-up. Nothing permanent.'

'I never thought you'd know about Alice Cooper,' I said.

'I met him once,' he revealed to my surprise. 'My dad played with him at a charity golf tournament. It's his major passion.'

I laughed out loud. This was getting too ridiculous for words. Finally his eyes abandoned mine and strayed further afield over to my undressed body. I realised with a jolt that my knickers were rather transparent and that I hadn't showered when I'd got home in the early hours of the morning. But I didn't feel threatened, or aroused; Neil was safe. He held no sexual charge for me.

'You really like it?'

'I think so, it does look pretty, striking, although . . .'

'Although what?'

'It's just that teardrop tattoos have a story behind them, haven't they?' he said hesitantly.

'What sort of story?'

'I'm surprised you don't know. I thought it was one of those things that everyone knew.'

'What?' I asked him again, impatiently.

'People get them in jail when they've killed someone.'

'Oh shit!' I cried.

Neil went pale, mistaking my frenzied laughter for anger.

'Well,' I said, 'maybe I've fucked up, but it's too late now and I haven't been to jail and I haven't killed anyone. Yet. Now piss off and let me put some clothes on.'

Neil retreated back past the door and I was left with my thoughts.

It had been a mad, spur-of-the-moment decision, I knew, and now I was stuck with it.

I was the girl with the teardrop tattoo, and my life would never be the same again.

2

Bright Lights, Big City

The bed was too narrow and, as he shifted aside to lean over and extend an arm to the floor to reach his trousers, the quilt was pulled aside, uncovering me. The coldness of the morning interrupted my daydreaming. I was taken aback by how hairy the top of his shoulders looked.

What was his name again?

Peter? Mark? For the life of me, I couldn't remember. It had been a commonplace name. Even the sex had been unmemorable, and I recalled how, after he'd fallen asleep shortly after lifting himself away from me following his rapid climax, I had to reach for some much-needed relief using my own fingers.

David.

That was it.

'Cigarette?' He offered me one as he lit up his own.

'No thanks.'

We'd been flirting on and off for a few weeks at the pub in Cambridge Circus we both regularly visited, and yesterday evening I had given in almost out of lassitude and followed him home to his shared flat in Hackney. Maybe his lukewarm performance had been a direct response to my own evident lack of enthusiasm.

Had I even been attracted to him? Living in London

often made me do irrational things, and this was just the last in a series of minor mistakes I'd been involved in. After fumbling kisses in the dark once we'd got past the front door and undressing each other, I'd quickly realised David was hoping to fuck me bareback and I'd loudly stood my ground and insisted he use a condom. The fool didn't even have any in the flat or his room. Fortunately, I still had one secreted away at the bottom of my bag. The fact that a woman would think of carrying protection somehow excited his fancy and he was rock hard in a moment. Not for long, though.

As he puffed away on his cigarette with a smug look on his face, ignoring me altogether, I decided it was time to draw a line under the mediocrity of the whole thing. I rose from the bed in silence, bending over to pick up my scattered items of clothing, and quickly dressed.

'Don't you want to take a shower, have breakfast together?' David suggested.

'Not really.'

I'd been in London for a little while, living the independent life I'd so long dreamed of. And I wasn't any happier. Following my graduation from Sussex University, I'd decided to stay down by the coast for the summer rather than returning home. The fact that Liana had also opted to remain in Brighton had been a strong factor.

Neil had disappeared home and was sensibly spending a few months away from distractions to concentrate on his graduate job applications. He'd even found a friend to fill his space for a few months, a computer engineering student who spent all of his time online gaming and rarely left his bedroom.

To my surprise, my parents hadn't raised any objections to my ongoing absence and volunteered to provide me with a small allowance for a further six months while I found my feet. I imagined they had grown used to living on their own by now after my three years away and felt no urgency at the prospect of having a now-tattooed daughter back in the family fold.

However, Liana and Nick had now been dating for well over a year and, at the end of the summer, Liana decided to move in with him. I could no longer afford to stay in the flat we had shared for what now felt like an eternity and I just didn't have either the energy or the willpower to begin the endless round of interviews for prospective new tenants to share the premises and make ends meet, in all likelihood first- or second-year students who would prove as gormless as I had been at that age and no company at all.

So I ended up moving to London. My time to try the bright lights and the big city. A distant second cousin had initially allowed me to crash on her sofa in Mill Hill, but the suburb's distance from the heart of town was too much of a strain on my finances and my sense of adventure, and after I'd found a part-time waitressing job I managed a flat-share in Dalston.

With my literature degree, I'd been hopeful of finding work in maybe a bookshop, but it seemed I was one of a thousand applicants for every vacancy and no doubt my pesky facial tattoo was no help.

The real problem was that I now realised I didn't know what I truly wanted from life. I had never been particularly ambitious or assertive. Love hadn't crossed my path yet and I was beginning to believe that, even if it did, I would not be capable of recognising it. The real thing. Men I dated were a disappointment, intimacy such a fleeting sensation and all too often a let-down. Welcome to the real world, Lily!

I kept in touch with Liana, we visited one another when we could and spoke regularly on the phone, but I had begun to sense the darker side of her personality, which I had observed during the course of her and Nick's initial encounter, was gradually coming to the fore. From a distance I observed with unease as new acquaintances introduced her to a curious new world, involving BDSM and somewhat more clandestine activities she was wary of sharing with me.

On one of her visits to the capital, she did allow me to tag along with her and her companion for the evening, an older guy with a creepy taste for leather. I accompanied them to an underground club opposite the old Smithfield Market where it seemed almost anything went.

Liana hadn't revealed the dress code to me until we arrived and she removed her coat. She wore a lace bodysuit that was totally sheer with no underwear beneath it. Her nipples pointed through the fabric so obviously that the girl on the door, who seemed to know her well, suggested that Liana could double as a coat rack. She accessorised with black gloves and a bowtie around her neck in a strange fabric I had never seen before, but which many of the other party-goers were wearing.

Latex, Liana explained, and I saw much more of it when curiosity got the better of me and I followed her and her leather-clad friend through to the bar. A bevy of fierce-looking women on the dance floor were dressed in the same stuff.

I soon forgot the latex when I set eyes on the men these women were with. One had a guy attached to a leash, cowering at her feet like a dog. Another man was standing next to them waiting to be served at the bar. He was wearing just a rubber G-string with a pink pouch at the front that covered his genitals. One of the women asked him why he was taking so long to fetch their drinks, and I watched in horror as she raised something she was holding in her hand and brought it slapping down against his buttock to hurry him along.

'What the fuck is this place, Liana?' I asked.

'You'll like it,' she replied. 'Trust me.'

As the evening progressed, I witnessed stranger and stranger behaviour. Liana spent most of the evening on the dance floor, leaving me to creep across to the area that she called the dungeon for a better look. There I saw men and women bent over all kinds of furniture in various states of nudity, each of them with a partner who seemed to be torturing them in one way or another. A man in a leather kilt was repeatedly bringing his hand down on a woman's buttocks and she was moaning loud enough to raise the roof.

It was a little like watching a horror film. I saw things that I didn't want to see, yet I couldn't bring myself to look away. There was some part of me that felt an odd kind of connection with the people in the dungeon. What I witnessed didn't arouse me exactly, but it spiked my interest, and to Liana's amusement I asked her if she'd like to go back again the following weekend and then the one after that.

I was weirdly fascinated by the assorted goings-on in the club, which ranged from the bizarre to the hardcore. I had no desire to participate and preferred to indulge the voyeur in me, remaining on the perimeter of the activities, which helped me get noticed by one of the organisers. A couple of weeks later, I was offered a part-time job with the club, attending to the cloakroom and other minor chores two or three nights a week.

'You look as if you're observing everything and making careful mental notes,' she had said to me. 'That's good. We might need a chronicler one day.'

She was an imposing woman, dressed on that initial evening in a red latex cat suit, her dark-brown hair floating all the way down her back and gliding against the shiny surface of her costume. She was all curves, her strong legs delineated by the costume and emphasised by her impossibly high heels. She appeared to be acting as the mistress of ceremony for tonight's entertainment, mingling with the crowds, encouraging, suggesting, prodding, her voice hoarse and confidential, soothing one moment and harsh the next as she ordered the men and women in attendance around as if they were her own personal puppets. Everyone referred to her as 'She', and it felt almost dangerous to even enquire as to her real name.

I was stunned and in awe of her worldliness and acquiesced immediately when she offered me the job.

'You'll have to wear something else, though,' she pointed out. I didn't have any of the fetish-themed clothing that the club preferred everyone to don, so I usually borrowed a simple black dress from Liana.

'I don't think I own anything appropriate,' I remarked with regret.

'Not to worry,' she replied, looking me up and down as if taking my modest measurements. 'I think we can conjure something up that will suit you. Your skin is so pale, and I love the way you wear your hair.'

I was one of the few girls I knew who still sported the hair they were born with. Jet black, it reached right down to the small of my back as I hadn't had it cut since I'd reached my teens.

By then, I'd found a day job assisting at the counter at a music shop in Denmark Street, London's old Tin Pan Alley, just off Charing Cross Road. Music had always been one of my passions, maybe even my only passion. I'd had ten years or so of cello lessons and had even taught myself to play the guitar, although for some reason I'd not picked up an instrument since I'd left home. The store sold and hired instruments and also stocked sheet music.

With my job there and the part-time hours at the fetish club, I was financially secure for the first time in my adult life, not that I had expensive tastes or a costly way of life. I didn't begrudge the lack of free time, finding both activities enjoyable and a welcome contrast to one another. It was like living in two different worlds and it made life interesting.

London was a forest of possibilities and I wanted to sample every single one of them. I wanted loud music and white lights, to be alone in a crowd and be a part of an unthinking multitude, to have picnics in Regent's Park or Hyde Park or Hackney Downs, wander for hours on end down Brick Lane or the warrens of the Camden Town markets, carouse in Hoxton and meditate in the early morning on the slopes of Primrose Hill, shop for exotic vegetables in Brixton market, halal meat in Southall or kosher patisseries in Golders Green.

But, first of all, I treated myself to another, larger tattoo across my right shoulder: a multicoloured landscape of wild orchids. And I got my ears pierced and adorned by a welter of small, thin steel rings. Some days I would add a fake nose ring to compound my overall goth look, alongside a darker shade of crimson for my lipstick.

Lily of London was born in earnest.

Little did I know how violins would make a mess of all my carefully improvised plans.

I had been working at the shop in Denmark Street for almost three months when, shortly after we'd opened at ten in the morning, this serious-looking and rather handsome – if curiously detached – middle-aged guy walked in and enquired about violin rentals.

We normally traded in violins, but most of our demand was for electric guitars and bass guitars, so none of our stock was actually on display in the window, but was kept behind the till in a glass-fronted cabinet.

The man seemed anxious, as if he had come to the wrong place, but he gifted me with a broad, warm smile when I pointed out the tall unit standing behind me and confirmed we also hired instruments in addition to selling them.

My first instinct with men is to look at their fingers and I can usually recognise a musician from miles away. He wasn't one, but his fingers were the right length and thin enough. It made me wonder what he did for a living, but it was a bit too early to ask as I unlocked the cabinet with one of the keys from the heavy bunch we kept chained to the cash register.

He advised me the violin he was seeking to hire was not for personal use, which confirmed the fact that he didn't actually play, and politely enquired whether I happened to play myself. The friend on whose behalf he was there worked in the classical field. I mentioned in passing that I was more of a rock'n'roll sort of gal, which raised a faint smile.

When I handed over one of the instruments we had available, he picked it up carefully, almost weighing it, calmly watching with fascination how the shop's strip lighting reflected against the orange burnish of its wood, then passed his fingers sensually across its body as if it were a woman.

I shivered before I could stop myself. No man had ever caressed me the way he was caressing that violin, and I suddenly felt both terribly aroused and jealous at the same time. He briefly looked up from his examination and our eyes met. It felt as if he had X-ray vision and could see right through my clothes. He looked pensive for a brief moment, as if he was speculating about the appearance of my concealed nudity. I blushed and looked away.

The fleeting connection we had shared broke and he turned back to the violin, telling me he wished to arrange the rental we had discussed earlier, and I then had to busy myself with the paperwork and the necessary calculations.

He filled out the forms and settled the deposit and the rental fees by credit card. His name was Dominik.

I watched him stride out of the shop onto a windy

Denmark Street and soon he was lost in the ebb and flow of the crowds.

That night, back in my small room at the shared flat, I lay alone in bed, feeling cold but too lazy to get up and switch on the heater. I wondered endlessly about the woman Dominik had been getting the violin for, with my imagination veering off in all sorts of directions. I couldn't understand my agitation. Why had such an insignificant encounter triggered such curious reactions in me?

It was a night full of uncommon dreams. But no nightmares.

David, who worked for a big firm of accountants a few streets away from the Denmark Street shop, rang me the next morning, suggesting we go on a date. I swiftly turned him down. It was as if this brief encounter with a total stranger had opened a window in my mind to new possibilities, to life being different. It made no sense, I knew as I argued with myself, but that was just the way I felt. And I didn't have a clue as to what the next step should be.

It happened with the next violin to cross my path.

I had spent several weeks since my encounter with the enigmatic Dominik immersing myself in music again. I'd made a visit to my parents' house to touch base, as I did occasionally for the sake of propriety, and taken advantage of the trip to pick up my old guitar and a couple of boxes of LPs and CDs I had left in my bedroom there, records I had spent much of my teenage years singing and dancing to in splendid isolation, and which had felt alien once I had left for Brighton and uni.

It was like getting back on a bike again and my guitar-playing chops returned, rusty but not too unmelodic, even if I could only strum a few dozen tunes properly. But the music of Alice Cooper, Kiss, Free, Iron Maiden, Def Leppard and all my old favourites was truly joyful all over again as I reacquainted myself with their loud sounds, albeit on headphones in deference to my flatmates.

I would rush home from work whenever I wasn't part-timing at the fetish club and spent whole evenings in my room listening to the forgotten music of my youth. Initially I had never been keen on punk but now, listening to much of it with a new perspective, I discovered a new appeal in the songs of the Clash and the Jam and others which I had seldom seen before.

I was communing with music again and it was a blissful feeling. Like finding something that had been lost for ages.

Dominik returned the rental violin on one of my days off a fortnight later so I never saw him again. Maybe it was for the best.

It was late on a grey Saturday afternoon and Jonno, one of the other assistants at the store, and I were eager to close. It had been a miserable sort of day, drizzly, with customers few and far between and mostly indecisive or rude.

A man came through the door and the two of us heaved a sigh of exasperation – we probably wouldn't be able to close down for another quarter of an hour or more until we had dealt with him. Jonno ignored the new customer and walked down the stairs to the basement, leaving me to deal with the man.

He was in his mid or possibly late forties, dark-haired

and melancholy, wearing a brown corduroy jacket and clean, tapered jeans, a combination that somehow seemed just right for him. Under one arm he was holding a battered black violin case.

I had always been unimpressed by the blank canvas of younger men's faces. Older men were different: the life they had led could sometimes be deciphered in their features. As if the experiences and the emotions they had confronted had formed them, given them an added layer of attraction. Not all of them, of course. I had, for example, never been attracted to most of my school teachers or even the dashing lecturers at university. But this man was different. His face was like a book that I wished to read, a fascinating combination of sorrow and animal magnetism that took me by surprise and hit me in the gut.

He looked at me enquiringly and I could see how his gaze settled on my small tattoo. But it wasn't a look of disapproval, which I often got from older people, but one of gentle amusement and fascination.

'I was told your shop sometimes acquired second-hand instruments. Another store a few doors away said you might.' He raised the violin case he was holding onto the glass counter behind which I stood.

'We do,' I replied. 'But only the managers are in a position to appraise them, and neither of them is in today. You would have to come back, I'm afraid.'

'Oh,' he said.

And just stood there.

Surely he could wait until Monday. He didn't look like a person in need of urgent cash.

'I can look at it if you want. Give you my personal

opinion. Maybe even a rough valuation, though I can't guarantee the shop's owners would make an offer if you came around again,' I said.

'It's not a question of money,' the man said. 'I just sort of wanted it to find a new owner. Someone who would enjoy playing it. It was my wife's.'

'Your wife?'

'She recently passed away.'

'I'm sorry.'

'I'd even be happy to give it away if I knew if would end up with someone who could make good use of it,' he added, almost apologetically.

'That's a nice thing to do,' I said. 'Why don't you come back next week? I'm sure we'll find a way.'

He was about to pick up the case from the counter, but I leaned forward, took hold of it and unzipped it. The violin was in good condition, not an antique, but a good-looking and well-maintained instrument.

'I'm confident we could find a buyer for this,' I told him.

His features relaxed. 'That would be nice.'

I passed the violin case back to him.

Our fingers touched. His skin was warm, and surprisingly soft.

'I'm Lily,' I said.

'Leonard.'

He did return the following week, and agreed a reasonable price with one of the owners. Both parties appeared satisfied with the outcome. I sold the instrument at a small profit just under a fortnight later to a young student about to begin her first year at the Royal College of Music.

As part of the initial transaction, Leonard had been

obliged to sign some necessary paperwork and I had his email address on record as a result. Following the sale, I thought it would be nice to inform him who had ended up with his wife's violin. I knew the outcome would please him.

We began to correspond.

Initially, our exchanges were mostly about music. What he liked, what I didn't. Our memories of certain pieces or even songs – he was a surprising fount of knowledge about rock 'n' roll from all eras, although we heartily disagreed about the Clash, whom I had recently learned to appreciate so much more, but whom Leonard had a particular disdain for.

Nor was he much enamoured of heavy metal in all its varied incarnations, which made for a healthy exchange of views that we both enjoyed, although I was often irritated by his frequent conclusion to an argument whereby I would come to increasingly appreciate his tastes and side with his sharp opinions as I grew older.

On some days we would exchange up to a dozen emails, and soon I began looking forward to getting up in the morning and rushing to see my messages and invariably finding Leonard's final mail of the day, usually sent around the stroke of midnight. He was a faithful creature of habits.

Inevitably, certain personal subjects were never discussed: his late wife and the circumstances of her death, our sexual selves or why we had somehow connected in such a special way, the oddity of our increasing closeness, or the fact we stood two decades apart.

But as we jauntily skirted around them, the concentric circle of our unsaid words tightened and every successive mail seemed more charged than the one before. Although neither of us mentioned it openly, we were both becoming aware of the elephant in the room, that if we were to carry on conversing in this way we would have to meet up soon, for the first time since he had left the shop after selling his wife's violin and never expected to see me again, as it should have been in a right and proper world.

Leonard travelled a lot. He worked in the export trade, a field I barely understood despite his efforts at educating me. He was away a week or more every month, and while our exchange of emails continued while he was out of the country, it often took on an extra urgency as I sensed his loneliness as he wrote his rambling words in the darkness of foreign hotel rooms and the anonymity of airport lounges. It wasn't that he was gloomy; his mails were often wonderfully humorous, as he described the people he had to work with or the idiosyncrasies of the overseas cities he was passing through.

Our separate loneliness brought us together.

Our mails crossed across the electronic wasteland.

Maybe we could meet up for a coffee? Would be nice to be able to chat and have a longer and uninterrupted conversation.

I'll be in London next week. Would you like to actually get together in person?

He was in an identikit Marriott hotel room somewhere in the US Midwest and I was in the Denmark Street shop's basement as we both pressed SEND.

Life is sometimes an unlikely tissue of coincidences.

43

*

Ten days later, we had agreed an evening and a place, the bar of a large international hotel near Marble Arch. He'd pointed out that in a pub we wouldn't be able to hear each other speak.

I hadn't told a soul that I was planning on meeting up with Leonard. Certainly not Jonno, nor Neil, who I still spoke to from time to time. Not even Liana, with whom I remained in frequent telephone contact, if only to compare the diverging paths our lives were taking. I hadn't told anyone that we had met or been exchanging emails. I knew that Neil would be disapproving, Jonno would tease me and Liana just wouldn't understand. She would have found the age gap wonderfully rebellious, but would have thought Leonard too sensible and not nearly charismatic enough for her tastes, which clearly tended towards the extreme.

After spending a good ten minutes staring dismally into my wardrobe and wondering what would be an appropriate outfit to wear to meet a man twice my age in a central London hotel, I opted for simply dressing as myself in a pair of black jeans, flat ankle boots and a pale-blue cardigan to ward off the chill. The cardigan was cut wide at the neck and so displayed the orchid tattoo on my shoulder.

Now was not the time to try to be something that I wasn't or to slip into a cocktail dress and pretend to be twenty-eight instead of twenty-one. I wanted Leonard to be fully aware of the situation. The difference between us.

For Liana, getting dressed was a ritual. She chose her clothes based on the way that the fabric felt in her hands or wrapped around her body, and had once described shopping as a sexual experience.

For me it was a chore. Despite my goth leanings I still felt like a fish in the wrong water, as if I hadn't quite yet figured out where I fitted into the world and I didn't know what skin to put on when I left the house. Surprisingly, I now felt most comfortable in my latex at the fetish club. At least there I knew exactly what role I was expected to play and the rules on looking the part were perfectly clear.

Meeting Leonard was an entirely different situation. There were no rules for this.

He was sitting on a high stool at one end of the long, polished mahogany bar when I arrived. He hadn't seen me enter, and was leaning forward with both elbows resting on the bench in front of him, typing into a smart phone with a look of intense concentration on his face. He was wearing suit trousers and a white business shirt with the sleeves rolled up, as if he had just come from an important meeting. His jacket was hung over the back of the chair.

His salt-and-pepper hair was wavy and he wore it just a raffish inch too long for a man of his age. It was not affectation, just a natural way of showing he didn't follow fashion or convention and was at ease in his own skin. There was always a faint curl lurking at the corner of his lips, and I was unsure whether it was the sketch of a smile or the actual way he looked at most things with a degree of irony. An aura of peace emanated from him and it made me feel warm.

This is his life, I thought. Hotel bars and emails. I wondered briefly how many other women he engaged with in this way. Surely it couldn't just be me. Did he have dates booked every night of the week with strangers that he met in shops or online to distract him from the loneliness of international business travel?

He raised his glass to his lips and took a sip. Gin and tonic, I noticed as I saw the small bottle of soft drink next to him. Slimline. His glass was full of ice and I imagined how cold the tips of his fingers must be.

Finally he looked up and smiled.

'Lily,' he said, 'good to see you.'

He slipped his phone into his jacket pocket, slid off his seat and touched his hand lightly against my arm. I leaned forward and kissed his cheek.

'Come, sit down,' he added, pulling the seat next to him out. 'I'll get you a drink.'

He had barely looked up before one of the bartenders hurried over to take our order.

'I'll have a whisky sour,' I said, feigning confidence and ignoring the look the waitress gave Leonard as she asked him if he'd like another round. She called him 'darling' and brushed her fingertips against his for a moment too long as she handed him back his change.

At my choice of drink he had raised an eyebrow and tried but failed to suppress a smile. I wasn't even sure what a whisky sour was. I'd once overheard Liana ordering one when she was out on a date with a third-year student that I knew she had been trying to impress in her own, nonchalant way. It had arrived with a bright red cherry floating on the top of the glass and I remembered how inviting Liana's mouth had looked as she had taken the sugared cherry between her lips and pulled the stalk off with her fingertips. The third-year student hadn't stood a chance.

I hoped that I might be able to mimic a similar effect, but

when the drink I arrived I was too shy to attempt to be sexy and just left the cherry floating like a lost buoy.

Our knees brushed as I hoisted myself onto the bar stool. I always felt so small sitting up high, like a child with my feet dangling in mid-air a foot or two off the ground. Leonard was easily over six foot and lounging comfortably.

'Would you prefer to sit on one of the couches?' he asked politely as I squirmed, trying to get comfortable.

'Sure,' I replied breezily, eyeing the sofas with some trepidation. Two enormous leather monstrosities sat in the front of the bar area, with a sleek glass table the size of a small island between them.

Leonard picked up his jacket and folded it over his arm. I lost my balance briefly as I tried to stretch my leg out to reach the floor and he caught me by the elbow as I almost fell against him.

'Not accustomed to whisky?' he asked as he pulled me upright.

'Not accustomed to bar stools,' I replied. 'I prefer to sit closer to the ground.'

There was an awkward moment when we reached the couches and it became apparent that we could not sit either on opposite ends or on opposite sofas, as both of those options would put us so far apart we would need to shout or have a conversation in semaphore. Instead we would have to sit directly alongside each other with the rounded edges of the cushions pushing us even closer together, practically snuggling like a real couple.

From this angle I was able to study his profile. Square jaw, not a hint of stubble, and a recent nick from shaving that I felt a sudden desire to press my lips against. He had the slightest flecks of grey hair running down behind his ears and in the lock that fell stubbornly over his forehead. It occurred to me that he was older than Liana's father. Her parents had been teenagers when they had her. I was glad that my parents had me late, and my own father was in his late fifties so at least I did not have that comparison in my mind's eye.

'How was America?' I asked him.

'Fine,' he replied. 'The travelling isn't as glamorous as it sounds. The inside of chain hotels is the same the world over.'

We continued to make small talk and he quizzed me about my life in London and how I had ended up in the city working in a music shop after growing up as I had in suburban Berkshire. Eventually I found myself relaxing and opening up to him in a way that I hadn't before with anyone else.

Leonard was a good listener. And it made a nice change from most of the men I dated who talked endlessly about themselves. Partly, I knew that was my fault as I had a habit of encouraging others to talk to draw attention away from myself, but it was still nice to speak to someone who was actually interested in me. The real me. Not my bad-girl exterior or the good girl that was hidden beneath it, but the whole package: Lily. He was the first person I'd met who didn't ask me about any of my tattoos. Few things annoyed me more than being asked what my teardrop tattoo meant and why I had got it.

Afterwards, I realised with a sharp stab of shame that he had barely talked at all, other than to ask me questions. I had nattered on all evening.

Briefly, as we wound down for the night, I thought he might ask me up to a room that he might have booked in anticipation of bedding me, but instead he volunteered to walk me to the Tube. He first offered to pay for a taxi, but I told him that I enjoyed walking through the city at night, so instead he escorted me to Tottenham Court Road station and kissed me goodbye on the cheek. He laid a hand gently on my waist as he did so.

I waved goodbye with a skip in my step. Walking away from him, it occurred to me that our evening had left me feeling lighter, as though some burden had been lifted from my shoulders. Someone understood me at last.

As soon as I arrived home, I emailed him. I was afraid that if I waited any longer, I would lose my nerve.

> So nice to see you. Shall we do it again soon?

He was only in London for two more evenings, so we met up again the very next night. This time he took me to dinner in Chinatown, and we ate honey-glazed spare ribs and crispy fried seaweed in a restaurant on the corner of Newport Place and Lisle Street. We stayed until all of the other tables were empty and the waiters seemed on the verge of throwing us out. Once we'd worked our way through the extensive menu we ordered more and more bottles of beer.

By my third or fourth (or was it my fifth?) Asahi, I was simultaneously merry and depressed. Leonard would shortly be taking a flight to another international destination and I would be left to my ordinary life in London without him. He would only be gone for a week, to a conference in

Berlin. But still, the differences between us and the fact that our relationship was so odd and so far physically unconsummated meant that Leonard was like a butterfly in my hand. If I closed my eyes for a moment, I might open them again to find he had disappeared entirely. The thought made me blue.

The bill was presented between two fortune cookies. His was empty. Mine just said, *Stop searching*.

'What on earth does that mean?' I said.

'I think the waiters just didn't like us,' he laughed. 'You're not superstitious, are you, sensible Miss Lily?'

'I'm not very superstitious. But I'm not always sensible, either.' I screwed up the piece of paper with its italic font and tossed it into my bag.

A chill was in the air as we stepped out onto the narrow cobbled street with its rows of red flags and lanterns winking in the darkness. I huddled into the collar of my biker jacket.

He hadn't brought a coat along and pushed his hands into his jeans pockets to keep them warm.

I leaned towards him, and took one of his hands in mine.

'Shall we?' I said, stepping off the kerb with my hand linked with his, as if this added contact was nothing.

We walked like that through Soho, past the sex shops and the parade of coffee bars and noisy clubs, and briefly I thought of Liana and wondered what she would say when I eventually confided in her about Leonard. Until then I would hold this moment, and his hand, tight, like a secret.

His whole body tightened when I kissed him.

'Oh, Lily,' he said, breaking away from me. 'I can't kiss you now. You might regret it in the morning.'

'I won't. I know that I won't.'

I tried to kiss him again and he caught my chin in his hand.

'Believe me. It's not that I don't want to. I do. More than anything.'

'Then why not?' I asked. I was hurt now, and rejected, and I wanted to stamp my foot.

'You should be with someone your own age. This is crazy. I'm sorry. I shouldn't have met with you again. This is my fault entirely.'

'I don't want someone my own age,' I insisted. 'I want you.'

'Lily . . . Go home and sleep. Then talk to me in the morning.'

He kissed my cheek lightly and then turned and walked away.

That night I slept fitfully and not before sliding a hand under the covers and between my legs and orchestrating a blissful orgasm. Alcohol dulled my senses and always made my climaxes harder to reach, and as the wave of pleasure that I strained for seemed almost in sight but still torturously far away, I imagined Leonard's hands caressing my breasts and his tongue rasping against my nipples and the sound of his voice whispering terrible things into my ear and the heat of his breath against my skin. I came hard, thinking of him.

In the morning I felt somehow as if he knew what I had been thinking of as I had touched myself under the sheets the night before.

I rolled over and reached for my phone to check my emails as had become my habit since we had begun corresponding. Now I looked for Leonard's emails before I thought to do anything else, and on the rare mornings that I didn't receive one something felt at odds, as if I was wearing shoes with no socks on underneath.

His name flashed dark in my inbox and I smiled as I clicked on the message:

?

Just a single question mark.

The images that had soothed me to sleep flashed back into my mind.

I replied.

I still want you.

And pressed send.

His reply came just a few minutes later.

Come to the hotel.

He sent a cab to pick me up and within thirty minutes I was speeding across London and towards his hotel room. I felt every eye was on me as I strode past the concierge's desk and to the elevator, quickly stepping in and pressing the button to the fourteenth floor as Leonard had directed.

A 'Do not Disturb' sign was hung on the door, though it was slightly ajar.

I pushed it open and stepped inside.

Leonard was sitting in a white chair by the window, waiting for me.

'Close the latch,' he said. His voice was hoarse. 'And come here.'

I did as he instructed.

'Lily,' he said slowly, as if my name were a benediction. I stood between his knees, facing him, and he leaned forward and traced his finger along my jaw. 'You're so beautiful.'

I didn't know what to say, so I said nothing.

'Are you sure about this?'

'I'm here, aren't I?' I replied.

'That you are.'

He took me into his arms and lifted me into his lap. I nestled against his chest. Then raised my lips to his and kissed him in the way that I had been longing to since I had first set eyes on him.

His mouth was firm against mine, but his kisses were patient. He didn't push his tongue straight down my throat in the way that the boys I kissed at university parties and nightclubs did, and neither did he begin to fumble at my bra as though my breasts might evaporate into thin air if he didn't get a glance at them immediately.

Leonard continued to cradle me in his arms and kiss me softly until I became restless, and I took a handful of his hair in my hand, tipping his head back and biting his lower lip gently.

He pulled me away and laughed.

'No need to be so feisty,' he said. 'I'm not flying out until eight tonight. We have all day.'

'Fuck me,' I whispered.

Last night's climax had barely taken the edge off the deep well of desire that seemed to have been building up inside me for a lifetime. My pussy throbbed and all I wanted was for Leonard to fill me until there wasn't any room for anything else. I didn't want a single thought or feeling to cross my mind besides the sensation of him deep inside me. Cock, fingers, I didn't care.

'Please,' I said.

'Be careful what you wish for. You might regret it.'

'I won't regret it,' I replied firmly.

'Oh God, Lily, the things you do to a man . . .'

He stood up with me still in his arms and laid me down gently on the bed.

'But I'm not going to fuck you yet,' he said, 'even if you do want me to. Patience, my darling.'

I tried to sit up to pull him back towards me, but he pressed his hand against my chest and pushed me back down onto the bed. Then he was lifting up my skirt and peeling down my knickers and I forgot where I was and all the things I wanted to say as soon as his tongue flicked lightly against me and his finger slid into my pussy.

'You're so tight . . .'

'More,' I begged. 'Please.'

'All in good time,' he replied.

Then he was lifting my T-shirt over my head. 'Arms up,' he instructed, as I wriggled to get out of my clothing.

He didn't bother to unclip my bra at the back. Just pulled the cups down so that my breasts spilled out. He pulled and twisted my nipples in his fingers until I gasped.

'Too much?' he asked. He had curled up alongside me and was running his hands over my body, closely observing the way that I tensed or twitched or moaned in response to his caresses.

'No, not too much, more,' I said, and he squeezed harder.

No one had ever actually asked me what I liked or what I wanted before, and Leonard's interest in my pleasure was extraordinarily freeing. It was also the first time that I could recall going to bed with someone in broad daylight and without a drop of alcohol to lubricate my senses and lower my inhibitions. But his obvious desire for me and his confidence must have affected both of us because I couldn't have cared less how I looked or what Leonard thought of the things that turned me on.

He laughed when he noticed how I responded to his words.

'You like it when I talk dirty? I never would have guessed.'

'I love the sound of your voice,' I replied.

It was true. Leonard could have read the newspaper out loud to me and even each syllable of the money matters section when spoken in his throaty tone with its edge of humour and hint of lasciviousness would have made me arch my back and squirm against the bedspread.

'I want you to come for me.'

His voice deepened when he said this and his fingers found their way lower down, where he experimented until he discovered the exact rhythm that would drive me over the edge.

He leaned forward and scooped me tighter against him so that I was caught in his embrace as I began to tense and reach the cusp of an orgasm.

'That's it . . . Once you've come for me, Lily, I'm going to fuck you. But not before then. Do you want to feel my cock inside you, filling you up?'

'Oh God,' I moaned as I felt my muscles spasm and I convulsed against him and then collapsed, limp into his arms.

'Good girl,' he whispered.

He was still fully dressed. His stubble scratched my cheek lightly as he bent his head to kiss me again.

'Now,' he said, 'how many more times can you do that for me before I have to catch a plane?'

That day he introduced me to more sexual positions than I knew existed, let alone had considered before. My favourites were the variations in which I could see him and watch the range of expressions that raced across his face as he truly let himself go.

Most of the time he hung onto an element of reserve, a persona of either careless nonchalance or all-knowing Lothario who was utterly certain of his ability to bring me to orgasm. But when he was deep inside me and on the verge of his own release, there was something animal about him, as if the real Leonard was straining on a leash and he would show me flashes of feeling so intense that I trembled.

And I decided to set about finding a way to get him to let go.

'My darling girl, you don't know what you're doing,' he said as I pushed him down onto the bed and then rode him, holding his wrists down over his head.

When he said that, I just pushed down harder, even though I knew that the grip of my small hands was pitiful against his strong arms. It gave me a thrill to turn the tables and be the one on top for a change.

The hotel hadn't allowed him to check out in the late evening, so he had another night booked and paid for, and instead of commuting back to my own lonely bed in Dalston after Leonard showered and packed his bag hurriedly, I stretched out like a starfish and wallowed in the lingering damp patches and the scents of our lovemaking. The scent of him and me, together.

'Oh, Lily,' he said as he kissed me goodbye. 'What am I going to do with you?'

3

Eighty Days of Leonard

Of course it felt good being with Leonard.

But it also felt wrong in a thousand ways.

On the one hand, I now knew what it was to be with a man and not with a boy. There was nothing tentative about his lovemaking, or callow, or inexperienced. His gestures were determined, his appreciation of the moment intense and patient, and I found myself at ease with him like I had never felt with anyone else before. I would have expected no less from a man who was more than double my age.

But, on the other hand, I also knew he was not the sort of man I could take home to my parents or openly advertise to friends and acquaintances as my new boyfriend without attracting much in the way of disapproval. Not that I had any intention of parading him around. I enjoyed the clandestine nature of our relationship. I liked having a secret lover.

By common agreement, we would meet in hotel bars, none of which were in geographical proximity to our places of work. Sometimes we would go to his empty office where we would feverishly fuck on the carpet behind locked doors, while on other occasions we would take shelter in a hotel room close to one of the airports if he was flying out on business the next day. My flat-share was out of bounds. I never saw his house in Blackheath, and neither of us ever suggested it as a venue for our dates. It was as if our relationship was in a vacuum and it suited us both. It never occurred to me that he might be embarrassed to be seen with me, my teardrop, piercings and all-black wardrobe.

Because of the frequency of his trips abroad, he often arranged for me to join him in Paris, Amsterdam or Barcelona on a Friday night after his business had been completed and we would spend the weekend together before returning to London on the final Sunday-night flight.

This proved problematic and I found myself quite unpopular with the other assistants at the music shop in Denmark Street when I frequently elected to forego work on a Saturday under the pretext of family circumstances. I think Jonno guessed a man of some sort must be involved – he invariably signed me off on the rotas with a knowing wink.

The folk at the fetish club and the imperious She seemed less concerned, as they had a bevy of part-time helpers at their beck and call. In any case, I was careful to make myself available on any weekend when Leonard was not on the tail end of a business trip, as I would then spend most evenings with him during the actual week in London.

'You're never home, or answer your phone, these days,' Neil remarked one day, a month or so after I'd first got together with Leonard, as we sat indifferently nibbling at sandwiches at the nearby Pret A Manger, nursing our coffees alongside.

'Just busy, you know.'

'Busy doing what?' he queried.

'I've met someone,' I revealed.

The look on his face betrayed his disappointment. He had repeatedly tried to convince me, since he had also moved up to London, that we should go out on a date, but I had insisted it would be better to just remain good friends.

'Do I know him?' he asked.

'No.' And I left it at that.

How could I tell a boy of barely twenty-one who innocently yearned after me that I was sleeping with a man who was old enough to be his father, or even mine. That I enjoyed the age difference between us. That our gap in years made me feel feminine and desirable in a way that I never felt dating people my own age. That I had grown used to Leonard's worldliness and the comparative coarseness of his skin and the way the wrinkles around his eyes when he laughed or smiled made me feel joyful. The way we could both sustain lengthy silences when we were together or, alternately, talk for hours about everything and nothing and he could sit calmly, watching me and listening to me talk about my past life, and appear genuinely fascinated by the humdrum of my day-to-day existence. I knew such revelations would only hurt Neil further, so I kept them to myself.

The conversation with Neil quickly petered out after that and, anyway, we both had to go back to work, me to Denmark Street and him to Chancery Lane where he was doing an internship with a big PR firm.

A DHL van was parked outside the shop and a large delivery was taking place when I got back.

Heavy boxes were being passed from hand to hand in a

steady relay as some of the other staff carried the new consignment of guitars from the US factory down to the shop's basement. I joined the fray, although I heard the familiar message signal on the phone buried deep at the bottom of my jeans pocket. It was a quarter of an hour later when I had the chance to read it.

Leonard. This time it would be Paris. The reference code for the electronic ticket for Eurostar was attached and the name and address of the hotel we would be staying at. He'd been in Greece and Turkey all week, but had arranged a stop-over in the French capital on the way back to spend the time with me. I'd been hoping he might fly me to Istanbul, but I reckoned Paris was as good as the Grand Bazaar.

I made a quick call to the club and managed to swap the coming Saturday for a couple of weekday nights.

Later that afternoon, as I was daydreaming of Paris and what sharing it with Leonard would be like, three men walked into the store. They were speaking to each other in a language I couldn't recognise – but then, I didn't know or speak any foreign languages.

Two of the men were thin and tall like beanpoles, while the third was of medium height, a bit stocky, built like a swimmer with powerful shoulders. They all seemed to be wearing our regulation customer outer wear: black leather jackets, T-shirts and jeans. The swarthier one addressed me, fortunately in English.

'My friends here would like to have a look at the Gibsons you might have in stock.' His accent had something of the Scandinavian about it, harmonious but guttural.

'New instruments or second-hand ones?' I asked.

'Both,' he confirmed after conferring with his friends.

And, seeing me intrigued by the language they were speaking in, he said, 'They're from Iceland.'

'Ah,' I remarked, my curiosity satisfied.

'Me too,' he went on. 'But I left the island ages ago. Been in England nearly ten years now.'

I nodded.

'I'm with another band now, but I used to play with these two back home when we were younger. I'm Dagur Sigurdarsson. But you can just call me Dagur.' He extended his hand and we shook a hello.

'Lily.'

He had a lovely smile, with pearl-white teeth.

I busied myself with his friends while Dagur wandered around the shop examining our varied stock. One of the Icelandic musicians took an immediate liking to a Dobro and asked me to take it down from the far wall. I'd connected the instrument to a practice amplifier we kept permanently plugged in for tests and demonstrations, and a ripple of melodious notes tinged with country-and-western rhythms rang out through the store.

Ever since I'd been working at the music store I knew there was no need for any kind of salesmanship or words of encouragement. Musicians know their own mind and personal opinions wouldn't be taken into account. At any rate, the guitar player quickly agreed to acquire the instrument and gave me his credit card while I passed the heavy Dobro to Jonno to reunite it with its case and pack it.

I handed over the till and credit-card receipts to the buyer whom Dagur had rejoined.

'Anything I might interest you in?' I brazenly asked Dagur, feeling as if I were on a roll.

'I'm a drummer,' he pointed out.

I blushed, though of course I had no way of knowing what instrument he played. The store did not stock percussion. In the world of music, that was a specialist area which other stores catered for.

He theatrically blew me a kiss as he walked out of the door.

'You didn't know who he was, did you?' Jonno said to me. He was smirking from ear to ear.

'The drummer? Should I?'

'He's from the Holy Criminals.'

'Viggo Franck's band?'

'Yeah. That one. Not really my thing, but most girls go crazy for them.'

Not having gone crazy for them seemed to have raised me in Jonno's estimation.

I shrugged, playing up my nonchalance to impress him, though secretly I was chuffed to have sold a guitar to a bona fide rock star, or his friends at least.

But the thrill of Dagur passed quickly, and I returned to my thoughts of Paris. And Leonard.

A full day of work on my feet in the music shop had left me worn out, so by the time I arrived for my shift at the fetish club I was frazzled, light-headed and jittery from consuming too many energy drinks to push myself through.

I tried not to double up as it was just too exhausting, but I'd had to make some sacrifices in order to keep my dates with Leonard as well as keep my employers happy, and one of those sacrifices was losing sleep having to work for whole days and nights on the hop. I'd started in Denmark Street at ten a.m. and wouldn't be home from the fetish club until six a.m. the following morning.

The underground club felt surreal at the best of times, but tonight it was practically a dream world. Thursday nights were always quieter than Saturdays and so we tended to get more of the couples who came out purely to make use of the equipment and the anonymity that the club provided. The thud of floggers and the crack of whips on bare skin and the resulting screams really had a way of travelling, so I could easily understand why people came to the club rather than risk waking the neighbours with their unusual nocturnal practices.

Periodically one of the other club workers would take over on the counter to give me a chance to go to the toilet or take a cigarette break if I wished, though I didn't smoke. Invariably I spent these snatches of time in the play areas, observing the interactions between the club's guests.

Somehow I could never quite get used to the sight of women being tied up and effectively beaten. Often I thought of Nick and Liana together on the night that I'd accidentally witnessed. Even though I'd been aroused during certain moments, the thought of my friend in pain, particularly at the hand of a man, horrified me. I knew that each interaction was negotiated in painstaking detail and over the course of an entire relationship and that often it was the person on the receiving end of a paddle who had pleaded to be treated that way. There were plenty of dominants who got a release of sorts from having a partner at their beck and call, but also many who inflicted more pain because they were asked to and enjoyed the enthusiastic response of their submissive.

Richard was the club's only male Dungeon Master, whose job it was to give advice and keep an eye on the patrons and make sure that newcomers were following the rules. He had tried to explain the intricacies of the dynamic between doms and subs to me, and all the variations that I found so fascinating.

'You don't need to understand it,' he said that night, as he watched me watching a man caning a woman's arse so hard that she jumped and cried out in pain with each strike. 'So long as you respect everyone's right to do what they please with their own body.'

'Of course,' I replied. 'Each to their own. I know that. I just don't see what they get out of it.'

'Have you ever had your hair pulled? Or someone slap your butt?'

I mentally ran through my limited catalogue of sexual memories. So many were blurred by the passing of time and often the presence of alcohol. I remembered vaguely that a guy at a house party in my second year of uni had tugged at my hair as he kissed me and had nipped at my lower lip and then slid his hands under my skirt and smacked my arse. We were in the kitchen at the time and he'd been leaning against the refrigerator when I approached to get another bottle of beer and he'd taken me into his arms. When he had pulled on my pony tail and bit my lip, I'd just presumed that he was unskilled and clumsy, but slapping my bum had been the final straw. I'd been thoroughly insulted and had pushed him off and walked away. Who did he think he was? Someone starring in a rap video? Liana had chortled heartily when I'd told her.

'You need to lighten up,' she'd said. 'Objectification can be hot.'

I'd been shocked at the time, but hadn't given it much thought since. Liana was always trying to get a reaction from me anyway.

At any rate, I had resolved never to attend parties wearing a pony tail again.

Richard brought me back to the present.

'What do you think about dommes and their male subs and slaves then?' he quizzed.

He signalled over to She, who looked like something out of a superhero film with her gleaming latex catsuit and towering stilettos. She stood with her back as straight as a broomstick and her dark hair piled on top of her head in a slick bun that made her appear even taller. Her legs were spread slightly apart so that she seemed totally grounded, not crossed at the ankles or teetering precariously in the way that so many women balanced on their high heels. In each of her hands she held a shining silver bracelet studded with diamante jewels that sparkled in the light. Attached to each bracelet was a long chain, and attached to the end of each chain was a man on all fours staring at the floor and clad in just a pair of rubber hot pants with 'She's Slave' printed across their arse cheeks in hot-pink lettering. Mostly She ignored her slaves, but every now and again she would give one of their chains a tug and a smile would pass over her face.

'That's different,' I said firmly.

'How is it different? Why is it different?'

'I don't know. It just is.'

Richard's questions were beginning to make me feel uncomfortable.

The front desk was dead quiet when I returned to my place behind the counter. I had hoped that we would have a busy patch to distract me from the thoughts crowding into my mind, but it was getting late and past the time that most of our patrons arrived, unless they'd been to a house party or another club beforehand.

I had no moral reservations about women cowering down to men, providing that everyone involved was an adult, fully aware of what they were getting themselves in to, and doing it for enjoyment's sake, even if I couldn't relate to the pleasure that they experienced or the mindset that drove them.

I could more easily understand the dynamic between She and her slaves. That seemed to be more like a different sort of government than a sexual game. Like a matriarchal society with She as Cleopatra. And that was a system that I could appreciate. In fact, the feminist in me thought it entirely sensible. Men in power had been screwing things up for centuries.

Leonard sometimes gave me instructions in bed. Or held me in place when I wriggled away from an intense sensation. But he was so gentle, and it always seemed that he could somehow read my mind and was giving me what I wanted rather than forcing me to acquiesce for his own gratification. And more often than not, he looked at me as if I was something to be worshipped. Sometimes so intensely that it made me look away. I didn't feel that I was worthy of the sort of attention that She received. But I was certainly not a chattel to be used.

I could no sooner imagine Leonard wanting to whip me until I screamed or tie me so that I couldn't move any more than I could imagine Neil doing it.

A vision of Neil dressed in full leather regalia and looming over me with a riding crop flashed into my mind and I laughed out loud.

'Maybe it's time for you to go home,' piped Sherry, the girl who was helping with cloakroom duty tonight and who had caught me giggling to myself as she popped out for a cigarette. 'Nearly closing anyway and I'll cover for you. You look shattered.'

Sherry wasn't her real name, any more than She was She's real name. Most of the club's staff and the guests used pseudonyms or 'scene names' to refer to the fetish side of themselves. Partly this was a way to preserve anonymity and avoid any trouble that the unveiling of their private lives might cause, and partly it was a way to step from one persona into another, like putting on a new pair of shoes or changing into a party dress.

When I signed onto the club's payroll, I had been asked what I wanted to call myself and after little more than a moment's thought I had decided to stick with Lily. I'd had so much trouble figuring out my own identity that I had no wish to add any more complications to it now. I didn't want to be fragmented into the good-girl Lily and the bad-girl Lily, pre-tattoo Lily and post-tattoo Lily, Berkshire Lily and London Lily.

Right then I decided that I would just be Lily. The club was one place where I felt that I was truly free to be myself, whatever that was on any given night, and I didn't want to confuse matters by giving another name to some identity that I felt was the 'real me'. I wanted to be me all the time. Just plain old Lily.

London was just beginning to stir when I changed out of my latex waistcoat and into plain jeans, a sweatshirt and old trainers for the journey back to Dalston. It was just gone five a.m. and always a strange time of the morning, when half the people on the street had just woken up and the other half were on their way home to bed. The streets were inevitably full of oddballs when I headed home from the fetish club so I walked quickly, my head down, careful not to make eye contact with anyone. I wasn't particularly afraid. Just couldn't be bothered with the hassle of being harassed. Later the suits would be out in full force, but for now I was surrounded by drunks, tramps and council workers and it was a funny mixture that, combined with the early hour, seemed to bring out the worst in people.

Even the fresh air and brisk though short walk to Farringdon station couldn't empty my mind of the questions that had flooded it that night. I was worried about Liana. We'd naturally fallen out of touch a little – we lived in different cities now and recently I had been so wrapped up in Leonard.

She was still with Nick as far as I knew, but the last time we spoke it had been clear there was some tension between the two of them and she had hinted in passing that she had been spending more time with a group of people who Nick wasn't keen on. That was what had worried me.

Not long after I had begun working at the fetish club, I realised that Liana was by nature a sub, or at least had experimented in that area even if she didn't necessarily see herself as that. We had never discussed it directly, but I felt fairly sure that Nick was her dominant, and once I had got used to the idea and saw the two of them together I had developed an appreciation for him. He was discreet and clearly very affectionate towards her, and she always seemed happy when they were together. For as long as Nick was in the picture I was certain that he would take care of her.

But the thought that the two of them might have fallen out, leaving Liana to her own devices, made me panic.

She was the sort of person who was forever throwing caution to the wind in favour of chasing the next thrill. Liana followed her body where I followed my heart, and she was the type of person that I could imagine might easily take things too far and go down a perilous road.

By far the majority of doms on the scene were perfectly normal individuals who cared a great deal about their play partners, and the majority of submissives were equally well-balanced ordinary people who simply happened to enjoy a different sort of sex than the average, but there were a few folk who hung around the perimeters and were best avoided.

Every section of society has its fair share of extremists. Richard had been the first to warn me of the possible pitfalls to look for if I was supervising the fetish club's play area or keeping an eye on unsavoury-looking patrons to determine if they needed to be thrown out. Single men in cheap military jackets who stood too close to the play area were the stereotype, but it took all sorts, and it was the manipulative ones who managed to hold up a veneer of respectability that I worried about where Liana was concerned.

She wasn't stupid, but she was reckless. And she was my dearest friend.

I vowed then that as soon as I was back from this weekend in Paris I would make some time to catch up with her. I would tell her all about Leonard and confess my latest set of secrets, and hope that she still felt close enough to me to return the favour.

Until then, I would forget all about the underground club and the eternal fascination that world held for me. Even the parts of it that I didn't fully understand yet. And instead I would focus on Leonard.

I hurried home to rest and to pack.

Leonard had a life before me. But it wasn't one I wanted to hear about. There had been a wife, manifold adventures and much more. And I was jealous of it.

I sought my own adventures. A voice inside was screaming out that I deserved them, lots of them, and somehow this made me feel awkward when my feelings for Leonard took over and all I could do was daydream about an unlikely future together. My heart was his, but my soul was torn.

The room was on the top floor of a small hotel situated between the left bank of the Seine and the Boulevard Saint Germain. Leonard told me later that the famous French singer and dissolute Serge Gainsbourg had lived on the same street just a hundred yards away. You could even see the gated courtyard of his building from our window if you stretched your neck.

The train had been delayed under the Channel Tunnel for half an hour and it was already dark when I reached my destination.

The elderly man on reception looked up from his newspaper and just nodded when I mentioned Leonard's name.

I had texted him when the train had drawn in to the Gare du Nord and he had given me his room number. I was just carrying an overnight bag with a single change of clothes and toiletries.

Leonard was sitting on the bed reading a paperback, wearing his usual dark slacks and a T-shirt. His smile as he greeted me was full of warmth. He dropped the book as I walked in. The door had been left unlocked.

'Bonjour, Mademoiselle Lily,' he said. 'Bienvenue à Paris.'

'Hey, Monsieur Leonard. I'm pleased to be here . . .' I was about to try to say something witty, albeit not in French, but words failed me. There was a sense of serenity about him, in this small, badly lit room, as he looked up at me.

'Hungry? Most places wont be serving dinner this late,' he said, 'but I'm sure we can find something, a snack maybe. There's a stall that does nice crêpes near the Odeon Métro.'

'No need; I had a sandwich on the train, and I have a few apples in my bag.'

He rose and took me in his arms.

It felt odd, being with him here. On other occasions we'd entered rooms together, knowing all too well that we were planning to fuck. All of our previous meetings had been overshadowed by an immediate lust. We had never begun with small talk. But arriving separately like this, there was a sense of anticlimax, of doubt also, as if the whole process we were going through was artificial. I dropped my bag to the ground.

Leonard pulled me closer to him and kissed my cheek, with his tongue lingering lovingly across my minuscule tattoo, as if tasting it. He kept his eyes open, and I forced myself to do the same, although my initial instinct was to close them and surrender to his amorous intentions.

He undid the buttons on my light summer jacket and helped me slip my arms out of it as I held them up to ease his task. I could feel the fleeting touch of his breath caress my face, and tried to kiss him but he took a step back.

'No,' he said. 'First I want to undress you.'

I nodded obediently. He had visibly been rehearsing this moment, established its ritual. And I was willing to oblige. My mind flitted back to thoughts of the club and the conversation I'd had with Richard. But this was different. Even when he told me what to do. We were equals, indulging in mutual pleasure that sometimes varied in its form.

'Slowly,' he added and slipped down to his knees and began unlacing the knee-high boots I was wearing, giving me a full-on view of the top of his head as he concentrated on the task.

From my elevated perspective, his wild, untamed curls were a thick symphony of black and white threads spreading towards every direction of the compass. I felt, all of a sudden, like burying my hands in that luxurious garden of hair, but held back for fear of interrupting the solemn way in which he wished to unveil me, one lace, one garment, one lingering whisper at a time.

Below the window of our hotel room, I could hear the muted sounds of passers-by in the street, words I could not understand in a foreign language, like the murmur of a distant chorus to my agonisingly slow unveiling by this tender man I still knew so little about.

What did he see in me? I wondered. I knew I was

imperfect, a work still in progress, with so much of my life ahead of me, so many adventures to come. But I also knew that moments like these would be ones to cherish for ever, to hold onto in the fathomless storage vaults of my fevered brain cells and that they would affect me strongly until the day I died. Why was it that with Leonard I had these terrible intimations of mortality, a greater picture? Was it because of the gap in our ages, the fact that one day it was inevitable he would die and I would still be young?

Damn, I was taking this all too seriously.

The thin socks I wore under the boots came off, and then my tights and finally my knickers, leaving me fully exposed and, with a deep sigh, Leonard buried his face into my midriff, catching the intimate scent of me, releasing the warmth. It was both a solemn and an obscene moment and it was then I realised that he also was recording every gesture and visual of our ritual and storing it away. For future memories? For later gratification?

I tried to put myself inside his mind. Small Lily, with her modest breasts, her pale complexion, her jet black hair falling to her waist, her brazen, gaudy tattoo across her shoulder blade, her unkempt bush of curls, the tear beneath her eye. This was a man who had known women, many more than I had known men. What attracted him to me? Maybe it was the fact we were both lonely, even in the midst of crowds. They say opposites attract, but I sensed right then this was just another cliché, and what drew us to each other were the similarities, the emptiness inside, the silences, the desperate will to share our flaws, that's what made us special.

I was standing there with my legs apart, now just wearing

the thin cotton bodice that ended up halfway down my belly and Leonard was at my feet, like a supplicant at the altar, gazing soulfully at my pussy.

With one hand he gently parted my lips, opening me up, now ceremonially unveiling my pinkness and he dipped his tongue deep inside. I shuddered, as he began to orchestrate the steady rise of my desire, every single touch, every lick, a calculated assault on my defences, teasing my nerve endings, reaching deep into my soul and releasing all of the inhibitions that I had built, tearing them down. And then his tongue flicked upwards and wrapped itself around my clit, generating further waves of pleasure shooting across every inch of my body. I felt light on my feet. Leonard's other hand extended behind me and firmly cupped my arse cheeks, steadying me, holding me tight against him.

I closed my eyes and abandoned myself to the flow.

My cunt was on fire. My mind was captive in a circle of flames.

It was an exquisite form of torture, as every sinew in my body called out silently for some form of release.

I was certain that Leonard was aware of the turmoil he had created and the way he clouded my mind and controlled my body, but he affected to be unaware. I knew I was wetter than wet and wondered what I tasted like to him.

His tongue kept on teasing me, his hot lips wedded to my opening, caressing, playing, lingering with mischief as I imperceptibly widened the angle between my legs to encourage his steady advances.

His teeth.

Nipping my lips with care and attention, pulling, delicately biting into their fragile flesh, then delving deeper, higher, seizing hold of the inflamed bud of my clit, licking it first and then nibbling carefully at its increasing hardness until finally I couldn't bear the tension, the need, the razor-sharp anguish that veered between pain and transcendence and I breathlessly called out his name.

'Fuck me, Leonard. Now!'

He drew back, got up from his knees and I pushed him backwards onto the bed and began undoing his trousers, a pull on the zip, then unthreading the crisp leather belt, eager to pull out his dark cock, to satisfy my own voracious appetite, to feel the pulse of his life beat inside of my mouth as he expanded to fill me and quickly move him down to my pussy which was now screaming out for him, like a beggar in desperate search of sustenance, to make me whole again.

But Leonard was never one to rush, and even as we fucked and thrashed, there was always the deliberateness, the patience, the slow and rehearsed way he savoured our moments together, never rushing, thrusting metronomically, slow, slow, quick, quick, slow, and the juggling with the successive variations in speed and intensity as he continued his clever manipulation of my aroused senses, all the time observing the steady progress of my orgasm with his eyes wide open and that curious half-glimpse of a smile. I knew the way he looked at me when we fucked wasn't self-satisfaction, but just a thorough appreciation of the way we melded and responded to each other in the throes of passion.

He was so unlike others I had been with.

And even after we had finished making love and lay sprawled across the undone bed in a tangle of sheets and limbs, still catching our breath and allowing the waves of lust to steadily ebb away, he was by no means in a hurry to cover himself up as others would have done, unashamed at the way his body was on display to my observant eyes, and almost proud of its random imperfections, a fold here, a crease, a thin scar across his shoulder.

I loved Leonard's body. Though I wondered if maybe what he saw in me was youth. If I was not Lily to him, but simply a source of rejuvenation.

'You're wrong,' he said quietly to me one morning when I mentioned this. It was in Barcelona, and it would be the last time I joined him in Europe. 'It's not a case of me wanting to leech on your youth. Far from it. It's just that being with you makes me feel alive.'

I delighted in those lazy mornings in foreign cities and often nameless hotels, as we awakened and he allowed me to contemplate the spectacle of his body as we caressed intimately on the bed. His penis fascinated me, whether at rest or in full flight while we fucked, and he immodestly accepted my stringent gaze as I memorised its every fold and ridge and shade, and the way it jutted away from his body and lay against his thigh, almost like a creature with its own volition.

Leonard would joke with me that I was acting like a doctor as I examined him.

Or maybe I was trying to read between the lines of his body the life he had lived before me. All in all, it was a strange feeling.

Similarly, he confessed how much he loved watching me and how my nakedness pleased him. I could see it in his eyes anyway, the way he stared at me when I moved around the room dressing and undressing under his gaze.

In Amsterdam, our hotel-room window looked out on the Singel Canal, cobbled pathways buffeted by the thin rain and a parade of bikes parked by the edge of the water and trees fluttering in the breeze, and Leonard fed me raspberries and chocolate in bed as if I was an indolent Roman vestal spread across the bed and there for the spoiling, and later for the taking as he then unceremoniously stuffed my pussy with the final square of dark chocolate and waited until it melted before sucking the ensuing paste out of me with relish. Laughing my head off, I soon ended up kissing him and tasting myself alongside the strong, fragrant flavour of the cocoa as our lips met.

It was also in Amsterdam that he slipped a flower in my ebony black hair to celebrate spring and asked me to wear a flowing white skirt that floated all the way down to my feet and my Doc Martens boots and begged me to wander outside, arm in arm with him, pantiless.

'Do it for me,' he asked. And I indulged him.

In a small jeweller's shop close to the Dam, he bought me a fine gold ankle chain which he locked in place with a miniature key which he then put swiftly into his pocket. Had I been collared? I immediately wondered, thinking suddenly of Liana. No, it wasn't like that between us. But then what did he mean by it?

'So you always think of me,' he said. 'When I'm gone. After Leonard . . . It almost sounds like an existential play, doesn't it?'

I began to panic and to protest, but Leonard was firm.

'This can't last, Lily. I'm not a fool. It mustn't last.

Anyway, it's inevitable, you will tire of me, meet someone younger, who will prove less boring and with whom you won't have qualms about being seen in public with. You'll see.'

I opened my mouth to disagree, but Leonard put his fingers to my lips and wouldn't allow me to say another word.

'It's not up for negotiation,' he concluded, a cloud of sadness now enveloping us. 'Don't kid yourself. It's how it will be, how it should have been.'

His fingers moved away from my mouth and he kissed me on my forehead.

Two weeks later we were in Barcelona. He was travelling back from the Middle East. The lobby of the hotel we stayed at was all straight lines and mirrors and as we checked in together, having arranged to meet up at the airport and taken a cab into the city together, the uniformed staff on duty at reception gave us a knowing look. We were dressed in entirely different styles, Leonard in his usual dark-blue business suit and me in a frayed leather jacket, leggings and knee-high boots. Most of the guys on duty were probably only a few years older than me and I thought I could read disapproval in their eyes. Perhaps Leonard sensed it too. He could have tried to come up with a throwaway excuse, maybe pretend I was his daughter, but as he signed us in, he insolently confirmed that indeed we were together and would have no need of two separate beds when one of the clerks suggested it. For my part, I was blushing all the way down to my roots, but I was beginning to understand the perils of our situation. Until then, my feelings for Leonard had obscured the reality we were wading through as we blithely pretended to be a couple.

A couple who had little in common. Neither friends nor even musical tastes.

Walking down the Ramblas from Plaza Catalunya, I was overcome by fear and the prospect of happiness receding and, in the throes of panic, I told Leonard I loved him and that nothing else mattered. We made a detour by the large covered food market to gaze in wonder at the colours of the fruit, and the exotic spreads of fish and meat scattered across the dripping marble counters.

Later, on our way back to the hotel on Condal, we passed the caged birds on display in the pet market and I felt like crying. It was irrational, but it was like a blanket of fog falling on us and cutting us off from the city as we stepped along silently, both prey to moody thoughts and pre-monitions of darker tomorrows.

That night we fucked like savages, almost ripping each other apart, rage over-spilling as our bodies made contact like prize fighters in a ring. I scratched him. He bruised me. And neither of us felt it necessary to apologise. Words had become useless.

The following day we had the morning free before our late-afternoon return flight to London and so we visited Parc Güell. The endless flight of stairs leading to its gates saw us both breathless. But the view from the top was unforgettable, and with the city unfolding below us in the sun we held hands in public for the first time and sat on a stone bench and kissed as a posse of bespectacled nuns guided a group of young children past our embrace and looked at us both sideways and disapprovingly.

*

After those too-brief few days in Barcelona, a crazy collage of passion and self-doubt and moments of awkwardness and silences that lasted too long and too many words spoken or left unspoken, we parted for our longest absence so far. Nearly a whole month.

I woke the morning after my flight back to London and rolled onto my belly, stretching for my phone as I always did to check my messages. Leonard usually replied after midnight, and I always left his last message until first thing in the morning. It had become a habit, and then a superstition. If I woke in the middle of the night knowing that a missive from Leonard was likely waiting for me, I left it until dawn broke and my alarm went off, fearing that the absence of his name in my inbox would darken my day.

That morning, my mailbox was indeed empty, bereft. Along with my heart. He'd been doing a lot of travelling lately. Maybe he was simply stuck at another airport somewhere out of range. Or perhaps he had mistakenly left his charger in his checked luggage.

But I knew that Leonard was a creature of habit, and he hadn't emailed me for a reason.

I resolved not to send him anything until he first communicated with me. That was the way that we did things. And I would not go clutching after him like some lovesick school girl.

Instead, I tried to distract myself by resurrecting my old life and routine. Lily before Leonard.

I began by contacting my friends, but Liana's number just dialled out over and over, and a week went by and she still hadn't returned my calls. My worry for her, combined with my fear that I had lost Leonard for good, turned into a hard knot within my stomach that threatened to overtake the rest of my life, so that I was gloomy at the music shop and pensive at the fetish club, even though both my employers were pleased to have me available for more shifts.

Neither Jonno nor She enquired after my state of mind, probably presuming that the reason for my suddenly frequent appearances was the same as the reason for my initial disappearance. Man trouble.

A couple of weeks after I got back, I called Neil, just for the comfort of an old friend's voice.

'Lily!' he cried into the phone, after barely two rings.

He sounded jauntier than I had heard him before.

'You're in a good mood,' I said.

'I got the job!' he shouted enthusiastically. 'As an accounts manager.'

I vaguely remembered that he had interviewed at the PR firm where he was interning and struggled to bring the details to mind. A pang of guilt sharply assaulted my mind. I had been so wrapped up in myself I hadn't been paying any attention to the lives of my friends.

'Wow, good for you,' I said. Neil was the first person among my peer group who had actually found what we deemed to be a proper job since graduating. The rest of us were just floating around, working in summer jobs that had somehow carried on whilst wondering what to do next.

'So what will you be doing?' I asked, forcing cheerfulness. Maybe speaking to him was just the ticket to distract me from my troubles.

'Account management. In the planning department,' he explained. 'It's not a senior position, but I'll be working on some campaigns and stuff. Next step the company car maybe . . . I'm on my way, Lily. Isn't it great?'

'Oh,' I replied. Somehow I had presumed that he'd end up in accounts. Checking off invoices or running payroll.

'How are you doing, honey? It's been ages.'

'I'm good,' I lied. 'We should hang out again. You doing anything tonight?'

'Can't tonight. Work thing. And tomorrow. Next week?'

'Sure,' I said, and with a loose promise to see each other soon, we hung up the call.

I was pleased for him, but our conversation had left me feeling even lonelier. The old Neil that I knew seemed to have been replaced by a newer version that I was out of touch with and unused to.

Where had I gone wrong? I wished for the old days, for the ease of university life and the structure of exams to study for and lectures to go to and the burden of real life in the outside world always looming, but in some faraway future that would surely take forever to actually knock on our doors.

Even an Alice Cooper record on repeat failed to shake the blues out of me.

With a sinking heart, I refreshed the button on my browser again and checked my inbox.

Still nothing.

Leonard had gone silent. And I felt, with all the inflexible certainty of youth, that an important page of my life had been turned.

4

Eighty Days of Dagur

For weeks I wandered aimless through a thick fog of guilt, still wondering whether I had done the right thing. Or ruminating on the possibility that it had not been my decision alone and that, somehow, Leonard had talked me into it.

It was as if during the eighty days that our relationship had lasted – and I knew this was the exact number of days every time I looked up in the morning at the wall calendar taped above my small writing desk in my bedroom – he had gradually been sowing the seeds of doubt, feeding me one crumb at a time the manifold reasons we could not last. Until the day the cup overflowed and we were obliged to break things off. The more I reflected on it, the more it seemed that way.

So, in a sense, he had planned our coming apart from the moment we had first met, in order to spare me future pain. It only made me love him even more as all this became clear.

Time and time again, I felt like dialling his number, but never did because of the unexplainable fear that he might be doing so at the very same moment and that our calls would cross each other, cancel themselves out. My whole body rebelled against this necessary separation.

After work at the instrument store, I often walked further

afield and silently haunted the bars we had frequented in the hope of catching a glimpse of him there, with a terrible anguish in the pit of my stomach that I would eventually come across him, in quiet conversation with another girl of my age, which would have marked him out as a proper bastard and manipulator. Or maybe I was hoping I would, because such a discovery would then mute the pain that was eating away at me. In any case, there was no sign of him. Had I known where he lived, I would have willingly, and with no fear of embarrassment, camped outside his Blackheath residence until I caught sight of him. I was in turmoil, emotions fighting emotions, feeling hollow and lost.

With bad timing, there was no work at the fetish club for a few weeks while the premises were being redecorated, so all my evenings were free and business at the store was slow, so I had all the time in the world to spend with my contaminated thoughts, allowing every tiny epiphany I had shared with Leonard to simmer away: the way his fingers had drawn a lingering trail of saliva across the flowers of my tattoo as he solemnly traced them that time he had undressed me in a hotel room that looked over the Heathrow approach road and we then fucked to the rhythm of the passing cars roaring by on the motorway right below; the tremulous, warm ripple of his breath as his mouth approached my nipples; the pressure of his fingers holding my arse cheeks apart as he rode me from behind; the worlds of silence that often peppered our conversations. It was like a dam of memories bursting, and what had once been intensely pleasurable was now metamorphosing, one steady step at a time, into pain when I evoked it.

I finally got through to Liana. She was still living in

Brighton, but was now no longer involved with Nick and she hinted that she had moved on to another relationship, although she was somewhat secretive about it. She had found a job working for a local firm of lawyers and, having discovered, as I had, that English Lit degrees were thirteen to the dozen and no great help in finding employment, was contemplating some additional legal studies. I really felt I needed to talk to someone, and Liana had once been my closest confidante. We agreed I'd take the train down to the coast the next Saturday morning.

There was a steady drizzle colouring the day grey as I stepped off the train and left the station. Liana had moved into a bedsit in Hove and had explained how to reach it by public transport, but I elected to take a cab. The travelling with Leonard had given me a taste for creature comforts.

Seeing Liana was a shock. Her once lustrous brown hair was bedraggled, as if she had not combed it for days, and her features sunk. We shared a similar pale complexion, but today she looked like a Halloween rag doll.

'Going through a bit of a bad patch,' she said, noting the look of dismay on my face.

'Damn,' I said. 'And there I was hoping coming to see you would bring me some cheer.'

'Join the happy-go-lucky club,' she remarked as we walked upstairs to the kitchen for an injection of caffeine.

'A man?' she enquired.

'How did you guess?'

'You know me, I'm psychic.' She attempted a feeble smile.

My heart sank. Exchanging bad-luck stories was not my idea of a comforting weekend with a mate.

As it turned out, our stories were quite different. I was no longer with Leonard, while Liana was still navigating the ragged edges of an on–off relationship with a man who, it appeared, was also older than her. I was too vulnerable to admit to her how much older than me Leonard had been, and she was similarly non-specific, although I guessed her guy was in his early forties. That was about the only thing in common with our stories.

If I had thought my own tale of woe was special, I was unprepared for hers.

'He's a dom,' Liana said.

I knew it.

'A good one?' I asked.

'In some ways.'

She explained to me a little of the dynamic that she shared with her dom, whose name she refused even to mention. Perhaps she thought that I would report him to the police. As she told me more, I thought that I probably would report him to the police, but I'd rather skin him alive myself first.

'I thought Nick was a dom too?' I said, puzzled. 'Your dom.'

Liana sighed.

'That was the problem. I thought so too. But I didn't really understand myself either then, it was all so new . . .'

'So Nick's not a dom? What about all the rope and stuff?'

I remembered that crazy night when we had ourselves tattooed and her encounter with Nick and what I had been a witness to. How she had been tied up and used so roughly and the ecstatic look that had spread across her features as Nick had enjoyed her response, and how I had briefly realised this was the real Liana I was seeing in action, a stranger whose deep-seated desires and motivations were so different to mine.

Although we still remained in touch, our visits and then our phone calls had gradually became fewer and fewer and I realised that we had slowly begun to drift apart after that night. Even if my education in the avenues of sexual tastes had broadened since then, we'd never quite managed to patch things up between us – perhaps because we had never talked about it.

It was complicated, but then as I'd grown and had a serious relationship of my own, I'd come to realise that few things are straightforward.

'Yes,' Liana continued to explain. 'Nick liked rope. He's an artist. He thought rope was pretty. But that was about it.'

'It looked pretty intense to me.'

'Yeah, but you were high, Lily, and had never seen anything like it before. It really wasn't that big a deal.'

'So you're into other stuff besides rope? And Nick isn't? That's why you broke up?'

'I guess that's the short version.'

'We have all day. Why don't you tell me the long version?' I slipped out of my chair and flicked the kettle on again.

'Nick didn't enjoy hurting me. Or even just making me uncomfortable. He's really quite a softie.'

'You wanted him to hurt you?'

'I am submissive after all. You may as well get used to it.'

'Sorry,' I said. 'I'm not judging you. Just trying to understand.'

'I'm not really into pain per se. But I am into power play. The D/s dynamic.'

I nodded, encouraging her to continue. I'd seen people playing at the clubs, but hadn't actually got to know any couples intimately so wasn't totally familiar with the mind-set behind the sex.

'It's in the trust bond between two people, you see. The spanking, flogging, all of that is just how it manifests itself physically . . . but all kinds of other things can be involved. Throat fucking, fire play, hot wax, needles, electro torture . . .'

A wicked smile crossed her face when she saw me wince. The old Liana that I knew was hidden away in there some-where beneath her glum exterior. She still loved to shock.

'That all sounds painful.'

'Nah. Not when you do it right. A good dom warms their sub up first, so by the time you get to the harder stuff it's not bad, or painful, unless you want it to be. You should give it a go sometime. You do work in a fetish club after all.'

'It's not really my thing.'

'You never know until you try. And some things aren't what they seem. Fire, for instance, feels like a warm hug. And wax is quite cosy, so long as you use the right candles so it's not too hot.'

'Hmm.' I wasn't convinced. 'But what do you get out of it? Just the sensation alone?'

'Not exactly. There's something almost spiritual in it. When you find the right person, and you really let yourself go, it brings on a sort of trance. And it's so freeing, to leave all the responsibility in someone else's hands, to be allowed to be so totally uninhibited like that. To enjoy things that people say shouldn't be enjoyed. To play with danger. You must have seen it at the club. Don't you ever let yourself go?'

I shook my head.

'Then you haven't lived. When he pulls my hair, spits in my face, it takes every thought out of my head. Every worry. It's like I've been peeled back and he has my soul sitting in his palm, like a butterfly. As if he's really seeing me. Not all the bullshit that I've built up over the years. The fake confidence and the bravado. It's like he's seeing the real me. And then the aftercare, when I'm totally broken down and he pulls me into his lap and cradles me like a child . . .'

The hot tea burned my throat when I took too big a gulp. Liana was waxing lyrical and now had a slightly dreamy expression on her face. As much as I was glad that she felt able to confide in me about all of this, it creeped me out a little. Kinky people could be very intense sometimes.

'What's gone wrong, then? If it's so great, why the long face?'

'It worked with Nick and I for a while. I think I was born submissive. I've always been this way. And he was the first to bring it out of me. Initially it was great, and I loved it. But after a while I started to want more. Things that he couldn't give me.'

'He didn't like the harder stuff? Couldn't he just do it anyway, for you?'

'We tried that for a while. Didn't really work though. There's a difference between someone using you because they really want to and because they know you want them to. It switched everything around. I felt like I was topping from the bottom all the time. And I knew he wasn't really into it. So then we agreed that I could play with other people. Just to get that release.'

'And he got jealous?'

She stirred another teaspoon of sugar into her tea. I'd watched her dissolve five spoonfuls in her mug so far, and she was mainlining gingernuts one after the other. Liana was on a sugar binge.

'Not exactly. It's not uncommon to have more than one play partner. I'd go to the clubs and whatnot regularly, and be flogged by the Dungeon Master, or people we knew who were into it. It was a release for them, and for me. Nick wasn't jealous. But as I stopped seeing him as my dom, my feelings changed. Then we started to bicker. And then I met someone else.'

'The guy that you're seeing now?'

'No, one of his friends, actually. We only saw each other a few times. But just clicked instantly. Have you ever had that with someone? That immediate connection? Like love at first sight, but not love.'

I thought of Leonard and the way it had felt as though we'd known each other for ever as soon as we met. The way that he'd known exactly how to touch me, without any instruction.

'Yes. I know what you mean.'

'His name was Alice.'

'Funny name for a guy,' I said.

'Yeah,' she laughed. 'That was how we got talking, actually, because he reminded me of you. I know how you still love Alice Cooper, even if you tried to pretend not to . . . He spelled it differently. American. A-L-Y-S-S. But

I called him Alice. We had some amazing sessions together. So intense. Perfect, you know . . .'

She was getting that far-away look in her eyes again. Sub-space, I had heard it called in the club, when people went into a trance while they were really being flogged or tied up. Liana hadn't had a tendency to space out before. I wondered if unleashing her submissive side had made her more dreamy in general.

'But Alyss moved away,' she continued. 'Back to America. He was only in the UK for a few weeks on holiday. These sorts of relationships get so intense so quickly. Because of the level of trust and the communication involved. It's like you have a bond that no one else can really understand or appreciate. Like you're alone together on your own island.'

Again I thought of Leonard, and how the privacy that we both imposed on our relationship because of the age difference made us closer. Because we were sharing a secret.

'Makes sense.' I nodded.

'Alyss encouraged me to move on. Find a new play partner. And I did. And I was trying to get over him so I jumped into it a bit quicker than I should have. Played hard. Pretended I could handle things that I couldn't really. I wanted to be the tough girl, the strong one. To be invincible. So I couldn't be hurt again. And I met the guy I'm seeing now who likes to play hard but sometimes too hard. And he won't stop. And now he wants to control everything, and I don't like it, but I can't seem to get out of it, and I don't know what to do.'

'Oh, honey,' I said, jumping up and putting my arm around her as tears began to leak down her face and she briskly brushed them away. 'You've always been strong. You don't need to prove yourself to anyone.'

She buried her head in my shoulder and sobbed.

In contrast, the story of my encounter with Leonard and its commonplace outcome paled. I had meant to tell Liana everything, but in the end I just said I'd broken up with someone. My misery seemed pathetic next to hers.

We spent most of the weekend drowning our sorrows, hopping between familiar haunts from our student years and window shopping, sneering at clothes we could neither afford nor would ever wear, and the women crowding the Brighton streets who could. Not that our superiority over them was any consolation to our rumpled distress.

On a drunken impulse, shortly before I was due to catch my mid-afternoon train back to London on Sunday, we agreed to cut each other's hair. I trimmed Liana's to page-boy effect and she savaged mine until I had a boyish bob that barely reached my shoulders. Gazing at myself in the spotty mirror of her bathroom afterwards I barely recognised myself.

'Not too short?' Liana asked me.

'It'll grow back,' I said. 'You?'

She brushed her hands through her scalp.

'Either he'll kill me or he'll find a way to punish me for doing it,' she said. 'He always says he loves my long hair and I'm not to touch it.'

Her face had gone deathly pale.

'You should have told me.'

'It's OK,' she said, shrugging. 'He'll get over it.'

*

Back in London, Neil was similarly unsympathetic to my plight.

'It's a bit creepy, Lily,' he replied, when I told him I had been involved with an older man.

'Why?'

'I don't know. It just is.'

'Try and explain why to me?' I insisted.

'He's . . . old enough to be your dad. Don't you ever look down while you're . . . you know . . . and think . . . ?' He was carefully trying to choose the right words to express his indignation.

'No, I don't think anything of the sort. Leonard is not my father. He's just a man who happens to be a bit older than me.'

'A bit older!' he exclaimed. 'He's more than twice your age. And . . . Leonard, that's an old man's name.'

I laughed out loud, confronted by Neil's prejudices.

'You just don't understand. If the attraction is mutual, age is neither here nor there.'

'But . . .' he spluttered.

'Anyway, it's over now and I can see you're clearly not willing to provide me with a shoulder to cry on.' I slipped off the barstool.

'Lily!'

'Fuck you, Neil.'

He'd changed. He wasn't the Neil that I knew any longer, so it was easy to walk away. Nowadays he spent more and more time at work and each time we saw each other he looked more like an advertising executive and less like my old friend. Tonight he'd arrived in a sharp new suit with his tie half loosened and I'd briefly imagined tearing it off him and tethering him to the chair with it to show him that he wasn't all that just because he worked in the West End.

Neil had been no help. It was just me and my memories, good old Lily and her sadness. I knew I would manage. Time would pass by and the image of Leonard's face would become more and more unclear as his features faded. Hopefully the feelings he had evoked would also grow fainter and life would continue. Just a blip, I thought. I was determined to make a go of things, and if Leonard had encouraged me to see others, like Liana's man Alyss had, to extravagantly sample life and its box of delights and what it had to offer while I was still young, I would. Not that I felt young; right now I felt like a million years old.

I'd seen a Holy Criminals gig advertised in *Time Out* and, on a whim, tried to get a ticket but it was sold out. When I mentioned it to Jonno at the shop, he told me he knew someone in their management's office and volunteered to give her a call to try to get me on the guest list, although he joked that I'd never expressed any interest in the band until their drummer had come into the shop with his Icelandic buddies.

I arrived at the venue with my warpaint on – dark-purple lipstick, thick black eyeliner and short hair gelled – and wearing leather from top to bottom alongside my Doc Marten boots that Leonard had never liked. My name was on the list at the door as promised, and I was even allowed a plus one, although I had come alone. Jonno was not a fan of the controversial Viggo Franck and his band either.

I was even given an all-access badge, which allowed me to visit backstage.

I noticed Viggo immediately, all wild hair and tight

trousers. He was in a corner, surrounded by women lapping up every one of his dubious witticisms. I moved to the other end of the Green Room, where the drinks were generously laid out on a long table, with fruit, meats and cheese in abundance. I was clumsily balancing my plastic glass of red wine and a plate in which I had piled up crisps, nuts and an egg-and-cress sandwich, when someone brushed against me. I turned round.

'I like your hair short.'

'I didn't think you'd recognise me.'

'I never forget a teardrop,' Dagur said.

I was allowed to watch the whole gig from the stage wings with some of the other hangers-on. The set was powerful and theatrical, even if the music still wasn't on my precise wavelength.

Afterwards, Viggo retreated to his dressing room with a couple of tall short-skirted blondes in his wake. Dagur, still dripping with sweat, shirtless and exhibiting a splendid tattoo of a horse carved dark and deep into the taut skin of his back, approached me and winked. There was nothing sleazy about the way he did so, it was just a complicit way of smiling at me.

Nevertheless, I moved closer to him and, with slow deliberation, ran my hand over his brow. He kissed me. His lips were firm and demanding and when I leaned into his arms, he responded by placing just one hand lightly on each of my hips and holding me still so that he could continue to concentrate on pleasuring my mouth. He didn't try to grope me or take advantage of his position too soon, and his way of keeping me simultaneously aroused but also at arm's length attracted me like a moth to a flame.

*

The next morning I woke up in his bed. He had turned the heating on full and when I blinked my eyes open to welcome in the day, he pulled the covers off the bed leaving me naked and exposed to his wandering eye as I stretched lazily across his futon mattress. His apartment was practically bereft of furniture and the enormous low bed with its crisp white sheets and black walnut frame dominated the whole room.

'That's better,' he said, when he'd removed the sheet that I had pulled around my shoulders in the night. 'I want to see you.'

He had already brought me a cup of coffee on a tray and a plate of sliced fruit with a spoonful of honey dribbled over the top. Next to the cup of black coffee was a little jug of cream.

I could definitely get used to this. Guys my own age weren't likely to bring me breakfast in bed. They were just too worried that the slightest kindness would make a girl think that a rock on the finger and a white picket fence was just around the corner.

Older men weren't like that. They were nicer to women. Took it all a bit less seriously. I liked that.

Dagur was in his early thirties, I guessed. Maybe a little younger. He looked reasonably ordinary with his clothes on, though I supposed that might have been because he was always in the shadow of the charismatic Viggo Franck. But naked he was beautiful. Almost entirely hairless, muscled, and with that tattoo that rippled when he walked. I was getting wet again just thinking about it.

'What are you doing tomorrow, babe?' he asked. He was

sitting down on the edge of the bed with a laptop balanced on his knees. Every now and again he would reach over and idly stroke my ankle until I wriggled all the way down the bed so that my legs were hanging off the edge behind him and his hand was resting just below my pussy instead of on my calf.

He looked up and grinned.

'Oh, like that, is it?' he said, moving on top of me and slipping a finger inside me, casually moving it around until I began to moan and grind against him. The sheet scratched against my back as I slid further down the bed to push his hand in deeper. Last night had been good, but it wasn't enough. I wanted Dagur to fill me again, fill all the parts of me that Leonard had left empty.

His laptop clattered onto the floor.

'More,' I said, 'I want to feel more . . .'

My feet found purchase on the floor and I pressed down to gain traction as I wrapped my hand around his wrist and pulled, guiding him.

'You're too tight for that, babe.'

'Try harder,' I insisted, pushing his fist inside further. 'Fill me.'

Dagur's eyes flashed and in an instant he had me pushed hard against the bed with my legs over my head and his fingers slipping in and out of my cunt. He curved his hand around to ease its passage and I winced as his fourth finger slipped in and stopped abruptly at the knuckle.

'Relax,' he said. He leaned forward and stroked my cheek with extraordinary gentleness. Then he reached under the bed and pulled out a bottle of lube. It smelled strongly of cinnamon and was cold and wet against my skin.

'Why don't you try?' he said.

'Me?'

'Yes. I want to watch you fist yourself.'

He took my palm and pressed it against his own, coiling his fingers over mine to indicate how much smaller my hands were than his.

'I'm not sure that I can . . .' My mind tried to conjure up the appropriate image, but it just didn't seem possible.

'I'll help you,' he said, then slid his hand out of me slowly and took hold of my wrist to guide me in. His fingers were damp and sticky.

'Have you tried DP?' he asked, as I slipped one finger, then two, then three, then four inside.

'DP?'

'Double penetration. Two men at once.'

'No,' I breathed, almost overcome with the thought that my entire hand was millimeters away from sliding into my vagina. My surprise had almost overtaken my arousal and for a moment I was distracted, imagining the physical possibilities.

I'd never had a threesome. But I knew that Liana had – her first boyfriend had wanted to experiment with his bi side and had invited a friend along one night, with her permission. Liana had told me how after she'd watched the two men suck each other off, they had agree to both fill her. She had straddled one and the other had kneeled behind and entered her anally. When she related the story I had imagined how she must have felt, like a queen, riding two of them at once.

She'd laughed when I told her that. And now I understood why. Most likely such a situation for her would have meant a double loss of power. I saw it the other way around. Having two men looking at me longingly, worshipping my body, touching me the way that I asked them to. After she'd left, I'd disappeared into my bedroom and fantasised about it with the door firmly closed and my hand between my legs.

'But you like the idea, don't you?' Dagur asked again. 'I can see how wet you're getting. Does it turn you on, thinking of two men's cocks inside you?'

He had bent his head to whisper directly into my ear. His Icelandic lilt lent a rough, hard note to his words that made me catch my breath, and forget all the other distractions rushing around in my mind as my body throbbed with a sudden rush of desire. If I hadn't already been lying down, then Dagur's voice would have made me weak-kneed and light-headed. Leonard had been the first man to make me realise how much I enjoyed the sound of dirty words spoken aloud, but he wasn't the last.

'Oh God, yes,' I replied. Every nerve ending beneath my skin strained for release.

'Well, I can't give you that now, but this will be close enough.'

His hand locked around the base of my thumb and wrist and he pushed gently until I felt myself open and I slid all the way inside.

'Wow,' I said, in wonder. The inside of my opening was not as I had expected. I was tight at my entrance, but inside, totally accommodating. I stretched and twisted my hand, exploring. For a moment I closed my eyes, ignored Dagur entirely and sank into the sensation of my fist pressing inside me, filling me to the brim.

When I opened my eyes, Dagur was staring at me with shining eyes.

He made a growling sound in the back of his throat and flipped me over onto my side, pressing my knees up against my chest and holding my wrist firmly in place.

'More,' I moaned. Even my fist wasn't enough. Would never be enough to fill all the blank spaces inside me that Leonard had left behind.

I squirmed as Dagur tugged at my breasts, grabbing and twisting each of them in his palm, kneading my flesh roughly as though he had lost control of his own senses. His teeth were sharp against my skin as he brought his mouth to my bare neck and nipped.

'I'll give you more,' he croaked. His voice was ragged. His finger pressed against my arsehole until that opening too gave way for him, inviting him in.

'Oh God, you're so tight,' he whispered as he began to move his finger in circles and then added another.

'More,' I instructed, and Dagur let go of my wrist and fumbled under the bed again to find a condom. His hands were shaking almost as much as my body. Then he re-applied the pressure to my fist, pushing my hand deep inside again as his cock found its home deep within my arse and I cried aloud with the sheer overwhelming joy of it all.

The pressure of his cock brushed against my knuckles, separated from the bare skin of my hand only by the wall that stood between us, the separate entrances of my cunt and arse.

'Can you feel that?' I asked him as I slid my hand up and down to heighten the sensation.

'Fuck yes, I can feel that,' he said as he curled me up into a ball and took hold of a knot of my short hair and began to thrust faster and faster until his body tensed and tightened and I knew that beneath the thin skin of the condom his semen was flooding inside my anus.

His chest was slick with sweat when he collapsed against me and held me against him without bothering to remove his cock. He kissed me gently on the lips and ran his fingertips up and down my flank.

'Ow,' I said, as I pulled my hand free. My wrist ached from having been trapped in an uncomfortable position. Dagur took my hand and brought it to his lips and kissed the back as if he were greeting a princess.

'That was impressive,' he said. 'But you didn't come?'

'No,' I replied. I'd never seen the point in lying about it.

'It was strange. I could feel my muscles tensing as if I was going to come, but it was as if I was so full that I had no room to climax. Like I could tighten but not let go.'

'Interesting,' he mused. Then propped himself up on his elbow and shifted his weight so that he was leaning over me with his body pressed hard against mine. 'I'll fix that. If you just give me a minute or two to recover.'

He was true to his word, and we spent the rest of the day in bed together, a tangled heap of limbs in damp sheets.

It was early evening when I finally returned to my room in Dalston and crawled into bed to relax at last.

Any solace that I found in the pleasant ache of my body and the peace of my own company was lost in my worry for Liana that kept resurfacing no matter how many times I reminded myself that, like me, she was now a grown woman and had always been able to take care of herself, even if her behaviour didn't always tally with my own.

Finally, I resolved to phone her and check on her state of mind and, if necessary, attempt to cheer her up with news of my latest escapade.

'Oh, Lily,' she giggled, 'you slut!'

'How dare you, young lady!' I responded in the same tone, pretending I wasn't in on the joke.

'In the nicest possible way, of course,' she added. 'One minute you're all shacked up with your older lover boy and the next minute you're gallivanting off with a rock idol.' She sighed. 'I'm jealous. Though I would have gone for the lead singer or the guitarist. Drummers are definitely on the lowest rung of the groupie ladder, I reckon. Typical of you to start at the bottom. Do you plan to work your way up?'

'Talk about the pot calling the kettle black,' I pointed out. 'I'm not the one who likes being tied up and spanked.'

'Takes a slut to recognise a slut,' Liana concluded the banter. 'So, tell me everything. I want all the juicy details about your rock star. Was he wild?'

'Not that wild,' I reassured her. 'Though he did introduce me to a few new tricks.'

'He sounds like a beast,' she continued.

'Actually, he's rather nice, although I wouldn't call him the boyfriend type.'

'Or the white picket fence type, I guess?'

'Definitely not the marrying kind,' I confirmed.

'So, tell me about these new tricks. You never know, I might learn something.'

'I doubt that,' I laughed.

The weeks went by and Dagur and I continued to see

each other casually as his tour schedule and my work allowed. I quickly became inordinately fond of him during the time we spent together and enjoyed every single moment with him, both in and out of bed. He was fun to be with, an imaginative and energetic lover with a wicked sense of humour. In fact, a total contrast to Leonard whose melancholy inner life was never far from the surface, even when he was at his most expansive and joyous. When Dagur laughed, there was no holding back and the roar rising from his throat was anything but subtle, so full of life and un-censored. And when he fucked, he gave himself body and soul to the task, maybe a touch selfish but untiring and attentive to my responses and tremors, playing me like he did the drums with fire and precision, riding the rhythm, dictating the tempo, taking as much pleasure from his professional artistry as from the welter of physical sensations the lovemaking triggered inside his body.

He was not sentimental though.

Once he queried the ankle chain I still wore. The symbolic gift that meant that every time I looked down I was reminded of Leonard. 'Another guy?' he queried dis-tractedly. When I nodded, all he said was, 'I don't mind. I really don't, you know.'

Sex, for him, was a game, and one he enjoyed playing with gleeful abandon. As much as he enjoyed playing his drums, performing or eating. A basic need, which he indulged in wholeheartedly, quite free of reservations or afterthoughts.

Of course he liked me, but I had the sense that I could have been any girl. We were interchangeable, disposable, temporary harbour pleasures on an endless hedonistic road.

He would never hurt any of us, but neither would he make any promises of permanence or happy-ever-after to us. We were friends, fuck buddies. It didn't mean anything beyond the moment and the brief comfort of good sex between relative strangers.

'Sounds perfect,' Liana observed on the phone one evening. 'No hang-ups involved. Just enjoy it while it lasts,' she added.

'I don't know,' I said.

'So he's not ideal, but who is?' Liana queried.

Maybe, deep down, I didn't aspire to be a slut after all.

When Dagur was hard and loud and metronomic, pumping inside me like a Viking warrior unleashed, I yearned for Leonard's quiet gentleness, and when my horse-tattooed drummer had relaxed and wrapped his muscled arms around me in sensual embrace, I would be begging silently for one of those rare moments when Leonard's face loomed above me with his expression stuck in eternal contradiction, as if his soul was battling with his innate sensibility, and his thrusts accelerated, aligning themselves with the rise of my own pleasure, taking the pulse of my life and responding in perfect unison.

One night, after Dagur had arrived at my flat late after a gig in East London and we lay folded up against each other in my narrow double bed, my body still suffused with the inner glow of our earlier lovemaking, I woke suddenly in the early hours of the morning. It was still dark outside, and I must have been dreaming, my thoughts all in a jumble, people, events, things scattered randomly across the back screen of my sleeping mind. Dagur was lying on his side with his arm clamped affectionately over me, snoring lightly, a man sated and at peace with himself. I should have felt satisfied too, but when I looked up at him, I just began missing Leonard. Badly.

A case of the wrong man at the wrong time.

I wriggled out from under Dagur's grip, reached across to my bedside table, and picked up my phone. Calling up the contact list, I scrolled down to Leonard's number and my finger hovered over the 'call' button for an eternity, as my mind tripped the light fantastic between certainty and fear and a whole range of feelings in between.

Then it came to me that wherever he was – if he was still in Europe and not travelling somewhere else right now – it would be the middle of the night for him too and he didn't deserve to be wakened from his slumbers at such a bad hour when all I would say was likely to make little sense and not change anything about what held us apart and always would do.

I then thought I could send him a text message, but quickly came to the realisation that I would be quite in-capable of saying what I wanted to say properly, choosing the right words, conveying the precise feelings that were cutting me to shreds.

Maybe Leonard was, at the same moment, unable to sleep and also hesitating with his mobile phone in hand, sharing the same thoughts, juggling with the same doubts. I wanted to think so.

So I put the phone down on the floor by the bed, looked at Dagur's broad shoulders and listened to his breath. My hand slipped under the covers and reached down to his crotch. I cupped his balls in my hand, feeling their inert weight and quickly he stirred and rolled onto his back and his limp cock began to grow, just an inch away from my lingering fingers.

I slipped my head under the covers and took him into my mouth. In the darkness, surrounded by the sweet combined odours of our warmth, I sucked until he was fully erect and pulsing and then manoeuvred myself on top of him and deftly inserted his length inside me. His eyes were still closed, but I was sure he knew what was happening. I was riding him bareback and I didn't care.

He moaned. A lazy sigh of satisfaction. I thrust against him determined, hungry, burying his rigid cock deep inside me.

Again and again, until it almost felt I was fucking myself, using him as a prop. The way he no doubt felt when he fucked me or another fan or groupie, I speculated.

I already knew I wouldn't come this time. But I thirsted for his hardness to fill me, to split me apart until I screamed and the ghost of Leonard left the room, inconsequent, a thing of the past, someone I must forget if I was retain my emotional sanity. Hello, Dagur; goodbye, Leonard. That way, it almost sounded like the title of a song. Goodbye, Leonard, hello, rock 'n' roll.

Dagur was oblivious to my discontent. It was neither here nor there to him who initiated the sex between us, and the fact that I might wake in the early hours of the morning desperate to be filled was, in his mind, an ordinary and perfectly acceptable state of mind and nothing to be remarked upon, though he did insist that if we were going to carry on fucking unprotected, we would need to get ourselves tested. His attitude made me blush, but it also gave me a sense of confidence and freedom to more readily accept my own desire. Dagur merely frowned when I mentioned in jest that I had become a slut, as if he had never heard the word and couldn't conceive of such a thing. Unlike many other men, Dagur didn't believe there was such a thing as too much sex or too many partners. It was simply a necessary part of being alive.

I resolved to be more like him, and spend less time wondering about who I should and shouldn't be going to bed with and just get on with the business of enjoying myself.

So when he called and invited me to come along with him on a photo shoot his management had set up, I decided to throw caution to the wind and agreed.

'Aren't the whole band coming?' I asked Dagur, presuming that he must be doing promo with all the other members of the Holy Criminals.

'Actually, no,' he said. 'Promotional stuff goes through our manager, and he felt much of the publicity material that involved me was a bit out of date. He wants to refresh the portfolio. Viggo and the others all did new sessions weeks ago. I'm the only one left. I've been putting it off for ages, but our manager is getting a bit uptight.'

'Scared the camera will leech your soul?' I teased him.

'Guess I am. He's actually a well-known lenser. Better known for his fashion work. I heard about him through the gals in the management office. Today he might only be doing some test shots. Nothing formal. But I've always felt uncomfortable being snapped on my own; with the rest of the band it's OK, we fool around a bit. So the photographer suggested that I bring a friend . . .'

I was flattered that Dagur had thought of me. I'd imagined that he must have a slew of blonde-haired, nymphlike admirers who he would turn to first to hold his hand.

'Hi, I'm Grayson,' said the photographer in a chirpy voice as we arrived. His eyes landed on my teardrop tattoo, but he didn't remark upon it, and I liked him immediately.

I sipped a coffee and watched as Grayson set up the lights and shifted equipment around. For half an hour, following the initial set of Polaroids, Grayson shot away at great speed, circling Dagur like a buzzing bee, varying the pauses and instructions. Throughout, Dagur's smile was strained and fixed, his discomfort at being in the eye of the lens all too obvious.

'You have to relax, man,' Grayson said.

'How do I manage that?'

'Just do something that feels natural,' Grayson suggested. He didn't blink an eyelid as Dagur lifted his arms overhead and pulled off his long-sleeved T-shirt, then unbuckled his belt and unbuttoned his jeans and peeled them down his legs and over his feet and tossed his clothes in a heap to the side.

Dagur winked at me and then at the photographer, his sense of mischief relaxing him, his tenseness disappearing by the minute.

Grayson smiled. 'If that's what it takes,' he commented.

'It does, a hell of a lot,' Dagur said. 'I'll trust you and our manager to see that nothing compromising emerges from this, though.'

'You have my word for it,' the photographer said, resuming his dance around Dagur, who was now looser and less rigid.

Of course I had seen Dagur naked dozens of times before, but I'd never really observed him like this. Usually, when we undressed in front of each other, it was a matter of hastily tearing off clothes while embracing or rushing to dress again in the morning and hurry off to rehearsal or work. Undressing was never a ritual like it was with Leonard, one layer peeled slowly off before the next, as if each item of clothing represented another boiled-down emotion or inhibition removed, bringing us closer together one piece of fabric at a time, naked in mind as well as body.

But as Grayson focused a spotlight on the skin of Dagur's chest, I found myself evaluating him in a whole new light. Despite his powerful shoulders and the rippling muscles that spread across his back and torso, he looked strangely vulnerable when motionless and unaroused. His cock hung short and soft, nestling between his legs in a frame of dark hair. Weak. Fragile.

I leaned back in my chair and did not bother to politely hide how much I was enjoying watching Dagur caught in the glow of the camera lights like an insect under the glare of a microscope. As he responded to Grayson's instructions, I felt my nipples hardening and my panties beginning to dampen. I was grateful. With Dagur unclothed and me clothed and viewing the spectacle from afar, it was easy to fantasise that I had orchestrated the whole thing and now had my man trapped in the palm of my hand and subject to my every whim.

'You're enjoying this, aren't you?' Dagur asked as Grayson disappeared into another room to change his camera battery.

He slipped his hand under my singlet and gave my breast

a squeeze. I hadn't worn a bra that morning, on Dagur's advice. If I was going to have any skin photographed, then it was better if my flesh did not sport the deep-red lines that often appeared in response to the constriction of underwired lingerie.

'Hey,' I said, playfully slapping his hand away. 'Did I say you could do that?'

'Not interrupting, am I?' Grayson joked as he returned to the room just as Dagur was removing his hand from under my shirt.

I hadn't paid the photographer much attention earlier. He'd been friendly enough, but with the cool detachment of a professional who was simply doing a job. He'd seemed to blend into his equipment so that it was easy to forget that he was even human and not just an extension of one of his cameras.

Now, as I felt a warm flush heat my skin and Dagur's naked flank so close to my body, I looked at Grayson in a whole new light. He was in good shape too, I thought as I peered at his torso and tried to imagine how he looked under his clothes. He wore a tight T-shirt that stuck to him like a second skin and indicated he was lean beneath it, though not as muscular as Dagur who worked out regularly for the sake of the band's sex appeal. His jeans were low cut and too big for him, they sat loosely on his hips, displaying the occasional flash of his designer-branded boxer shorts when he moved.

By the time Grayson had asked Dagur if he wanted any shots together with me, my nipples were as hard as rocks and I was momentarily too embarrassed to remove my shirt as the effect that the two men were having on me would be immediately obvious.

Grayson did not appear to notice my rising ardour. His cool demeanour only served to increase the heat that was unfurling steadily like a flower blooming inside my body.

'That's great,' the photographer said. 'Great. Please, carry on, I'm just adjusting the lights.'

Dagur was sitting down on a striped black-and-white stool holding a pair of drum sticks and I slid behind him and straddled his back.

'God,' he said, craning his head around to catch my eye. 'You're wet.'

My pussy slid against the skin of his back as I moved closer against him and tightened the grip of my thighs around his waist.

His cock began to harden against my calf and, suddenly aware of the intimacy of our situation and the gaze of Grayson behind the lens of his camera, I started to giggle.

'Just pretend I'm not here,' Grayson called out, in a relaxed voice. 'Do what comes naturally.'

The temptation was too much for me. I didn't just want to imagine that I had Dagur trapped between my legs, a captive to his arousal, I wanted to have his image captured that way. I got down on my hands and knees in front of him and started to suck his cock. Forced him to lose control.

What would Liana think of me now? I wondered and smiled to myself, as much as I could smile with my mouth full. The lights continued to flash around us and I waited until I could feel Dagur about to explode in my mouth and then I leaped to my feet and took him by the hair and held him by the scruff of the neck as I turned to face the camera.

Grayson went mad then, snapping and flashing excitedly as I felt my face bathed from within with heat and emotion and Dagur dropped to the ground in front of me. He was growling with the pain of having the rise of his orgasm interrupted right before its release and I shook with the thrill of the power that I held over him.

It was then that I noticed the bulge in the photographer's trousers and lost my mind entirely.

'Put the camera down,' I instructed.

Grayson obeyed as if I was leading him by an invisible chain.

'Come here.'

He stepped towards me and I took hold of his crotch and squeezed.

'I want both of you,' I said. 'Now.'

'Whatever you say, young lady,' Grayson replied, as he fell to his knees.

5

Eighty Days of She

Dagur stirred.

His left leg was draped across my midriff as we all lay in a tangle of limbs across the patchwork spread of blankets and multicoloured sheets scattered across the studio floor. I turned on my side and came face to face with Grayson's elbow. I was sandwiched between the two men. Brushing sleep away like cobwebs from my mind, I gathered my wits and the night we had spent together came rushing back to me.

If Liana had affectionately called me a slut on the phone, then I was definitely one now, I reflected with a wry, self-satisfied smile. Two men in the same evening, at the same time.

But the thought didn't drag the slightest feeling of guilt or embarrassment to the forefront of my thoughts. On the contrary, I felt elated, fulfilled. It was an uncommon feeling for me.

A sentiment of freedom I couldn't recall experiencing before.

I shifted imperceptibly, hoping not to wake either Dagur or Grayson, who both seemed to be sleeping like innocents, the soft and firm cushion of their flesh hemming me in, protecting me in a dormant and exhilarating embrace.

I dived back with relish into my memories of the pre-
ceding night, poring forensically over it, gestures, rare words,
caresses, wonderful excesses, over and over, as if I was
searching for some form of justification for my uninhibited
actions. How, at times, my eyes closed and, swimming in a
whirlpool of sensations, I had deliberately tried to guess
which of the two men was inside me by his insistent rhythm
and muted sounds, or when both had been playing me
simultaneously in pleasingly unholy combinations and it
had felt like the most natural thing in the world, their
sexual alliance punctuating the ever-flowing rise of my
arousal like master craftsmen at work, turning the mechanics
of sex into a meticulously constructed work of art.

A pang of cramp began its insidious invasion of one of
my trapped feet and I was obliged to adjust my position
between the men's drowsy bodies. One of them groaned
and I felt his breath in my ear. I knew it was Dagur. I had
become familiar with the steps of his awakening over the
past few months. Soon, he would want to stretch his limbs
to every corner of the improvised bedding in which we
had found ourselves and would scratch his scalp a couple of
times before opening his eyes wide, coughing to clear his
throat, and, hey presto, he would be ready to get up and face
the new day. Unlike me, who could spend hours on end,
dozing, daydreaming, lazily lingering between the sheets,
he was a person who rose instantly, as if spending an extra
minute than was necessary in bed was a diabolical waste of
time.

Grayson was still inert on my other flank.

Dagur began to stretch, his elbow dug into my side. I
winced.

His movements dragged the sheet that was covering us away to the side and Grayson and I were unceremoniously uncovered. He was lying on his stomach, his square buttocks fully exposed.

'What a sight for sore eyes.'

The woman's voice came from behind us but I hadn't heard her walk into the studio. I turned my head in her direction.

It was She.

She was wearing an exquisite form-fitting silk kimono in powerful primary shades of red and pink, like an explosion of colour in the geometrical drabness of the photographic space.

Dagur dragged himself up on his elbows and faced her, oblivious of his nudity.

She gazed at him, her eyes lingering with appreciation on the spectacle of his long, soft cock flopping against the side of his thigh as he sat there with legs impudently opened, sustaining her examination. Grayson kept on sleeping.

Her eyes then turned towards me.

'You I know,' She said. 'So who's this hunk? Your boyfriend or one of Grayson's rough-hewn models?'

I was taken by surprise and dumbfounded.

Dagur rose to full height, looked around the studio to see where his clothes might be.

'I'm Dagur. From the Holy Criminals. Grayson has been commissioned by our management to take pictures of the band. Lily is a friend of mine. And you are?'

She smiled enigmatically.

'I see dear Grayson is still out cold in dreamland. He

sleeps like a baby after a good fuck. I live with him,' she declared.

Still stark naked, Dagur stepped over to her and formally shook her hand.

Back at the club, many of us had endlessly speculated and gossiped about She's 'civilian' life. She had always been a source of fascination for most of us, haughty, imperious, beautiful in a terribly cold and remote way, with hints of abominable cruelty lingering around her persona, whether in her stern dominatrix outfits or in functional, businesslike day-to-day clothing when she arrived some evenings and we caught sight of her before she changed and assumed her authoritarian mistress of ceremonies role. We knew she was not the owner of the club – two middle-aged hedge fund investors who would often wear drag on their rare visits to the place were – but she acted as if she did, and her word was gospel.

So was she Grayson's wife, companion, mistress, domme even?

My mind was reeling, not least because she knew who I was already and now loomed above me as I lay there naked next to the uncovered body of her man. There was little doubt about what had happened during the previous night.

But She didn't appear to be angry in the slightest. In fact, there was a hint of amusement on her perfectly painted lips.

She read my thoughts and reassured me.

'Don't you worry, Lily. He's allowed to play. With whoever and however many times he wishes. I'm not the jealous type. It's not that sort of relationship.'

'You know each other?' Dagur asked, slipping back into his jeans. He never bothered with underwear.

'My evening job at the fetish club,' I explained. 'We work together.'

'Quite a coincidence,' he said, now pulling his T-shirt on.

He glanced at his watch. 'Oh.'

'What?'

'I didn't realise what time it was already. I have rehearsals. Out in Maida Vale.'

'I can call you a cab,' She suggested.

'That would be great.'

He looked at me on the floor. 'You'll be all right, Lily?'

'Of course she will,' She said, holding her mobile phone up to her lips and ordering Dagur's cab. 'I can look after her. Don't you worry.'

He was out of the door a few minutes later, leaving me with She and the still-sleeping Grayson. I pulled a sheet over our bodies, blushing under She's insistent gaze.

'Your musician seems nice,' She said. 'Had I known, I might have joined you all. Could have been great fun.'

I opened my mouth but couldn't find the right words.

'So, was it good for you?' She continued.

'Hmmm . . . actually . . . yes,' I stammered.

She smiled broadly.

I couldn't help but warm to her now. It was as if she had suddenly unfrozen and was human again and not a remote ice goddess dictating her terms from faraway poles. She almost seemed glad I had slept with her man now that she knew the sex had been fulfilling and pleasurable. And the addition of Dagur to the equation lent a hedonistic touch to the whole improvised affair she clearly heartily approved of.

She stepped towards us, extended her hand and ruffled my hair, which I was allowing to grow long again, although it would take an age to reach the same length I'd enjoyed before Liana and I had succumbed to temptation and cut it in a bid to renew ourselves. She stubbed a bare toe in Grayson's ribs.

'Hey, Gray, wakey-wakey,' She whispered. Then, to me, 'There's a shower in the room over there.' She pointed to a door at the far end of the photographic studio.

I rose. She was almost a head or more taller than I was.

Grayson was waking up.

He wiped the sleep away from his eyes, saw me as I gingerly walked away towards the far door and looked up at She.

'Hi, you . . .'

'Good morning, Gray.'

From the corner of my eye, I saw her kneel down to his level and kiss him, while her hand wandered down to his crotch and grabbed his genitals and squeezed them.

'Ouch,' he complained.

'Just checking everything is still in working order,' She said, and squeezed harder, insolently demonstrating that she was in charge. Grayson blanched. 'For now,' she added.

I'd reached the bathroom door, and felt discretion was now the better part of valour. As the water came gushing out of the showerhead, it obscured any sounds that might filter through from the adjacent studio.

Whatever the curious vibe circulating between Grayson and She, I felt exuberant. Liberated. It was as if I had thrown an invisible set of chains to the four winds and freed myself.

I no longer felt any sense of jealousy knowing that I wasn't the only girl in Dagur's life, or that, as far as Grayson was concerned, I was just an additional plaything, a pleasing distraction. Knowing emotions were no longer on the menu gave me an infinite sense of freedom. I would enjoy the men, enjoy the sex, live for the moment, seize the day and all those clichés. Now I could genuinely try to forget Leonard. I would live my own life, embrace hedonism. Be real. Find myself even.

By mid-morning we had enjoyed copious cups of extra-strong, invigorating coffee and one of Grayson's assistants, a cadaverous young man clad all in black with a bulbous nose and shaven-headed, had run out to the high street and returned with a bag of hot croissants straight from the local patisserie's oven which all three of us scoffed with unfaked appetite. By the time I had emerged from the bathroom, whatever She and Grayson had been up to was over, although his face was pale and drawn, which it hadn't been when I had left them after he had awakened. I noticed that She's features were as cool, salon-tanned, calm and collected as ever.

She declared she had to go and do some paperwork at the club, and when I suggested I should leave with her, she protested and insisted I stay at the studio, that there was no rush for me to leave. She would be back after lunch and wanted to talk and maybe, in the meantime, I could help Grayson out with a project of his. She didn't say how. I had the day off from the Denmark Street music store, so I agreed. I was intrigued to hear what She wanted to discuss with me.

'I didn't realise you worked at the club,' Grayson said, shortly after She's departure. I was standing in the main room of the studio, glancing idly at some of the prints hung on the white walls: waif-like models in absurd, unpractical fashions; well-known celebrities with grins from ear to ear, and images of the bleak façades of derelict buildings in the rain. One of his assistants had now tidied up and there was no longer any trace of improvised bedding, or evidence of the night's frolics.

'I'm only there part-time, a couple or nights or so, so we've seldom spoken.'

'She can be distant and cold if she doesn't know you well,' Grayson remarked.

'How long have you been together?' I ventured to ask.

'Quite some time,' he replied. He was tidying up a table full of various lenses. 'You and the drummer?' he asked.

'Not long.'

'That's what I thought,' he commented.

'Did you?' All of a sudden I was annoyed by his presumption. He had changed into a pair of black jeans and a white-collared shirt that was open at the front displaying a thin chain with a cross attached to it that hung around his neck. He was barefoot.

'So how did you meet him?'

'How does one meet anyone?' I responded. 'We sort of . . . came together.'

He nodded.

'So, do you do this often?' I asked. 'Get involved with the people you photograph?'

'Not as much as you might think,' Grayson responded. 'Very rarely, in fact. I have some new lights I want to try out,' he continued. 'Would you like me to take some photos of you?'

I'd once read in a magazine that he was known as a photographer who didn't get out of bed for less than several thousand pounds a session and was much in demand. And now he was volunteering to take pictures of me. For free. Why not? I thought.

'Sure.'

I didn't flatter myself he was doing this to get into my pants. He already had, so to speak. It was just his way of being friendly. Post-coital photography. If it ended up with my sleeping with him again, this time without Dagur along for the ride, I actually didn't mind, although I was a bit nervous about the prospect of She returning to interrupt our activities, let alone joining us, a possibility I couldn't banish from my mind without a tremor of intrigued anticipation.

He summoned one of the two assistants who seemed eternally on beck and call in one of the adjoining rooms to the actual studio space. She rushed in, washed-out denim skirt, knee-high boots, grey knitted woollen top and cropped auburn hair, a lean and businesslike vision of speed and efficiency, carrying an assortment of cameras and lenses. She also doubled as his make-up girl. She gave me a fleeting glance and suggested touching me up. Neither of the assistants had been present yesterday, which had me wondering whether the threesome that had happened had not been entirely planned by Dagur.

The make-up she was proposing might partly conceal the teardrop so Grayson insisted it should remain visible, that it made me special, and he wasn't bothered by the fact that in any photo of my face it would draw immediate attention, become a focal point for the viewer.

Tom, his male assistant, joined us then, pulling along a rail laden with a selection of outfits, but again Grayson dismissed the idea. He was intent on photographing me as I was, wearing my own clothes and with my own, imperfect face. This made me feel at ease. I was not a professional model and was keen for the results to represent me as I was, not like a painted clown clad in exotic plumage. Lily unadorned. Tom retreated, impassive, to the side room with the movable wardrobe before returning again to the main space empty-handed.

Following the photographer's peremptory instructions, the two assistants ran around pulling screens, adjusting lights and setting up Grayson's equipment.

'First, I want to just capture your face, Lily,' Grayson proclaimed and he waved the two assistants away.

It was just me and him.

'Would you like some music?'

I nodded.

He connected an iPod to a set of small speakers.

From the little I knew of Grayson, I expected rock music, but the melodious strains of a classical melody emerged. I even recognised it from my distant cello lessons. Vivaldi's *Four Seasons*.

Reading my thoughts, Grayson remarked that he found classical music more soothing, that it established the right mood of intimacy. Maybe we could switch to rock 'n' roll later, he suggested.

'Do you want me to sit or stand?' I felt different without Dagur there. Now it was just me in front of the lens and in the absence of yesterday's erotic energy. I felt stranded on a beach of lights, not knowing which way to go or look, as Grayson began observing me, weighing me up, his eyes analytically measuring the angle between my eyebrows, the configuration of my cheekbones, reading the sheen of my skin, pinning my features down like a butterfly in his mind before casting his photographic net over me and capturing me like a fly in amber.

'Turn your head to the left a little. And stay still.'

He adjusted his lens and snapped a couple of shots.

'OK, now the other way. That's it.'

I blinked as the lights flashed brightly with each snap of his finger on the shutter.

'Take half a step back. A little less. Now to the right just half a step . . . no . . . back . . . no. Relax. Let me move you.'

He clasped my chin in his hands and tilted my head upwards and then downwards, right and then left, each time stepping away and taking more shots of my face from every conceivable angle.

His manner was antonymous to his behaviour the previous evening when, along with Dagur, he had seemingly abdicated any sense of control and had abandoned himself to my direction and had spent the night obliging my every command.

Today he spoke like a dictator and moved me around as if he were a sculptor and I were a piece of clay.

I didn't like it much. Having my every blink prescribed by another was not my cup of tea and I quickly became restless and struggled to stay still long enough for him to capture each image.

Soon he gave up on my face and began concentrating on my body.

'Would you mind removing your T-shirt?' he asked, and I laughed at the way he had so politely asked me to take off my clothes, considering that a few hours ago he'd seen me naked and stretched out in the most obscene positions imaginable. I pulled my T-shirt over my head and slipped my skirt off as well just to show him that I wasn't any more afraid to show him my naked body today than I had been yesterday. I hadn't expected to stay the night and my previous day's underwear was stuffed in the pocket of my handbag. Today I was bare.

Grayson did not seem in the slightest surprised by my demonstration. He presumably saw naked bodies daily so mine was nothing to him.

'Great. Now, arch your back a little more. No, less. Curve to the right,' he instructed.

The lights were too warm on my skin and beneath them I became hot and irritable. I shifted my weight from one foot to another and Grayson let out an exasperated sigh and laid a hand on each of my arms, pinning them firmly to my sides and shifted me back again.

I hissed at him and shook his weight off. 'All right, already! No need to shove.'

He dropped his hands from my side immediately and snatched up his camera.

'That's great, Lily,' he breathed. 'Do that again.'

'Do what again?' I could feel my lip curling up in anger. Celebrity photographer or not, I was well and truly tired of posing for him.

'Exactly like that. Be yourself. Show me Lily. Let it all out.'

I leaned forward and snarled into the camera lens.

'Fuck yes,' he cried. 'Do it again. Louder.'

The next time I clenched my hands into fists and I roared. I howled. It was as if I had opened my mouth and released every word that I had never spoken and every thought that I had ever locked away inside and let it fly from my belly through my throat and out into the universe where my cry could surely be heard across half of London.

I was invigorated.

'Push me,' he said.

'What?'

'Shove me. Scratch me. Beat me.'

At first I was tentative. He was holding a camera and the lens alone was probably worth thousands. The room was cramped with all the lights in it and filled with cords and the legs of tripods that could easily be tripped over. Also, I had no wish to actually hurt him or to be violent. Or did I? The thought of shoving a man – of being allowed to – gave me a thrill.

I reached my hands about to his chest and gripped his shirt and dragged him towards me.

'That's it. Great. Now push me away.'

He stumbled and quickly found his footing again as I pushed him backwards lightly.

'Harder,' he cried. His breathing had quickened. Grayson the professional was finally losing his cool.

His response excited me and I grabbed his shirt again and wrestled him down onto the ground. He flipped onto his back and continued shooting. With each movement I was careful to pause and let him capture my pose, realising that the pictures he was now taking were increasingly intimate. My breasts dangling over his face. My legs spread over his body. My pussy wettening in response to the heat of his gaze.

'Yes, yes, angrier, harder, come on, Lily,' he sputtered, encouraging me.

'Like this?'

I bent over, straddling him, holding his torso between the vice of my thighs, my pussy lips just tantalising inches away from his face, my fingers now digging into the soft skin of his shoulders.

'Try and look fiercer,' he whispered.

I shifted backwards a little to improve my angle of attack and tightened my lips in an expression of wrath and my buttocks bounced across his crotch. He was hard, his cock straining against the black denim of his jeans. I deliberately ground down on him, feeling overcome by the exhilarating sense of control this gave me over him.

His mouth opened and a soft moan rose to his throat. Throughout this time, he was clicking away, the lens now fixed on my face. I leaned closer, the pressure in my fingers increasing.

He squirmed briefly.

'Did that hurt?' I softened the pressure.

'It did,' he said breathlessly. 'But go on. Continue, Lily, it's good.'

I leaned over so that my breasts would move into focus from his perspective, my nipples grazing against the edges of his open shirt, enjoying the rough feel of the cotton brushing against their sensitive tips. I was also becoming aroused by the situation, but in an odd way, it didn't feel primarily sexual this time. It was the sensation of power I was holding over him that went to my head, making me feel intensely alive.

I don't know what came over me, but I lifted my hands away from his shoulders, briefly tempted by the idea of pressing my fingers into the delicate skin of his neck, but instead, almost instinctively I slapped his right cheek with the flat of my hand, summoning all the force I could muster. He was taken by surprise, allowed the camera he was holding to drop to his side and winced. But he didn't protest.

His eyes rolled back in an expression of pure pleasure. 'Oh fuck,' he said. 'Do that again.'

I did.

A tremor raced through his prone body beneath me, and I even suspected he might have come.

I took a deep breath. I was shocked by how much I was enjoying this, but didn't quite know what to do next.

My thoughts were interrupted by She's voice.

'Wow,' I heard her say behind me. 'You've quickly got the feel of him just right, haven't you?'

My face flushed.

'I . . . I . . .' I was hoping to explain that Grayson had encouraged me all along, that this was what he wanted. But I was speechless, trying to imagine how compromising the whole situation must look like to her. Me, stark naked, squatting over him, wantonly displayed and angrily slapping him in the face.

'If I didn't know better, I'd say I have a younger rival,' She said in a jocular manner. 'It's a good thing I'm not the jealous type,' she added.

She walked past us and faced me, towering over the tangle of our bodies on the studio floor.

'Very tasty,' she remarked.

There was no way I could cover up or conceal any part of my anatomy. Beneath me, Grayson just smiled at his companion, not looking in the slightest guilty.

'You're a natural, Lily,' she stated.

'A natural?'

'The way domination and control come to you instinctively. I'd bet the house on it.'

A less strained demeanour had returned to Grayson's features, following the excitable pink hue his face had adopted at the peak of our interaction.

'I'd agree with that,' he said.

And then, noting the puzzled look of interest on She's face, 'You'd never think it, eh? Such an innocent-looking young woman, but given a chance she would have flogged me in a shot.'

At the mere thought of the image this brought up in my mind, I turned scarlet but felt a quiet fire lighting up inside me. I had seen dominatrixes at play some evenings in the club and, however much I had found their rituals fascinating, they hadn't struck a deep chord. They were part of another world. But I now realised this was because I had not thought of myself in their situation, in their skin, controlling a man, firmly, roughly, decisively.

I disentangled myself from Grayson and rose to full height, still a head shorter than She who was looking at me with increasing interest. I hunted around for the clothes I had left on the sofa in the far corner of the studio. Grayson also lifted himself from the floor and brushed himself off.

He and She exchanged knowing looks and he then picked up the three cameras he had been using during our session and carried them to the sideroom.

'I want to see what we got,' he said.

Leaving me with She, who was carrying a bunch of shopping bags, all with designer names: Prada, Burberry, Agent Provocateur, Coco de Mer, as well as a couple of blank, anonymous carriers, which hinted at more secret purchases.

'Come and have a coffee with me,' She suggested, waving in the direction of the door.

I knew that if I consumed more coffee today, I would be unable to sleep for ages – the stimulus of the caffeine together with the realisation of the pleasure I had taken from dominating Grayson would keep my mind in a state of blissful effervescence – but I obediently followed her.

She switched on a gleaming, stainless-steel espresso machine and tuned to face me. Her eyes were surprisingly pale, a jigsaw of grey and emerald swirls. I wondered whether she used contact lenses as I didn't recall them being so striking before, not that I had ever been this close to her at the club.

'Tell me, Lily, how did it feel when Gray was under you? Try and explain your feelings, how it affected you. What went through your mind, what else you wanted to do to him, to hear him say? How did it turn you on?'

I paused for a long while before replying, and She didn't hurry me.

'It was a rush,' I said at last, though that didn't capture even half of the feelings that had flooded through me as Grayson had fallen to his knees in front of me and his expression had turned so ecstatic, so intoxicated, after I had slapped his face. And then the tone in his voice as he had begged me to do it again.

She nodded and then turned away from me, busying herself in the kitchen cupboards pulling out brightly coloured coffee cups and saucers, a sugar bowl and a box of chocolate biscuits. Her long, thin fingers were like spiders creeping into the box and when she removed a chocolate finger and placed it between her lips as if she were about to light a cigarette, I noticed that her fingernails were painted the same colour as her eyes, a luminous greyish green, the colour of the ocean on a cloudy day. She bit down hard on the biscuit and then licked her lip, catching the fragments of chocolate that had broken off and stuck to her lipstick with the tip of her tongue.

Finally she slid a piping-hot espresso in front of me on a saucer and I took a swift gulp to regain my equilibrium, burning my mouth in the process. She pulled out a barstool, indicating that I should sit down.

I pulled myself up onto the stool and with my legs now dangling off the side in mid-air, felt even more childish in the presence of her cool air of authority. She remained standing, and made no move to respond. Faced with her silence, I continued speaking.

'It was as if I had set something free. Like opening a cage and letting the real me fly out. And not being afraid of the consequences. As if I could do anything. I could break the rules. And it wouldn't be wrong. I wouldn't hurt anyone. Grayson would appreciate me, no matter what I did. No, more than that. It was like he was worshipping me. He loved it. I felt invincible. And so alive. Like I had him in the palm of my hand.'

She smiled wryly.

'And what did you want to do to him? Tell me,' she encouraged.

'I wanted to rub myself all over his face.' The words tumbled out of my mouth before I could think and I immediately wanted to take back what I'd said. Part of me knew that it was true, though, and wanted to crow with delight at the satisfaction of saying so out loud.

'And? What else? No need to blush, my dear.'

'I wished I'd had a cock. So I could choke him with it.'

She laughed, displaying two rows of gleaming white teeth.

'He would have liked that,' she said. 'And would you have liked to fuck him with it?'

'I hadn't thought of that,' I replied honestly. I conjured up the vision in my mind of Grayson on all fours in front of me, his face pressed into the carpet, my hand wrapped tightly in his hair and then imagined how it would feel to ride him. The thought sent a ripple of excitement pulsing through my body and my hand shook briefly, spilling a few drops of espresso over the tiny cup and onto the smooth surface of the marble bench top.

'I can see that you like the idea,' She mused. 'Have you ever worn a strap-on?'

'No.'

'Ever seen one?'

I shook my head.

'Then we have a lot of work to do.'

'Work?'

'Domination requires training. I am going to train you.'

It was an order, not an offer, and I meekly acquiesced.

'You're not on shift tonight, are you?'

'No,' I replied, 'Sherry's on tonight.'

'Good. We'll start at the club. Have you subbed before?'

'Never.' I felt horribly inexperienced. She was my employer, and I worked at a fetish club, and I had never so
much as tried even the most basic activities that our patrons
enjoyed.

'You've never been spanked? Tied up?'

I thought of Liana and grimaced.

'None of those things have ever appealed.'

'I understand why,' She said, 'I really do. But it's important to try it from the other side, so that you understand what
sort of sensations you're inflicting on your sub.' She paused
for a moment and smiled as a sudden, pleasant thought
occurred to her. 'I can make Gray dominate you,' she added.

I shuddered at the idea and She grinned wickedly.

'He would hate it,' she said. 'But he would do it.'

I had no doubt about that. The activities of the past
twenty-four hours had been just play-acting for both
Grayson and I. She was his domme. And ordering him to
dominate me might provide her with an ideal opportunity
to reassert her authority over both of us.

'First,' she said, 'let's find you an outfit. Gray is bound to
have something here that will be suitable. As you saw today,
he likes to bring the domme out of his female clientele.'

'What's in it for him?' I asked. I was suddenly curious,
and perplexed in the same way that I had been when Liana
had described to me the enjoyment she took from submission.

Some of the men at the club subbed just so they could get close to attractive women. Most of them were about as charismatic as a wet teabag. But Grayson was a good-looking guy, and I doubted that he'd have any trouble finding a date that he didn't need to kowtow to.

'Why don't you ask him?' she replied, heading towards the studio. Her kimono wrapped around her long legs as she walked, giving the impression that it was a living creature caressing her flesh. She was wearing matching silk slippers with a thin sole so that her steps were soundless on the wooden floor.

Grayson was sitting in an office chair in a small room attached to the studio, flicking through images on his computer screen. He was engrossed in his work and by turns his face lit up animatedly or dropped into a frown when he saw something that he wasn't satisfied with. He either hadn't heard us arrive or was ignoring us entirely.

'Lily wants to know what you get out of submission. Tell her.'

Pulling his attention from his work was a visible struggle, but it was a battle that She won before too long and he turned to give us his attention. And sighed.

'Sometimes people just are the way they are, you know. There's no reason.'

'You can do better than that, Gray,' She said. She sauntered up behind him and leaned over his back, running her fingernails up inside the front of his shirt and then circling his neck with her hands. The gesture could easily have been mistaken for a simple affectionate caress, but I could see his eyelids flutter closed and his breathing quicken as she tightened her grip and began to restrict his airway.

He made a noise in the back of his throat, half growl, half purr, certainly an expression of intense pleasure. As soon as Grayson began to relax into her grip, She stood back, leaving him unfulfilled, but not before reaching into his open shirt again and twisting one of his nipples so hard that he jumped.

'When the right buttons are pushed by the right person at the right time,' he said, 'there's an overwhelming desire to please, to be subsumed, to serve, and when pushed harder, to debase oneself or be debased, humiliated to better worship the domme, the mistress. Why? I don't really know. For me it doesn't feel like a choice. More like an instinctive response. Some believe that the loss of power is associated with the powerlessness of being a small child, with its safety and comfort and freedom from having to make a choice. I don't prescribe to that theory entirely. It's all a bit Freudian. But I agree that when I submit to She I feel safe, and comfortable, and free. It's relaxing to not have to make decisions. Not being responsible. And for some it's a way to enjoy pleasures that otherwise might provoke guilt or shame.'

'And dominating?' She asked. 'Tell her what you get out of dominating.'

'Nothing.' He laughed. 'Absolutely nothing. It's hard work, you know. If you want to explore your dominant side then you need to be prepared for some very hard work. There's a great deal of skill involved in beating someone properly, or tying them up. To know exactly what your sub's limits are and to push them just far enough but not too far. It's a great responsibility to hold someone's safety and their service. Some subs can be very demanding.'

She rolled her eyes.

'It's the eternal question,' She said. 'Who is really serving whom? But at the end of the day, we all do it because it gives us a thrill. Gray is right. It doesn't matter why. Now. Put this on.'

She threw me a black corset and a long stretch-lace pencil skirt with a Victorian style frill at the bottom. When I unrolled it I realised that not only was it see-through, but there was a hole at the back where my bum cheeks would peer through.

'I'm not wearing this!' I protested.

Grayson laughed. 'You reckon?'

She was standing with her hands on her hips, staring me down.

'I'll help you with the corset,' she said.

I peeled my clothes off for what felt like the tenth time in twenty-four hours and shimmied into the skirt.

'Turn around. Hands against the wall.'

She sounded like a cop from a TV drama and I had to admit that the thought of She clad in uniform and brandishing a baton and a pair of police-issue handcuffs was not unappealing.

The corset's steel boning pressed uncomfortably into my ribs as She pulled the laces tight.

'I can't breathe,' I complained.

'You'll get used to it,' she replied without a modicum of sympathy.

The club was just getting started when we arrived. A few couples stood at the bar nursing drinks and chatting to each other. It was early and the music was low to encourage conversation. As the night warmed up, the sounds of whips cutting through the air and paddles beating flesh would reverberate through the adjacent dungeon and blend into the heavier beats that the DJ would begin to play after midnight.

'Wow,' Richard, the club's Dungeon Master, whistled when he clocked my outfit and the towering heels that She had lent me. Usually I wore more sensible shoes when I was working and would stay behind the front counter most of the night.

'Mistress,' said a soft voice, near my feet. I looked down.

One of She's regular club slaves had approached, crawling on his hands and knees. He was naked besides his routine latex hotpants, which barely covered his arse, exposing an inch of bare crack and the curved, fleshy sides of each buttock. Tonight he was wearing a hot-pink pair with a white frill, which lent an extra layer of humiliation to the ensemble. On each of his nipples hung a clamp and a thin chain with a tiny bell attached to the end, which tinkled when he moved to warn of his approach.

At the sight of him prostrate in front of me, my nerve endings began to tingle and I felt my blood heating up and rushing through all of my limbs, as if I'd just gulped down a shot of whisky or necked a glass of champagne.

She appeared by my side. I hadn't noticed her gliding across the room, as silent as a shadow.

'Stuart is offering pony rides tonight,' she said, holding aloft a human-sized leather saddle and a riding crop. The saddle was pale tan and well used, with cracks running across the leather. It was padded underneath with sheep skin and had a high pommel for the rider to hold onto. Stuart lifted his back a little as if to invite me to climb aboard. He continued to stare at the floor.

'Go on then,' She said. 'Take him for a spin.'

I took the saddle gingerly from She's outstretched hand and leaned down to Stuart.

'May I?' I asked him. Domme or not, it seemed only polite to check first.

'Please, Mistress,' he replied.

The saddle slipped over his back easily, as if it had been made especially for him.

There was no dignified way to climb atop. My skirt was so tight it simply wouldn't stretch far enough for me to sit astride him unless I rolled the fabric all the way up to my waist so instead I kept my knees together and began to bend down to sit side saddle, hesitating before I lowered my full weight onto his back.

'Won't I hurt him?' I asked She.

'Trust me,' she replied, 'he doesn't mind.'

Stuart had raised his head and was sniffing the air eagerly as if he were a real pony.

She thwacked his arse with the crop and then handed it to me. I clenched my thighs to keep my balance as he jolted forward in response to the smack on his arse.

'Don't be long,' she said, 'I want you to try something when you return.'

For the first few steps I felt foolish. I was riding on the back of a grown man! Something I hadn't done since I was a child and had played horsey on the rare occasion that my father had time to spend with me after work before falling asleep.

But as I found my rhythm and noticed how the other

club-goers parted to allow us through, I began to enjoy myself. At first I was gentle with the riding crop, uncertain how to wield it or how hard I could bring it down on Stuart's skin without making him yelp, but after a few delicate taps I found my confidence and brought it down harder on the right side of his buttock which I could just reach without tipping myself off.

I had no desire whatsoever to fuck him. Even the idea of it seemed wholly wrong. Unimaginable. But I did want to grab his balls and bring him to his knees in front of me begging for my mercy.

We lurched back to She and when we arrived at the tips of her stiletto boots, Stuart stretched forward onto his flanks with his face flat on the floor. As I came to my feet I glanced down to thank him and saw the tip of his tongue flicking out and trailing along the front of her shoe. He was polishing her boots. With his mouth. She shifted her weight and lifted her foot infinitesimally to allow him better access.

'Now,' She said. 'Time for you to try how the other half lives.'

'Gray,' she cried out, beckoning the photographer over from his relaxed position leaning against the wall behind us where he was surveying our interaction with a wry smile on his face.

Tonight he was dressed in a pair of low-slung leather trousers with a studded belt and a pair of heavy silver boots. Over the top he wore a black mesh vest that clearly displayed his lean torso and also a pair of nipple clamps with a thick chain running horizontally across his chest connecting one nipple to the other.

He didn't appear to be discomfited in the slightest by the

contraption that made him vulnerable to a cruel tug at any moment that She decided to reach over and pull the chain.

Grayson took a moment too long to collect his thoughts and saunter across to us and, in a blink of an eye, She had one hand around his throat and the other hand resting on the chain, heavily enough to make both him and me wince as the teeth of the clamps bit into his nipples.

'Spank her,' she hissed.

I grimaced.

Spanking. Of course I had suspected it as soon as I'd seen the skirt that She had made me wear, but I had still hoped against hope that she might have something else in mind. Spanking was in my mind the most foolish and humiliating of all the submissive practices that I could think of. I found it distasteful and silly, a reminder of all the things that I disliked about tacky porn films and cheesy upstairs-downstairs erotic tales that inevitably involved a poorly dusted living room and a PVC-clad maid who needed to be punished.

Grayson seemed just as pleased about the whole idea as I was. She looked back and forth between us and grinned like the cat that got the cream.

'I'm waiting,' she said with an air of authority, giving his nipple chain another tug.

'On the bench,' Grayson turned to me and ordered.

I took another look at She's scarily impassive expression and complied. It might be humiliating, but it would be over quickly and I supposed that I would learn something. Half a dozen people had suggested to me that since I worked here I ought to at least have a basic understanding of how our customers got their kicks.

The first smack was fairly soft, but the shock of it made me jump. The second was harder and I had to stifle a low moan. I wouldn't give either She or Grayson the satisfaction of seeing me vulnerable. The third smack made a loud crack noise and, listening to the mumbled responses around me, I became aware that a crowd had gathered. It was no surprise. I'd never noticed Grayson at the club before and She only ever appeared when she was working, not as a participant. And no one had ever seen me getting involved either as a submissive or as a dominant, let alone both in one evening.

Blood rushed into my face, heating my cheeks, as I flushed with shame imagining how I must appear bent over the spanking bench with my head hanging low and limp like a doll's and my bare arse in the air and fully exposed to all and sundry. I was briefly grateful for the cut-out buttocks as I knew that no matter what, She would have insisted on my spanking being on bare flesh. Having just my arse exposed was humiliating, but nowhere near as bad as it would have been to shimmy my skirt up to my waist and display my legs and bare pussy to anyone who cared to look closely enough.

Grayson's breath was hot against my skin as he bent forward and whispered into my ear. 'Try to let go,' he said. 'Let yourself fall into it. It'll be easier.' He stroked a lock of my hair as he drew away. It was a simple gesture, but full of affection and reminded me that we were both unwilling partners in this exercise and I was not fighting against him. Just trying something new.

His next few blows were more rhythmic and I tried to follow his advice and relax into the sensation of his palm slapping against my skin. Eventually the slaps began to blend into each other and the impact was no longer painful, but more like being exposed to a source of heat. After the stroke he would cup my buttocks gently, as if he were catching the pain in his hand. I began to learn the pattern of his strokes and press back against him each time he rested his hand on my arse, to encourage him to keep it there longer. I also noticed that as I pushed forward and back to match his rhythm, I had begun unwittingly grinding against the rough leather padding that covered the bench.

Then I lost control and cried out as a much sharper blow landed from a smaller, cooler hand. She. Grayson's warm palm was quick to apply pressure to ease the sting.

Her voice was harsh in my ear.

'Think about how much he hates this,' She said. 'How he's only doing it to serve.'

I imagined She leaning over Grayson and directing each of his blows. The frustration on his face as his instincts warred with each other and his compulsion to submit to She won over everything else.

Briefly I felt almost drunk as I pictured how it would feel to have someone feel that way about me. How I would humiliate them, hurt them, debase them, care for them and hold them safely through it all.

'Oh,' I moaned, this time with pleasure, as Grayson brought his palm down on my flesh again.

'That's enough,' She said. 'I don't want her to enjoy herself too much. The night is still young and we have so many more treats in store . . .'

6

The Eye of the Lens

Neil held the door open for me, removed my coat and then gallantly pulled out my chair once we reached the restaurant's dining area.

He looked the picture of the London gentleman in a crisp white shirt with a grey waistcoat over the top, matching cigarette-cut suit trousers and pointed black shoes that shined like mirrors when they caught the light. His usually curly hair was slicked back into submission bar the one stubborn lock that had been falling over his left eye and irritating him for as long as we had known each other.

I leaned forward and tucked it back into the rest of his fringe. Neil took my hand and held it across the table.

'It's nice to see you, Lily,' he said. 'It's been too long.'

'Yes,' I murmured, pulling away and upsetting the flower arrangement that stood between us. Neil caught the falling vase just before it crashed over the pristine white tablecloth.

Our relationship had been strained and uneasy for the past few months since I had walked out on him after his unsympathetic reaction to my then recently ended romance with Leonard. I'd received a few emails and text messages from him, breezy updates about his new job and flat in Hoxton. I had read and swiftly deleted them all without responding.

The last time I'd spoken to Liana, she had surprised me by standing up for him.

'Don't be so hard on the guy,' she'd said. 'It's not his fault he's done well for himself.'

So when Neil called and invited me out to dinner, I agreed. He'd just been promoted and wanted to celebrate.

'But not with my workmates,' he'd added.

'How come?' I asked. 'Are they so bad?'

'Not bad, exactly,' he said. 'Just all so full of themselves sometimes. I want to spend a night not thinking or talking about PR for once. And see you.'

He'd taken me to Miyama, a Japanese restaurant in the City. He said it reminded him of Brighton and the time that Liana had blown a wad of her father's money taking us all out to dinner at the sushi restaurant near the pier where we drank too much sake and took all the chopstick wrappers off the tables and made them into origami swans and frogs.

We'd just begun on the sharer plate of sashimi delivered by a young Japanese man with thick black-framed glasses when Neil waved his chopsticks in front of my face to catch my attention.

'Earth to Lily,' he said. 'Your phone is ringing'. His voice brought me back to the present and the sound of my mobile. I'd been distracted, imagining how the waiter's flesh would look constricted by a web of rope. Images like that had begun jumping into my mind more and more often lately and I was sometimes a little disturbed by the frequency and intensity of my kinky thoughts. I shook my head slightly in a vain attempt to clear my mind.

'Nice ring tone,' Neil said, as I pulled my phone out of my bag. It was the *True Blood* theme, 'Bad Things' by Jace

Everett. Liana had programmed it into my settings when I'd been to visit her and I hadn't got around to changing it back.

Neil raised his eyebrows even higher when the word 'She' flashed up on the screen.

I answered immediately.

'Lily,' She said, and continued talking without so much as waiting for me to reply. 'Are you free tonight? Sherry's called in ill.'

'Ah.' I looked up at Neil. We'd only just received the first course and it seemed terribly rude of me to bow out now, though I could really have used the money from an extra shift. 'Sorry,' I said, 'I've got plans tonight.'

She huffed into the phone. 'Nothing you could move around? I really need you. I'd be truly grateful, Lily.'

'Actually, I'm with a friend.'

'Oh,' she said. I could hear the grin in her voice. 'By all means, bring him along. I'd be delighted to meet your "friend".'

I grimaced. She would eat Neil for breakfast and I shuddered to think of what he might think of her. If he'd thought that my relationship with an older man was weird, I couldn't imagine what he might think of the club and its inhabitants in their various states of dress and undress.

As if he knew that I was thinking of him, Neil waved his chopsticks in front of my face again.

'Hang on,' I said into the handset, taking a small measure of pleasure in the knowledge that She would be fuming at the interruption.

'If you have to go to work, Lily, it's OK. I understand,' Neil said.

'No, really, I—'

'Honestly. We can finish the sashimi and come back another time for the other courses.'

He wiped his mouth on the napkin and called the waiter over again to ask for the bill.

'Lily,' She hissed into the other end of the phone. 'Bring him with you.' The phone went dead. She had hung up before waiting to hear me agree.

She'd spoken loudly and I knew that Neil had been able to hear most of the conversation from across the table.

'You've been called into that club you work at?' he asked.

'Yeah. Someone's called in sick.'

'I could come with you. I haven't had a night out in ages.'

I sighed. 'It's really not your kind of place.'

'How do you know? And why can't you just give me a chance?' he replied angrily. 'You're always so pissed when people make presumptions about you, Lily, but you do the same thing to other people all the time.' He stabbed a chopstick into a stray piece of ginger and bit into it savagely.

'Fine,' I said, convinced that as soon as he set one foot in the place and looked around he would make a bolt for the door and I wouldn't hear from him again. Probably for the best, too. If he couldn't handle it, then maybe we should give up pretending to still have anything in common and just put our university friendship behind us and move on.

She looked as harried as I'd seen her when the taxi pulled up outside the club and she met us at the door. The Fox and Garter, another club in town that masqueraded as a pub with a dungeon hidden beneath it, had closed early due to a power failure and so it was extra busy tonight with all the punters who had come to us to continue their evening.

Neil's eyes widened as he took in She's sleek crimson catsuit, matching top-hat fascinator and higher-than-high heels. She was dressed as a ring master tonight and carried a whip by her side. Her arm was relaxed, but there was something about her manner that promised that the whip was not far away from cracking even when she was leaning nonchalantly against the wall seemingly without a care in the world.

'Well, hello, Lily's friend,' she said to him in her best Jessica Rabbit voice, running her eyes up and down his body as if she owned him.

I bristled at her approach and took Neil's hand in mine as we stepped inside.

'Oh,' She said, raising an eyebrow at my gesture. 'Like that, is it?'

'Yes,' I replied. 'It is like that. Come with me, Neil,' I added in the most authoritative tone I could muster and led him into the cloakroom.

His eyes darted here, there and everywhere as he caught a glimpse of the busy bar area and the people within who were dressed in all manner of costumes that all seemed quite ordinary to me now, but which were probably over-whelming to him. There were men in corsets, frilly skirts and high heels; women in military uniforms or lingerie; both sexes in latex body suits, and some with masks as well. Several women were topless and there was the obligatory man wearing just a cock ring with his flaccid penis bouncing as he walked.

'You're going to have to change,' I said to him abruptly. 'You'll stand out like a sore thumb in that.'

'OK,' he said meekly.

I unbuttoned his waistcoat and then his shirt. The fabric felt pleasantly rough beneath my fingers and without even meaning to, I found myself running my hands along the stiff cotton and fumbling with the buttons for longer than strictly necessary. He held his arms out as I slipped each garment off his shoulders and onto a hanger and then hung them on the rail.

Neil didn't move a muscle. He was like a doll, allowing me to move him back and forward as I wished. I hesitated before I moved down to his belt. The leather strap felt warm to the touch, in strong contrast to the cool metal buckle. Dagur had once let me bind his ankles together using his belt strap and I immediately pictured Neil in the same position, face down and lying uncomfortably on his erection while I ran my finger into his arse. The thought excited me and I fought to bring my mind back to the present. This was Neil, not Dagur, and I was at work, and any minute now he would panic and make a run for it.

'Are you wearing underwear?' I asked him in the most unfeeling and casual tone that I could muster.

He nodded.

A spare pair of the hot pants that She's slaves wore lay on the shelf behind me. They would most likely fit Neil, but I didn't want to see him in a pair of pants that said 'She's slave'. He didn't belong to her.

His boxers would do. They were designer-branded, black and forgettable. I looked him up and down. He had definitely been working out. Or maybe he'd always been built this way and I'd just never noticed. His naked torso was not at all unpleasant. The bulge in his shorts was un-mistakable, but he was a man, and the place was full of women in skimpy clothing. I didn't take his response to heart and no one in the club would be offended by his erection if it didn't shrink by the time we reached the bar.

Neil was a fish out of water and clearly had no clue how to behave in the sea of flesh that surrounded him, so I took him by the hand and led him down to the dungeon. I wasn't worried that Neil would do something inappropriate like gawk creepily or reach over and grab a stray breast that fell into his line of sight, as he was far too shy and well-mannered for that. But with his baby-faced good looks and air of innocence, he would be like catnip to She's troupe of dommes who were lined up and leaning against the bar like lionesses reclining at a waterhole, sleek and relaxed but ready to spring into action at any moment and only too eager to initiate a newcomer into the pleasures of a riding crop.

'Richard, thank God you're here,' I said to the Dungeon Master. Tonight he was shirtless and wearing a leather kilt with half a dozen pockets, each one containing a tool of the trade. It was the first time that I'd noticed he had a silver barbell through each of his nipples. He hadn't previously struck me as the type of guy who would sport a nipple piercing. He was short and bordering on fat, but had thick biceps and having seen him in action I knew that he had a fierce strength in his limbs that belied his gentle expression. Most of the experienced dominants – the ones that Liana would call 'good doms' – had a similar air of softness with a steely core beneath it. Those who were confident in their own power had no need to swagger around the club and show off their assertiveness or ability to suspend a willing sub from the ceiling at every opportunity.

'I'm always here for you, Lady Lily,' Richard replied. He'd started calling me Lady as an affectionate term of endearment ever since the night a few months ago now that I had ridden She's slave, Stuart, across the room on a saddle. Since then I had been learning more and more of the arts of domination and was particularly proud of the fact that I could surprise a room full of people by swinging a bull-whip longer than I was.

'What's that?' Neil asked, pointing at the pinwheel that poked out of one of the flaps on Richard's skirt and was glinting menacingly in the light. Curiosity had got the better of him.

I removed the instrument from Richard's pocket and held it up to Neil's face. He'd turned white.

'It's a pin wheel.'

'Looks like a mini pizza slicer. But sharper. Doesn't it . . . hurt?'

I had wondered the same thing the first time I'd seen a Wartenberg wheel, a device originally used to test nerve sensitivity in skin that had been abandoned by the medical profession in favour of more modern techniques and subverted by kinksters as a sensation sex toy. It was a particularly evil-looking device with a seven-inch-long handle and twenty or so radiating sharp pins at one end, but unlike most of the other implements that looked much softer than they were in reality, the pinwheel was much less evil in practice than it appeared. She had demonstrated one to me by rolling it over Grayson's skin after she'd flogged him. He had gone into spasms of delight, shivering and shuddering and moaning with each line that she drew across his hot skin. I'd loved watching the crisscross pattern that bloomed white and red and then faded, like a road map of pleasure and pain across his body.

Richard grinned from ear to ear.

'Not when it's used right,' he said. 'I'm sure the lady here would be happy to demonstrate.'

'I have to work,' I cut in, shooting Richard a fierce glance that I hoped indicated I wanted him to shut up. 'I was hoping you might keep an eye on Neil while I'm stuck behind the counter.'

Neil stared at me and then back at Richard. 'I can look after my—'

'Please, Richard,' I said, ignoring Neil's request for freedom.

'No problem. I'll keep him safe for you,' he replied.

Neil paled further at the notion that his safety might be in question, but by then I was well and truly late for my shift and too impatient to reassure him.

'Great,' I replied, and fled back to the front door with one final glance at his soft tanned skin and the snug fit of his boxer shorts.

It was one of the busiest shifts that I'd worked since I started at the club, and I didn't have a chance to check on Neil until we were closing up and Richard delivered him to me at the front desk.

His face was flushed and his eyes dilated.

'That was amazing,' he said, waving his arm wildly to flag down a passing black cab.

He had the slightly rabid punch-drunk look of someone who has just been tied up or spanked and I felt a stab of annoyance at Richard for not keeping a closer watch on him.

'Oh?' I said. 'Did you try anything?'

'No,' he said. 'But there was this girl that he did this stuff to and the way she looked . . .'

His face had taken on the far-away, dreamy look that Liana got when she was talking about what it was like to experience submission.

The driver tooted impatiently as Neil swung on the door loosely and stared at me.

I panicked.

'I think I left my jacket at the club,' I said. 'Go on. I'll get the Tube.'

His expression turned from pleasure to confusion. 'But you're wearing your—'

'I'll call you later, OK?' I interrupted.

I turned and ran.

Neil had returned to his old self by the time that I eventually relented and started answering his calls again. I wasn't sure what it was about his interest in the fetish side of my life that made me feel so uncomfortable, but I was pleased to find that he seemed to have dropped the subject and things between us were back to normal, other than the fact that every time I heard his voice the vision of him near naked in his boxer shorts with a pin wheel running over his body assaulted my mind.

My strange dreams hadn't subsided either, and now featured Neil instead of the hog-tied Japanese waiter who had filled the nocturnal images that had haunted my sleep for the few weeks after we visited Miyama.

Besides my restless nights, life was peaceful and time continued to fly by in a regular mix of days at the music shop and evenings at the club without any unusual episodes. I had been taking advantage of the ebb in my social and romantic life to complete as many shifts as I could and, despite my low wages, my savings had grown to a tidy sum. I took great satisfaction from watching the balance on my bank statements increase and carefully filed each crisp statement into my desk drawer as they arrived.

It had been a quiet evening at the club and I was changing back into my civilian clothes when She put her head around the corner of the staff changing room.

'Lily, can you give Gray a call? He wants to talk to you.'

I must have looked quizzical because she reassured me.

'Don't worry. Nothing weird. Just a project he's begun that you could help with.'

At least someone was expressing some form of interest in me. It had been ages since I'd heard from Leonard, while Dagur was overseas on a three-month tour with the band and was no doubt busy fending off the amorous attentions of exotic foreign women following every gig. I hadn't expected Dagur to call, message or send me postcards anyway. It wasn't his style.

I nodded.

I was uncertain about facing Grayson again on my own in the wake of our improvised threesome and that ambiguous photo session that had somehow ended up with me straddling him wildly, inadvertently pulling the lid off my hitherto dormant tendencies to dominate men. Somehow I wasn't quite reconciled with that new part of me yet. Yes, it attracted me and awakened a distinct fire inside, but on the other hand I still liked to be with men and be made love to in a traditional manner. Both instances provided me with pleasure.

I rang him the next evening, but was unable to meet up for at least a week as I couldn't take any days off at the music store and, on the few evenings I wasn't part-timing at the club, I just found myself too tired to budge from my sofa or my bed, recharging my batteries after weeks of hard work. Grayson didn't appear overly concerned and assured me that it could wait. It was something long term, he said.

We agreed on an early evening when I would travel to his East End studio straight from Denmark Street.

'Will She be there?' I asked him, out of curiosity.

'Is that what you all call her?' As if he didn't know.

'Yes.'

Grayson chuckled.

'No, the fearsome Ms Haggard will not be in attendance,' he said. 'She's catching up on her accounts at the club, I daresay. But you don't feel we need a chaperone, do you, Lily?'

'To keep me from spanking you?' I queried.

The roar of his laughter triumphantly rumbled down the telephone line.

'Has She been giving you lessons, by any chance?' Grayson ventured jokingly. 'Anyway, I'm willing to take my chances,' he concluded.

As I moved briskly from the autumnal chill rising from the nearby river into the warm building where Grayson both worked and lived, I loosened the thick grey cashmere scarf Leonard had bought me on Kalverstraat in Amsterdam and wiped my nose with a tissue. The cold had been biting outside. One of Grayson's assistants was busy tidying the studio floor from an earlier session, crumpling long sheets of paper, rolling up an assortment of rugs and methodically picking up random props and locking them up in a tall metal cabinet at the other end of the photographic space.

'Drink?' Grayson proposed.

'Just a coffee,' I suggested.

Grayson hailed his assistant and asked him to prepare the espressos and he left the room. All the main lights were off and we sat in one of the comfortable leather sofas against the far wall, with just a lone spot illuminating the circle of darkness we had taken refuge in.

'How's Dagur?'

'I shrugged 'I don't know.'

'What's up?'

'He's on tour with the band. Won't be back for a few months; it's a long one. Anyway, I hadn't seen that much of him before he left because he was busy rehearsing some new material.'

'So you were never really an "item"?'

'That's one way of putting it,' I replied. 'I don't think rock stars are all that keen on domesticity.'

'Pity,' Grayson said.

'Why?' I wondered if he was hoping to arrange another threesome.

'I'm looking for musicians.'

'What for?'

'A new project I was hoping you could help with.'

'I'm all ears.' The tall, thin assistant handed us our coffees and silently slipped away. Shortly after, I heard the front door close.

'I'm always busy,' he sighed, 'but lately it's mostly been

commissions. Well paid, of course, but not ultimately that satisfying,' he explained. I noticed he hadn't added any sugar to his espresso, unlike me who added sugar cubes into the coffee like a ship drops an anchor. 'It's been ages since I've done anything personal.'

I nodded. That was the problem with all the artists I knew, musical or otherwise. Either they had no money to enable them to do what they wanted or they had all the money in the world and no time for anything other than pleasing the masses.

'There's an important gallery in Southwark, with a branch in New York, and they've been at me for a long time to come up with a theme for a solo exhibition but I couldn't quite focus on the right angle, the subject. It could also be expanded into a book. The last one I put together was six years ago.'

'The walls in the rain?' There were prints on the far wall. They were striking, bleak, but somehow full of light.

'Yes, that was it. I could come up with more of the same, I suppose, but this time around I'm determined to concentrate on people. Not portraits, as such, but bodies. Something more personal.'

I remembered the passion in his eyes as the session that had so conveniently been interrupted by She's arrival had progressed, long before the original excuse of trying out some of his new equipment.

What could he possibly be thinking of now? I couldn't imagine anything more personal than our last photo session. And I knew I hadn't signed any form of model release at the time. However brave I was, I could just imagine my parents' faces if they came across nude photos of me. I swallowed hard, even though my curiosity was well triggered.

'So what about Dagur? You said you were sorry he was away. Somehow I don't think his management team would be keen on him disrobing for the lens. There's good publicity and bad publicity.'

'I know.' Grayson looked increasingly serious. 'But it made me think of musicians.' He fell silent.

'What about them?'

'Just this feeling that they're different from you and me. Like athletes. The way they plunge head first into the music, like athletes disappear into their sport. It makes you want to . . . catch their . . . essence. I'm probably confusing you?'

'Not at all. I know exactly what you mean.' I saw the same thing at the club with submissives and dominants going into sub or dom space.

'So, I was thinking of just taking a series of photos of musicians, well-known ones if I can convince any and unknowns too, of course. The images would be of them clothed and unclothed, with their instruments, probably all in black and white. I can see it all in my mind already, even though it's difficult to explain. There would be a progression, from mild images to eventually totally explicit ones, them making love to each other and their instruments. In your face. Shocking.'

His mind was on a roll, his eyes lighting up as he spoke.

'Of course,' he continued, 'their faces would be obscured, out of focus or out of frame if they so wished. And . . .' He hesitated.

'Yes?' I prompted Grayson.

'I have someone in mind for the final set. I came across her the other night at a function. Not actually the place I would ever have thought of seeing her. But it made me think she might agree to it. The classical violin player, Summer Zahova . . .'

'The girl with the red hair?'

'Exactly. She would be perfect. Something tells me she would be game. She gives the impression of a moth circling a flame when you meet her in real life. A fascinating young woman.'

'Did you ask her?'

'Not yet. We only met very briefly. I might still, but first I have to put together a whole portfolio with others so I know exactly what I'm seeking. I was thinking that Dagur might agree if the pictures were anonymous, or he might be willing to suggest others. Or maybe you have some contacts of your own, through the music store?'

'I don't know any customers well enough to really ask. Jonno might know . . . but I'm not sure. And Dagur – his horse tattoo makes him easily recognisable,' I pointed out.

'Those sort of things are never a problem. I have Photoshop for that.'

'I used to play cello. And some guitar, though I never made the professional grade,' I suddenly blurted out. It was as if the devil made me say it. Like that split second when I had decided to go with the teardrop.

'Did you?'

'I know I'm not a model, but I'd be willing to have a go. You wouldn't even have to pay me . . .'

Grayson smiled.

'I like the way you photograph,' he said. 'You're another person altogether under the eye of the lens. And when you go into domme space, it's almost the look I'm going for . . . Hmm . . .' He considered. 'It could work.'

'There's my own guitar,' I offered, 'but I have access to other instruments, through the shop.'

'Any limits?' Grayson looked me straight in the eyes.

'Limits?'

'How far would you be willing to go?'

I did not hesitate. I liked the idea of having Grayson capture my essence. Maybe his camera could work out who Lily really was, where I had failed.

'All the way. So long as my face isn't in shot.'

'Of course,' he said. 'No problem. It is a pity again about Dagur. I would have loved to get some couple shots. And I'm not sure how many of the musicians would be comfortable with that.' He paused, then, having thought about it again, 'Could you bring another friend along, maybe? He wouldn't have to be a musician, just someone you feel comfortable with. I have some vague ideas in mind I'd like to try, and I can just see you, holding the cello, him holding you . . .' He was already daydreaming the scene, conjuring it out of thin air.

I couldn't think of anyone right then, but I was certain I would come up with someone. Maybe one of the guys at the club would do it.

We had all spent the day stocktaking at the music shop, by far the least favourite part of my job there, ticking off the inventory against stock sheets and trying to locate boxes that had, over the past six months, been moved to nooks and crannies in the basement where they shouldn't have been stored. It was a tedious activity and, away from the shop floor, cold and dusty. At times like this I almost missed the argumentative customers I was often confronted with, who always knew better and whom we weren't even allowed to debate with, or the tedious ones who took an eternity to reach a decision about whether or not to purchase the instrument they had been toying with.

We'd drawn the steel shutters and secured the locks and all I could look forward to this evening was a stop by the supermarket to get some fresh bread and milk on my way home and a night in front of the TV. Jonno and the others were off to the pub, but I was in no mood for it. I was fidgety and on edge because the session with Grayson to get his book project started in earnest was now just a few days away. I had eventually asked Neil to come along with me. There wasn't anyone else that I trusted in the same way as I trusted Neil, besides maybe Richard the Dungeon Master, but I guessed Grayson would appreciate photographing someone younger and more nubile. I'd assured Neil the photos would be anonymous and hadn't detailed the possible extent of his involvement. All he knew was that I would be photographed and wanted a friend to be present to make me feel at ease. His initial reluctance had melted away when I mentioned that I would probably be nude for the latter part of the set, at which stage he blushed, looked at me incredulously as if he thought I was joking, and then hastily agreed to accompany me.

A fine drizzle was falling, blurring the West End lights and shop windows and I realised I had the wrong shoes on for this sort of weather, having chosen to wear thin ballet-like flats for convenience during the cumbersome stocktake. I looked up at the sky to see how thick the clouds were. He was standing outside on the edge of the narrow pavement holding a black umbrella over himself as he kept watch on our exit. At first, because of the semi darkness and the thin blanket of rain surrounding us, I didn't recognise him. Just another silhouette in the street. He could have been anyone.

'Lily!'

It was Leonard.

He looked much the same as the last time I had seen him, all those months ago. My heart jumped and my stomach clenched, or a combination of the two. Why was it Leonard had such an instant effect on me?

'It's been a long time . . .' I managed.

'I know. Things have been busy. Work, travel, all sorts of things,' he apologised.

The others from the shop hadn't lingered and had hurriedly moved on to the pub. Leonard and I stood in the rain looking at each other. I pulled the hood of my parka up, and he stepped towards me offering me the protection of the umbrella.

'Did you have any plans? Can we talk?'

'I was only going home. Sure.'

He moved to my side, the shadow of his large umbrella enveloping the two of us as we moved towards Charing Cross Road.

The nearest hotel bar, off Shaftesbury Avenue, held too many common memories, and all the pubs in the area would be too noisy at this hour to allow a decent conversation, so we ended up in a Soho coffee shop, tucked in a corner as far as possible from the other customers.

'I still think a lot about you.'

'Me too.'

Once again, the familiar core of sadness in his eyes reached out to me. I felt helpless, bereft of words. He attempted a feeble smile and his hand moved across the table and touched mine.

'You're so cold,' he remarked.

His hand was warm, like his body always was at night when I spooned up against him and revelled in the welcome mould of his contact.

'I know. I don't think I'll ever change,' I said. 'Cold hands, cold feet, cold arse. I've never quite been the ideal woman to take to bed, eh?'

'It never bothered me,' he said.

'I didn't think you wanted to see me again.'

'I never said that, Lily, you know it. If only I could summon the right words to explain how much you've come to mean to me, I would. I still want you, badly. And, like you, I don't care what other people say when they see us together. They just don't understand. But all I do know is that we would have no future and—'

I opened my mouth in protest, but with a quiet wave of his hand he silenced me and continued his short speech, as if he had carefully rehearsed it in front of a mirror and would not allow it to be interrupted.

'Like you,' he explained, 'I don't give a fuck about the opinion of others, but I know things wouldn't last. One day the age gap would begin weighing on your mind and you'd start questioning everything, and once the rot set in, it would poison you, us. And I would feel guilty having you waste some of the best years of your life on me, Lily. And that's one thing I can't accept. I want you to be happy. Even if it's without me. Call it respect, call it cowardice, call it whatever you want.'

Every single word hurt, like a dagger being twisted under my skin, every increment of pain causing a silent, agonising scream strangled at birth in the depths of my lungs.

It wasn't that different from the last conversation we'd had in Barcelona. So why had Leonard wanted to see me again, just to repeat the same things over and over?

'Why . . . ?'

His eyes looked down, avoiding my questioning gaze.

'I needed some . . . closure,' he said, the word like a whisper, discreet, defeated.

His free hand dug into the pocket of his jacket and he pulled out a handkerchief and unfolded it over the table.

A miniature golden key fell out. Bounced lightly against my saucer and settled.

The key to my ankle chain.

'Take it,' Leonard said.

I looked down, nonplussed, at the small key. This curious symbol of the freedom he was granting me, letting me go. For my own good, if I was to believe him. And I did.

He rose and kissed me delicately on the forehead. For a moment I thought he was going to kiss the teardrop too, but he hesitated, drew back and left the cafe, turning his back on me and not looking back.

My coffee had grown cold by then, but I slowly sipped it, angry at myself for not finding the articulacy to counter his arguments, to save our relationship, bitter at the set of circumstances that had brought us to this point and the tyranny of having been born at the wrong time. The coffee also tasted bitter. I'd forgotten the sugar.

'Please tell me you won't freak out.'

Neil was looking wide-eyed at the mess of photographic equipment and orange cables scattered around the studio floor as Grayson adjusted the lights and I just stood there in an intense circle of brightness while his female assistant hovered by my nose holding a light meter up to my face and barking information at Grayson.

He'd asked me to come wearing my normal style of clothing, in this case mostly black, in an attempt to capture what he called my natural 'vibe'. He wanted to keep the set simple. Neil was asked to stand by the side and just observe for now.

Grayson and his assistant exchanged some mumbled words and half a dozen different lenses were placed on a trestle table ready for use, while Grayson directed me to stand on a vast white sheet of paper that they had just unrolled, forming both a floor and a back wall against which I was about to be snapped.

And then it began, Grayson moving around me like a bee buzzing around a honey pot, as I stood there motionless and silent, increasingly dizzy from the sweep of the roving camera eyes and clicking of the lights.

This was so unlike the other time when the session had become a seduction, a game between me and him. Now I was unimportant and he was the one in control, seizing whatever image he wanted, the way my limbs stretched, a sinew in my neck, the angle between arms and body. It was no longer personal. Tirelessly, he clicked away with joyful abandon. After a moment, I just drifted away mentally, absent, and let him capture whatever it was that he thought he was seeing. How it could really be my essence when I felt so disembodied, I didn't know, but he seemed satisfied enough.

I was handed the guitar I had brought along and ordered to hold it in various different positions while Grayson captured the angles I formed with it, both natural and quite unnatural ones. I knew this was all preliminary work, approaches, guesswork. Taking pictures helped Grayson to think.

He stopped for breath.

'OK. I'd like to start on the nude stuff now. Can you take your top off?'

He was fiddling with a lens and not even looking at me as I pulled my T-shirt over my head. Again, I hadn't worn a bra, to avoid the straplines from an underwire digging into my skin that I knew would be fiddly to retouch.

The polished wood of the guitar against my bare chest was hard and inflexible. I turned my head and saw Grayson's assistant yawning and further back Neil, hypnotised by the view of my small, pale breasts, a faint flush travelling across his cheeks. The heat of his gaze made me acutely aware of my nudity in a way that the disinterested stares of Grayson and his assistant didn't. Despite my every effort to stay calm and collected, I could feel my nipples beginning to harden and a hot flush spreading into my cheeks. I looked away from Neil and back at the camera to try to distract myself.

'And your skirt?' Grayson asked, indicating that I should

remove it. A fluffy white robe lay within my reach so that I could protect my modesty between shots, but it seemed pointless to me. By the time I had my clothes off they'd seen everything there was to see anyway.

I was brought the cello, then a chair, and I sat down open-legged to accommodate the bulk of the instrument between my thighs while Grayson lay on the floor, looking all the way into me, no doubt seizing in his lens the contrast between my dark pubic hair or the shadow of my slit and the burnished orange glow of the instrument.

'Neil,' he said in a kindly tone, attempting to put him at ease in case he fled the room altogether and ruined his shots, 'I could use you now.'

Neil stepped closer, attentive to Grayson's instructions as he was now handed the guitar, and instructed to hold it so one of my nipples might be seen brushing against the taut strings from the camera's perspective.

Grayson looked into the viewer and frowned.

'Your shirt breaks up the lines of the shot. Could you take it off?'

There was a short hesitation and Neil obeyed.

Seeing the doubt pouring across his face, Grayson quickly reassured him. 'Don't worry, neither of your faces will be seen in any of the photos. They will be compositions. Flesh against flesh, skin textures, just unknown bodies and the way they commune with the instruments. Trust me.'

Next Neil's hand was against my bare shoulder. His fingers drew a pattern against the small of my back. His arm brushed against my stomach. His mouth trailed barely inches away from my opening. His lips lingered in the gap between my belly button and the midriff of the guitar held tight against my body.

I relaxed against him, enjoying the gentle pleasure of his touch.

Grayson frowned again.

'No,' he said. 'This isn't right.'

The warm and comforting scent of Neil's skin had made me drowsy and I struggled to focus my thoughts and concentrate on whatever pose Grayson wanted from us next.

He crouched down and looked me straight in the eyes.

'Lily,' he said, lifting his voice at the last syllable, like a question.

'Yes?'

'Can you domme him, please?'

'What?'

'I need your essence. This is all very nice but it isn't working. The instruments aren't really you.'

'But Neil's not—' I protested.

'Yes, that's fine,' Neil jumped in.

I spluttered.

'It's for art, Lily, and we've come this far,' he added hurriedly, his hoarse voice down to a whisper.

I was outnumbered. And seeing as I'd already agreed to take my clothes off and had been captured in many explicit poses, I couldn't think of any reason to explain why I didn't want to dominate Neil in front of the camera. Or at all, I told myself fiercely.

'I'm not in the mood,' I protested weakly, but Grayson's assistant had already received her orders and rushed out of the room to retrieve extra props, probably straight from She's dressing room.

A suede flogger was pushed into my hand. Grayson had corrected the lighting and positioned Neil up against the wall with his arms outstretched as if he was leaning against a St Andrew's cross.

Facing away from me, exposed and vulnerable, he didn't seem like Neil any more. I was free to admire the pert shape of his bare arse that had been hidden beneath his boxer shorts at the club. Liana had always said that Neil had a nice arse, and I had scoffed at her. Now I could see it in all its glory, I was acutely aware of the way his cheeks curved so roundly away from his back, the little dimple just above his crack, and the light dusting of ginger hair that looked so soft to touch.

Neil had an arse that would look good red. Marked.

I brought the flogger down on his bare cheeks and he jumped, though I hadn't hit him hard. Yet.

'Yes, that's it,' Grayson exclaimed. 'Pretend I'm not here. Carry on.'

At first, it was impossible to pretend he wasn't there. Domming for the camera was completely different to just sitting there like an object, exposed to Grayson's gaze. This felt theatrical, like it did at the club on the few occasions that I'd practised on She's slaves under her watchful tutelage. Now I was in control, and I loved it.

My blood began to pump hot in my veins. Neil was moaning under each strike of the flogger and I watched with pleasure every flash of red that appeared on his skin and then faded as I brought the soft lengths of suede down onto his arse, first one cheek and then the other, up his back and down his thighs, varying the tempo and pressure of my blows to match his in and out breaths and the subtle change in tone of his groans that told me how much he could take. It was like playing a drum. As if his body were a living instrument and I was its master.

Beads of sweat began to appear on my brow and on his sides. When I struck hard and then cupped his cheek to ease the sting, he relaxed against me and I was overcome by tenderness and wanted to take him into my arms and stroke him like a child.

Time stood still and I was aware of nothing but the rasp of Neil's breath and the sound of the flogger beating against his skin.

Until the moment Grayson took a deep breath, paused, handing his cameras to his ever-silent and expressionless assistant and declared he was done.

Both Neil and I had become Grayson's puppets, positioned left and right, straight and crooked, chastely and indecently, just another set of props like the instruments we had been using.

'You can get dressed again, guys.' In his eyes I could see he was still faraway, lost in the visions he had conjured. Until the next model, the next musician, came along and the dance would begin all over again.

Ignoring us altogether, Grayson retreated to one of the side rooms and the strong spotlights were switched off.

We were dismissed.

7

Snow White at the Ball

The grey shades of the city unfurled as the car sped north, soon making way for the orderly parades of semi-detached houses standing to attention behind well-tended front gardens that littered our steady path through London's suburbs.

We'd begun the journey from Grayson's studio when it was still light, but by the time we reached the open road, darkness had already fallen. Grayson was driving and She sat next to him in the front and dozed throughout the journey, creating an uncomfortable silence I was reluctant to break. The car radio was set low to a classical music station and the gentle, cushioned hum of wordless melodies lullabied us along.

I had met up with Grayson again in Shadwell a few days ago, where he'd invited me to see the finished pictures from the shoot with Neil. The photographs were rather beautiful. Our bodies fit together almost as if we were one person and the way the light reflected from our skin was haunting in its simplicity. A few shots showed just my hand, which seemed so small and fragile in stature but so powerful gripping the flogger, with the curve of Neil's buttock rising to meet the lengths of suede, like a promise of things to come.

I still felt a little uneasy about the level of intimacy that I had unintentionally displayed for the camera, but considering the quality of the finished product it seemed churlish to complain. We were just bodies. Skin. Flesh. The emotion that Grayson had captured in the photographs seemed so clear to me, but it was intangible. A figment of my imagination. I didn't have any ownership over the way that the viewer chose to interpret the way that our bodies melded together, the precise turn of my wrist, the bump in Neil's spine.

Neil had shrugged off the event when I tried to speak to him about it afterwards to check if he was OK. As if being flogged nude by a friend in front of a celebrity photographer was an everyday occurrence. Instinctively I felt that he was holding something back, but I wasn't sure what. Perhaps he was just embarrassed about how far things had gone. I was ashamed of my own behaviour. I'd been responsible for him and his first scene, but I'd fallen so far into my own head space I hadn't stopped to give Neil a safe word or to even check that he really knew what he was doing. The presence of Grayson, his assistant, the lights and the camera made it seem at the time as if it were just a set-up, a game we were acting out, but I knew that for me it had gone beyond that once I had begun to wield the whip. Despite the public show, it had felt natural. More natural than almost every other interaction I'd had with Neil. If Neil felt the same way, he didn't share the fact with me. It was easier not to talk about it.

After we'd been through the images and Grayson had given me a disc with my favourite shots, he took me on a tour around their apartment. For the first time I had been allowed into the house beyond the confines of the photographic studio and been surprised at how conventional the furnishings and the overall style of their living space actually was. It was as if they kept a strict demarcation line between their kink life and their existence as a couple. It made me realise how little I knew about them.

The size of She's walk-in wardrobe was the only unsurprising thing. When she pulled the sliding doors open, it was a veritable treasure trove of outfits, shoes and accessories, a deep cavern of delight, of assorted materials, textures, brash colours as well as racks of fearsome implements most of which I hadn't seen before and would surely not even know how to use properly.

Grayson had then invited me to the ball, and we had agreed She would dress me for the occasion.

'The ball takes place only once a year. It's very special,' She had told me, a broad, sensual smile spreading across the scarlet hue of her full lips.

'Has it got a name?'

'No, we just know it as the ball. It's a celebration of everything we enjoy and believe in. And the tickets are very exclusive. Most people don't even know it exists. I'm sure you'll enjoy it, Lily.'

'I hope so.'

'I think you're ready for it,' she said. 'Our little kink debutante. Your coming out.'

It made it all sound very formal, albeit alluring, but I knew it was best not to ask too many questions. This world I was gradually becoming part of was a domain of half-whispered secrets, of darkness hiding between the folds of the light. It wasn't just the physical pleasure that beckoned me in its direction, but also the sense of ritual, the conspiratorial togetherness that bound all its participants from the instant they changed into their other selves and stepped beyond that invisible curtain that separated the everyday life from the kingdom of the senses.

I returned on Saturday afternoon, several hours before we were due to hit the road, as instructed, so that She could make me over. The extra time proved unnecessary as my costume was extremely simple: a floor-length grey silk sheath dress that clung to my body like water with a short beaded train in the shape of a tear that ran behind as I walked.

'A teardrop, for our teardrop girl,' She said as she pulled up the discreet side zip.

'You had this made for me?' I asked.

'Well, of course.'

The dress might almost have passed muster for an ordinary night out if it hadn't been so low at the front and the back. The neck line cut savagely between my breasts all the way to my belly button and the back was cut even lower, displaying the curve of my rump. I was close to naked from the waist up.

To my amazement, She had arranged flat shoes for me to wear with the dress rather than the towering heels that I knew she preferred and that most of the other dommes wore to events. She presented me with a pair of grey silk beaded slippers, lined with soft leather. They were so comfortable, I may as well have been walking barefoot.

'You'll be up all night,' She said, 'and I know you can't stand in heels for that long.' She sniffed, as if this were a great personality flaw. 'Besides,' She added, 'you don't need the false height. You're rare, Lily. A natural. You have more power when you're just being yourself.'

I wore my hair loose and, once She had finished glossing it and ironing out the frizz and any stray waves, it hung dead straight and heavy around my shoulders, like Cleopatra's bob. In my ears I wore a pair of long beaded pearl earrings, which swayed and flickered in the light as I walked.

She and Grayson wore matching red and gold military outfits sculpted to fit their bodies to the millimeter, as if they'd been fitted and measured that morning. Whatever their relationship was at home, Grayson wasn't accompanying her as one of her subs to the ball. The show that they put on for the rest of the world was one of equality. They were partners in kink.

With London now firmly in our rear-view mirror, Grayson's dark-green Saab was racing down straight country roads with alacrity. I saw a sign for the M25, which gave me a sense of how far we were, but we soon left it trailing in our wake as we reached a vast expanse of open fields. With just the glow of the headlights cutting through the night, we were like a ghost train chasing a will-o'-the-wisp through a swamp of darkness.

The low, cloudy horizon quickly raced to meet us and we took a turn onto a narrower road that led into woods. Five minutes later, we reached a high metal gate, where two burly attendants ticked our names off a set of checklists held against clipboards and waved us in. Grayson drove the car a hundred yards down the path beyond the property's entrance until the wall of trees finally parted and we emerged onto a vast clearing beyond which a towering mansion stood, its floodlit outline razor-sharp against the night sky.

The guests' cars were parked in a tidy half-circle in front of the large country house, with a handful of traditionally uniformed hired help on call to pick up the car keys and slot the incoming vehicles into the carefully organised pattern like pieces in a jigsaw.

She had woken up as we reached the front of the house, alerted by Grayson switching the radio off.

'Lovely. Truly lovely,' she remarked, looking up at the vast house that towered above them.

It could have been a scene out of *Brideshead Revisited* or any English upper-class property porn. There was no hint at the excesses and follies concealed within.

Grayson opened his door and I followed his example. He'd kept the engine running as the valet busied himself around the car and Grayson emerged from the Saab in full regalia and handed him the set of keys in exchange for a playing card. An ace of hearts, I noticed.

Only then did She make her exit from the car. Lazy, regal, like the queen of kink she was.

I could feel the gaze of other guests, arriving and disembarking from their own cars, linger on her as our trio moved together towards the house's front steps. Did I appear incongruous, a grey shadow, sandwiched as I was between those two aristocrats? I wondered.

The doors were wide open, and the sharp beat of techno music reverberated through the rooms all the way towards us like a gushing stream of sound.

We walked into a blinding pool of light as we finally passed the threshold and entered the house.

A large hallway opened up with a bevy of topless women in white Roman togas and silver belts all standing with trays of drinks at the bottom of a grandiose staircase, each with their hair held tight above their head in a severe chignon. I could not help noticing how opulent some were, while others were modest in size and so much less well-endowed. I noted, with a tightening of my throat, that they all displayed the same colour nipples, painted silver, matching the shade of their belts. For a brief instant, my mind in a whirl, I imagined how I might look with painted nipples.

As we passed the partly undressed young woman nearest to us, Grayson and She each picked up a glass of white wine, or maybe it was champagne, and I took hold of what appeared to be water unless they served vodka or gin in tall glasses here. My eyes were already darting around in all directions as we walked along, taking in the sights, the house, the guests, and nothing would have surprised me at this stage.

'Let's get the lay of the land,' Grayson suggested, taking both me and She by the hand. 'A bit of exploration before the fun begins.'

'The ball isn't always here?' I queried.

'No, it moves around. Seldom takes place at the same location twice,' She replied.

We moved on to a circular salon where guests jostled and congregated in small groups. A babble of indistinct conversation ebbed and flowed amongst the clink of the glasses and the swish and swirl of couture dresses, leather and latex under the glow of old-fashioned chandeliers.

So far it felt suitably lavish and classy, and anyone's idea of a bourgeois gathering of same-minded souls in a country mansion, or so I reckoned, had it not been for the half-naked waitresses stationed by the stairs and the elaborate assortment of clothing on parade, which added a curious sense of provocation to the proceedings. But the other guests appeared straightforward and, dare I say, normal, although I had long realised the corridors of BDSM were like a hall of mirrors and seductive depravity was always an inch away, skin deep behind the reassuring façade of everyday life.

A large French window at the back of the salon looked onto an endless garden, illuminated by a row of strong klieg lights, just like a *son et lumière* spectacle, with a variety of different-sized marquees which had been erected at regular intervals throughout the grounds. Beyond them lay a small wood, while the gardens to the left of the house were protected by a tall brick wall, with rows of barb wire across its top.

'Ah,' She exclaimed, pointing at the marquees. 'Our theatres for tonight.'

Grayson calmly nodded, downing his white wine with a greedy look of anticipation colouring his face.

We were still loitering without true purpose by the French windows when I felt the murmurs of the room shrink to a muted hush behind us. We all looked around.

A tall man in his late fifties, with a shock of abundant white hair and a pair of red-framed glasses, wearing an exquisitely tailored tuxedo whose shiny lapels caught a sharp reflection of the room's central chandelier, came surging head high through the crowd that parted at his approach.

Two steps behind him came a young woman. She was connected to him by a leash, which was itself attached to a dark collar circling her neck. In his other hand he held a minutely carved wooden walking stick with a metal pommel in the shape of a skull.

The woman was totally nude.

Apart from a pair of impossibly high-heeled and precarious leopard-skin-print shoes. And the collar around her neck, from which a small golden padlock hung.

I couldn't take my eyes off her. She was the most beautiful thing I had ever encountered. And thing was the right word. Her beauty had something of the unreal, the uncanny, about it, as if she had been manufactured to a most demanding specification and been brought to life just for this public display, so that we common mortals could wallow in our own imperfections.

Her face was like a mask of perfect beauty, serene, eyes green and distant, cheekbones gently rouged to emphasise their hand-carved precision, hair like pouring jade reaching down to her shoulder blades almost in a parody of a shampoo commercial, flowing, free, alive. Luscious red cupid lips in harmony with the rest of her make-up, strong, but elegant and discreet at the same time. Her breasts were high and firm and bouncing gently with every step she took behind her master, her long legs steady despite the awkward equilibrium imprinted by the tallness of her shoes, the back of her thighs tense and strong like whiplash string, her ankles delicate and poised, pillars for her movements.

Everyone gazed at her as the couple passed, ignoring our gazes.

She brushed against me as they headed towards the garden.

Her mons had been shaven to utter smoothness. But what caught my fevered imagination was the fact that she was also tattooed.

Just half a finger above her immaculately bare pussy, precisely centred, was the tattoo of a bar code, and next to it a number '1'.

Was it a real tattoo, or something temporary, the way I sometimes used to wear a detachable nose ring when I had felt particularly rebellious?

Gut feeling told me it was real. She was permanently marked. But already the couple was melting into the darkness of the garden, heading for one of the marquees, and all I could see was the white imprint of her naked arse as it swayed away, inviting questions and lust.

I caught my breath.

'Wow,' I said. 'She is beautiful.'

I was going to add something irrelevant, ask either She or Grayson questions about the striking couple, but She interrupted me.

'Ah, that Thomas. Why is he always so theatrical?'

A bell chimed.

The sound was light and playful and unlike any tolling church bell that I had ever heard.

'The shows are beginning,' Grayson said to me. 'You're going to love this.'

She had already begun to move towards the French windows, which had theatrically swung open at the sound of the bell, seemingly of their own accord.

Grayson took my hand and I followed him out into the garden.

The air was soft and warm and filled with the heady scent of tropical flowers, although the garden itself contained only a large field of grass on which the marquees sat, ringed by ordinary London plane trees.

'Where is that smell coming from?' I asked, inhaling deep gulps of air.

'The heaters, I think,' Grayson replied, 'although I'm not entirely sure. There's always been something a little magical about these parties.'

Tall glass cylinders, each containing a glowing flame, were dotted around the patio and the lawn and I noticed when I stood near one that every minute or so they hissed, exhaling a little scented vapour into the air.

'Your first night here too?' said a cool voice behind us as I was trying to decide whether the flames suspended in the heaters were real. From a distance, the glass cylinders were invisible so it looked as though a dozen tiny fires were suspended in the air across the lawn, as if the party had been gatecrashed by a dragon, or a group of marauding Vikings.

The voice belonged to a tall, blonde woman who was dressed in a bright red, blue and gold Wonder Woman outfit. When I looked closer, I realised that she was in fact completely naked and her costume was merely body paint. In one hand she held a lasso, and in the other, a long, dark wig.

'It was too scratchy to wear for long,' she confessed when she saw me staring at the length of hair in her hand. 'I've been looking for a pot plant to hide it in.'

I began to giggle, until Grayson shushed both of us.

'I'm Lauralynn,' she whispered into my ear as we slipped through the entrance of the first marquee and she slung the wig around a tent pole.

'Lily,' I replied, but it just came out as 'Lil . . .' as the last syllable was lost when my jaw dropped in response to the sight in front of us.

We had entered a forest.

The tent was full of large, squat trees. Each one of them with gnarled and twisted branches as if it were a hundred or more years old with roots that travelled far into the earth.

As my eyes adjusted to the dim lighting, I became aware that the twisted limbs of the trees were not all made of wood. Some were human. Each tree was covered with thick hessian rope and tied within each mess of rope was a naked human being. Some were suspended between branches as if trapped in a spider's web. Others were tied onto the base of the tree as if they were a part of it, melded to the very core of the trunk, blending with the roots. Yet others again hung in bundles from the branches' ends, as if they had sprouted there like fruit. In the very centre of the room hung a tree that wasn't buried in the earth at all but rather tied from the roof of the tent with ropes that ran all around it and then into the ground like roots. Tied to the base of the tree were a man and a woman, embracing. The rope ran from them over everything. Binding, twisting, connecting, joining, making the forest whole. One.

On the ceiling in glowing lights was the word *Earth* and below that the phrase *What constrains us also sets us free.*

'Wow,' Lauralynn said. 'Deep.'

I could have stayed and stared at the rope forest for an eternity. There was something peaceful about it. The faces of the nude and bound men and women were radiant and unblinking. They were like earthly angels.

But I could see the flash of red from Grayson's coat heading for the exit and hurried after him. She was no doubt miles ahead of us by now and I didn't want to miss anything.

Within the next tent was a large lake with a spotlight blazing into the very middle. It appeared to be completely empty. Not even a ripple decorated the surface of the water, yet I could see that Grayson and Lauralynn, along with the rest of the party-goers, were leaning over the pool and seemed captivated by whatever lay beneath the surface.

I crept to the rocky edge, again grateful that She had provided a loop on the train that attached to a bracelet on my wrist so that I could hold my dress off the ground to avoid ruining it.

Under the lake's surface lay twelve men. All of them blond, young, and virtually mirror images of each other in height and stature. They were arranged like the dial of a clock with their heads pointing into the centre. Only their chests were naked. From the hips down they were covered in a filmy white substance that moved in the water like seaweed. Their eyes were closed and for a brief and frightening moment I thought that they were all dead and we were viewing an underwater graveyard filled with beautiful corpses but then my eyes were drawn to the centre of the pond and I forgot everything else. In the middle, beneath the water, was another of the most beautiful women that I had ever seen. Her skin was so pale it had a gossamer quality to it and her cheekbones and eyebrows were so sharp they verged on alien. Her white-blonde hair fell around her shoulders and spread into the water like Medusa's crown.

She was cradled in the arms of another, much stronger-looking woman with short, cropped dark hair and an almost completely flat chest. Her hips were square like a man's, but her waist tapered like a woman's, and around her thighs she wore a white harness with a dildo attached to it.

So startling was the sight of the nude, still bodies within the lake that the occupants of the room had fallen completely silent. A hush spread over us like a wave.

Then a woman's voice, Russian, sprang from the loudspeakers.

'*My name is Luba*,' the voice said.

At the same time, the water began to churn. Each of the bodies rose into the air on platforms and when they were level with the surface, the platforms clicked together beneath them as if the water had become solid like ice.

The dark-haired woman pulled Luba to her feet and they began to dance. Around them the men pirouetted and swayed on their feet, worshipping the two women in the centre. The white costumes I'd thought were seaweed under water became like feathers that glowed when in the penumbra of the spotlight. They were birds. Swans. It was an erotic version of *Swan Lake*, and the two women in the centre were dancing a dance of death.

As the dance appeared to come to an end, Luba lay limp in the arms of the other woman, who had her hands twisted around her neck in a violent embrace as the two of them turned together this way and that. Just as the music stirred into a final encore, the dark-haired woman plunged the dildo into Luba's opening and she immediately sprang to life again and they kissed passionately. Then the panelled floor whirred once more and the platforms sank back into place, plunging the performers under the water again as they relaxed into stillness.

Applause rang through the room from the startled crowd as the spotlight switched off and in its place a message on the ceiling lit up, like it had in the previous room. This one read, *Water*, and beneath that: *What drowns us also sustains us.*

I heard the performance in the next marquee before I reached it. Over the rustling of costumes and the stifled chatter of the guests talking about the show in hushed tones came very clearly the sound of people fucking. Breathless moans and gasps, the high-pitched shriek of a woman coming and the deeper growl of a man reaching his own climax, the slapping of bodies together, the brush of skin on skin, screams that blended pain and pleasure in perfect unity.

The sight that met my eyes, though, was not what I expected. Instead of an ordinary orgy on a sea of beds, the couples were hanging from the ceiling and copulating in mid-air. Each of them wore a pair of wings and their lovemaking was both frantic and joyful, but more animal than human. The room smelled strongly of sex and, for the first time that evening, I felt a dart of interest inside in response to the bared breasts and cocks on vivid display. The other shows had seemed so ethereal that it had been difficult to relate to the participants and I had been intrigued but unaroused, as I would be if looking at nude sculptures or photographs. But in the presence of so many men and women happily fucking, I could feel my nipples hardening and my pussy getting wet.

'Holy shit,' said Lauralynn, who had once more appeared by my side. 'They're not attached to anything.'

I looked up. One pair of each couple, the one with the larger wings coloured in luminous dark violet, shades of black cherry or deep moss green, was securely harnessed to the tent ceiling, but the man or woman in his or her arms was completely loose and reliant on their partner to keep them safe. The unsecured partners wore flimsy pale-coloured wings in varying shades of pearly white, baby pink and cream.

'Fallen seraphs,' whispered Lauralynn. 'Saved by their demons. Cool.'

Someone else shushed her. It was Thomas, the man in the tuxedo with the woman attached to the chain.

Despite their precarious position, none of the 'seraphs' looked the least bit afraid.

The sign on the ceiling of this tent read, *Air: What makes us fall also helps us to rise.*

'Fire next, then,' Lauralynn said cheerily, ignoring the filthy look that Thomas gave her.

I remembered that Liana had once mentioned fire play, and said that it felt like a warm hug. Nonetheless, I wasn't prepared for what came next.

With my first step into the room I was plunged into darkness and total silence. As if all the people had vanished and it was just me in a void.

'Lauralynn?' I said softly. 'Grayson?'

There was no response.

Then a soft hand slipped into mine and a woman's voice said, 'Don't be afraid. Would you come to see my Mistress?'

I nodded, and then realised that the pitch darkness of the room made this an unreliable form of communication. 'OK,' I replied, tentatively.

The hand led me around the room to what appeared, in the little that I could see, to be an alcove with a bed in it. Upon the bed I could barely make out the outline of another person. A woman. She seemed to be wearing a mask of some sort, and just the pale skin of her jaw and the shape of her mouth was visible in the darkness.

'You will need to remove your dress,' she said. Her voice was warm and inviting, and I trusted her. 'And tie your hair back.' A hairband was pushed into my hand, and then both women helped to hoist me onto the bed where I lay flat on my belly and relaxed, enjoying the feeling of the fabric cover pressing against my bare breasts and legs.

A sense of warmth pervaded the room. Then the warmth became hotter and I heard the *whoosh* of an open flame nearby. The heat increased as the flame slapped down on my body and snapped away again so quickly that by the time I had jumped in response to the impact it was gone again. Another wave of heat rolled over my back as the woman drew her fire wand over my buttocks and back without touching the skin.

Her breath was soft as she bent and whispered into my ear. 'Is there a particular shape that calls to you?' she asked.

The words came out of my mouth before I'd even thought about it. 'A tear,' I replied.

Something cool trailed over my skin. Then the wand beat down on it again and I sucked in a gasp of air as the fire lit up the lighter fluid that the woman had applied and it blazed over my skin in the shape of a teardrop. It went out again as fast as it spread, too fast to burn. My heart pumped so quickly it felt as though it would burst out of my chest and I was filled with an overwhelming sense of happiness, as though all of my worries had been blasted away in the heat.

I collapsed back onto the bed and heard another *whoosh* as the flame was extinguished and the alcove went quiet again. The women let me lie still until I regained my senses and then helped me up to stand and get into my dress again.

'I can't see,' I said, as they led me back into the pitch-black main room.

'Follow the flames,' they replied in unison.

Every few seconds a guest in another part of the room would burst into fire and slowly I made my way through the tent guided by human candles.

The ceiling lights flashed and another phrase appeared. *Fire: What burns us also brings us light.*

Lauralynn was waiting for me as I stepped out of the tent exit and back into the garden.

'Lily, is it?' I nodded in recognition and agreement. 'I hope you don't mind my hanging around,' she said. 'My partner couldn't make it tonight and I'm here solo. You seem like the kind of girl I'd get along with.'

She was grinning like the Cheshire cat. In her red lace-up knee-length stiletto boots, the only part of her costume that wasn't painted on, and me in my flat slippers, she was easily a foot taller than me and my eyes drew exactly level with her breasts and the gold loops that adorned her nipples. In the centre of each ring sparkled a tiny ruby and I wondered if she had decorated herself especially tonight to match the outfit or if she always wore them like that.

'Not at all,' I replied. 'I seem to have lost my friends too,' I added. Grayson and She had long disappeared.

'Are the shows finished, then?' I asked. They'd all been amazing, but somehow I still felt as though there would be something more. A climax of sorts.

'There's the fifth element,' Lauralynn said. 'In the middle tent, I think.'

It was the largest tent of them all and sat directly in the centre of the other four but, until she pointed it out, I hadn't noticed that we had been travelling around the shows in a circle and were yet to go through the middle.

'What's the fifth element?' I asked, struggling to remember the little philosophy that we had covered in my literature degree. All I could think of was the Bruce Willis film.

'It's Aether. Everything else,' Lauralynn mused. 'The energy that drives the world. I wonder what they'll make of that. Let's go and see.'

She strode away and I rushed to keep up with her, admiring her rear as she walked. Lauralynn was also a beautiful girl but, with her thick limbs and broad smile, she seemed much more real than the dancer Luba, or the leopard-shoed woman that Thomas was leading around.

The final tent was a playroom. She and Grayson were both already at work. Grayson, I was surprised to see, was domming on this occasion. He was flogging one of the beautiful male dancers who had earlier been submerged underwater in a swan costume. The man was hanging from the ceiling with his toes resting on the ground and taking just enough weight so that he could support himself safely with his arms stretched over his head and his hands tied at the wrists.

Both of them were deeply into the scene and it was captivating to watch. Grayson had removed his shirt and his red military jacket hung open, exposing his sweat-streaked chest. He rained blows down on the other man's skin in perfect hypnotic rhythm.

'Didn't expect that, did you?' said She, who had melted out of the crowd and appeared by my side.

'No.' I shook my head but kept my eyes glued onto the sight of the dancer and the muscles in his flesh that twitched in response to each impact.

'You should always expect the unexpected,' she said. 'People are almost never as sure about their own desires as they might first appear. Dynamics shift and change. Now,' she added, 'I think it's your turn.'

I followed her gaze across the room to where a whole bevy of swan dancers stood. One was blindfolded, another on his knees in supplication with his wrists in cuffs in front of him. Another sat on a chair with his legs spread open and his ankles tied to the chair legs. He had a beautiful cock, which lay sleeping nestled against his thigh.

Each of them had a different sign held in his arms or pinned to his forehead. The man in the chair with his cock out held a note that said, *Eat Me*. The man wearing the blindfold held a note that said, *Beat Me*. And the one with his hands tied in front said, *Make Me Beg*.

'Wow,' I said to She. 'I feel like Alice in Wonderland.'

She laughed, and it was a sound of pure pleasure that matched the general happiness and vibe of the evening.

The room was lit softly and furnished with everything from silk throws and fur rugs to beds of nails and hard leather couches. Everywhere around me people were engaging in both their darkest and their lightest fantasies, in an environment where everything was normal and, for one of the first times in my life, I felt completely and utterly free.

'May I?' I asked the blindfolded man as I picked up the flogger that he held in his open arms. The flogger was made of rope, folded over into equal lengths and then tied at the top making a heavy but extraordinarily soft weapon. It would not be soft when it landed on his flesh, though, I knew.

'Of course, Mistress,' he said in response, and a broad smile crossed his face.

The room faded away into nothing as I began to swing. First gently, warming him up. Then harder.

'He's a proper pain slut, Lily, you can really whack him,' She called out.

It was true. His body jolted with pleasure the harder I hit him and when I really cracked, he moaned with delight.

I ran the flat of my hand over his skin, caressing his flank and the curve of his arse, and then bent my head and whispered into his ear, 'Put your hand up if it's too much, OK?' He nodded, and I noticed that he was now sporting a prominent erection. I reached down and stroked that, too, running my nails lightly over the length and head of his cock and then giving his balls a hard tug. A drop of pre-cum dripped from the tip of his penis and I caught it with my finger and ran it over his lips, then pulled his hair back and kissed him savagely.

Many dommes preferred not to touch their subs at all,

and certainly not in any kind of sexual way. But I wasn't like that. I could be cruel, but I liked it best when I knew that I was bringing pleasure. This had not endeared me to She's crew of pro-dommes at the club. I avoided playing in front of them as I knew that I didn't fit in. I longed to have a connection with the person that I tortured, to feel affection for them, not to have them debase themselves for me as easily as they would for anyone in a catsuit and a pair of heels, simply because they wanted to be treated like scum.

Here, though, in the final show room at this strange celebration of sensuality under the sign on the ceiling that read, *Love, Kink, Sex, Magic,* I felt that I could do whatever I liked.

I turned, though, when I heard a sharp, disapproving hiss coming from the corner near where She had been watching.

It was Neil.

He looked crestfallen. His mouth was stretched into a tight grimace and his eyes displayed an expression of deep disappointment.

I stood stock-still and let the makeshift whip drop to my side. The blindfolded man was leaning towards me, straining for some sign of comfort or for me to tell him what was coming next. Out of compassion and instinct, I reached forward and touched his arm to soothe him.

Neil took one look at the final gesture of tenderness that I bestowed on the dancer and fled from the tent. I tried to take after him but the room was a mess of bodies and furniture and half-clothed waiters and waitresses carrying trays of cocktails and Neil was already gone from the room by the time that I had made it even halfway across.

When I turned back to find She and ask her what the

hell was going on and why on earth they had invited Neil without asking me, I saw that she was on her knees in front of the seated dancer who had been holding the 'Eat Me' sign and she was giving him a blow-job. Her red lips snaked up and down his cock, leaving a trail of lipstick on his flesh with each stroke.

She on her knees.

Neil running from me.

Me running after Neil.

Everything had turned upside down. I was torn up inside. On the one hand the ball had given me such a sense of joy and openness and made me feel so at home with my desires, but Neil's reaction had made all of that disappear again. Was he shocked and disgusted with me or maybe just jealous? I didn't know what to think.

It was Lauralynn who gave me a ride home in the end.

'Come on,' she said, after watching the exchange. 'I'm not in much of a party mood myself tonight.'

'Missing someone?' I asked her, out of politeness, though my mind was busy working through everything that had happened.

'Yes,' she said. She sounded unsure of herself, a tone that was at odds with her confident demeanour. 'This guy I'm seeing . . . And I'm not usually even that into men. I don't know what's come over me. Love, eh?' she added. 'You can't count on it for much, but you can count on it to take you by surprise.'

I almost refused the ride home when I realised that it was going to be on the back of a motorcycle. A sleek black machine that promised danger at every turn. But it was either that or wait for She and Grayson, and I couldn't face talking to either of them until I had spoken to Neil. So I pulled on the helmet that Lauralynn gave me and hoisted myself up behind her. She'd lent me her jeans, too, for extra protection against the cold while she straddled the bike completely nude from the waist down, wearing just a biker jacket and her knee-high red boots.

Dressed like that we were begging to be pulled over, but we made it back all the way to Dalston without any problems. Lauralynn even stopped at a service station to fill up with gas and seemed to take particular delight in the look on the late-night attendant's face as he tried to work out whether her blue pants were painted on or not.

It was close to dawn by the time we pulled up outside my flat. The mode of travel had prevented us from talking at all so I'd spent the whole journey with thoughts of Neil running through my head and tears streaming down my face.

Lauralynn gave me her number as I thanked her for the lift.

'Drop me a line sometime,' she said in a thick American accent. 'Really. You look like you could do with someone to talk to.'

I was only capable of nodding by that stage and a few meagre words of gratitude.

Another day passed, and night had fallen again by the time I woke up.

Neil hadn't called. He didn't pick up when I phoned so I left him a message: 'We need to talk. Whatever you thought that was with the guy at the ball, it wasn't that. Just call me, OK?'

I didn't even know what it was that had happened that night. Or what Neil thought about it.

But he did call back, only minutes after I had ended the message on his voicemail. And we arranged to meet.

'That first time, the other week, with the photographer, it felt like a game,' Neil said. 'It was fun, playful . . . and special. It was you and me.'

'Did you enjoy it?' I asked him. 'The feel of the flogger?'

He nodded.

We were in the dark and smoky bowels of a shady Soho drinking club, just off Shaftesbury Avenue, that he had become a member of since receiving another promotion to executive level. I would never have pegged Neil as the sort of guy who would join a club, let alone one where tobacco fumes hung down from the low ceiling like a semi-permanent curtain of nicotine. Leonard and I had sometimes taken drinks in slightly more fashionable clubs in the area, but this place, which didn't even have a name over its door, just a grimy buzzer, felt as if it had stepped straight out of the 1950s up to and including the permanent five o'clock shadows and the total indifference of the two bartenders. But it felt cozy, intimate, the sort of place where secrets could be kept and revealed.

Neil was proving full of surprises.

He looked up at me.

'I did, Lily,' he stated. He held my gaze. 'A lot. You know I've always been so fond of you. Lusted after you. Even thought I was a little bit in love with you.'

I made a gesture to silence him, but he resolutely continued.

'Please, allow me to speak.'

I lowered my hand.

'Every time I saw you with another guy, I felt like death warmed over, jealous, bitterly envious and I began to think you were out of my league, that you would always see me as just a friend or a brother, not a man and a potential lover.'

Again I wanted to say something, but the forlorn look on his face suggested it would be best for me to remain silent for now.

'Surely you realised, if only from the way I hung around you and Liana, always there, at your beck and call, like some harmless pet,' he continued.

'I thought it was Liana you were pursuing,' I said. I was lying. I had always been aware of Neil's interest in me. It had been obvious from the moment we'd been introduced.

'No.'

'I'm sorry.'

'But you can't regulate the rules of attraction any more than you can fight the tide,' Neil said. 'And I kept harbouring some hope against hope that one day you would tire of the others, no longer be so influenced by Liana's wildness and come to appreciate my ordinariness. You were the first person from uni I re-established contact with when I came to work in London. No one else really mattered.'

'I'm flattered.'

'Do you remember the day in Brighton after you got the tattoo and showed it to me?'

'What about it?'

'I was shocked, but at the same time, I loved it. I thought it was downright beautiful, unconventional and daring, of course, but it just fitted in so exquisitely with your personality, that innate talent you have for surprising people, friends. It almost felt inevitable that you would have that tattoo on your face. As if everything in your life had been leading up to it. It had been preordained.'

'Perhaps it had,' I opined.

'I sometimes thought about you at night in my bedroom at the flat, knowing you were just a few walls away, and the focus of my imagination was never on any anything else but always the teardrop, Lily.'

'Oh.'

'Anyway, it was always you and that day we had the session with your photographer, Grayson, it was as if you opened the door to a whole other world.'

I wondered briefly whether Neil was evoking the intimacy we had shared being positioned nude and in explicit poses or the fact I had quickly taken control once Grayson had suggested that I domme him and found him surprisingly willing to bend to my compulsions and desires.

'It was a photography session, Neil. Play-acting for the camera. You mustn't read too much into it.' As the words came out of my mouth I wanted to take them back. I hadn't been play-acting. It had been much more than that for me.

'I know,' he said. 'You can't imagine how many days and nights I had dreamed of experiencing something like that with you. It was a constant preoccupation, ever since I heard about that club that you worked at and found out what happened there. I'm not stupid, Lily, I can use the Internet. I always wondered if you were like that, more than just a door girl, but I never knew for sure until you whipped me. Being with you was an ambition that dominated my waking days throughout my three years in Brighton. Or should I say my nights? Trying to visualise it, how it would feel, how it would happen, how you would feel, but never in a month of Sundays could I have guessed it would take the turn it did.'

'You mean me . . . taking over?' I ventured, aware we were beginning to tread on awkward ground.

'Not just that . . .' He hesitated.

'What?'

'It's . . . the way I . . . reacted to it.' He was stumbling over words, straining to say the right thing as if it was a matter of life and death.

'It made you feel uncomfortable?' I queried.

'That's just it,' he replied. 'It didn't. It felt as if you were the one controlling me, using me, toying with me and my body. My mind, too. And the more it went on, the more I sort of wanted you to go further. It was over so quickly, though, when Grayson had the shots he wanted. I wanted it to go on and on but I couldn't tell you. I was too afraid that you didn't feel the same way. And this had never happened when I'd been with girls before, not, I hasten to say, that there were that many before you. From the moment you took your first strike and your voice sort of went hoarse and you began to command me, it awakened something inside me. As if it had always been present but carefully hidden away. It confused me. Because I didn't expect to react in that way. It's difficult to explain. It seemed as if our roles had been reversed and, after the initial moment of shock, I wanted more, mentally accepted it felt right. I felt divided, bathing in the glow of lust requited while also yearning to be controlled, lose all control.'

I sighed. Had I been right to unveil my base nature to someone who had once been a friend? Open Pandora's Box?

'At the ball,' Neil continued, 'I saw you playing with others, it was as if you shone. And in the pit of my stomach I was aching to become one of those men who were just bound and waiting for your touch, and had you noticed me, I would have fallen straight to my knees and volunteered to become your slave, your dog, and accept any treatment, however degrading and humiliating, if only to become part of your life, Lily. I wanted to be owned by you, even if part of me rebelled against the very idea.

'But then I saw you kiss him. The other man. And that was something that you never gave me and I couldn't watch. That's why I ran away at the ball, Lily. I felt as if I no longer knew myself. Didn't know whether I wanted you to beat me or to make love to me. I didn't know what I wanted. I don't know what I want. It's scary.'

He looked away, a genuine sense of confusion colouring his features. I could see how torn he was between his feelings for me and the submissive instincts I had somehow unveiled. It seemed I had inadvertently opened a door and he was increasingly uncertain whether he actually wanted to close it.

'What do you want me say?'

I was angry at Neil now. And at myself.

Leonard.

Dagur.

Grayson.

She.

Why had life become so complicated?

8

Walking on the Wild Side

Life goes on.

I was beginning to understand my nature better, but I knew I still had much to learn.

She's lessons in life, the way she uncannily homed in on those desires that lay at the core of me, a budding friendship with the lovely Lauralynn, my increasingly rare nights with Dagur when he was in town and not on the road with Viggo and the band, the awkward attentions of Neil, the ambiguous nature of my dealings with Grayson and the still sharp, painful memories of Leonard all buzzed around inside my mind until things made neither head nor tail.

I felt I was no longer the same girl who had come to London straight from university, but I was still not the finished article. I was a work in progress, struggling with a welter of contradictions. As a teenager, I had of course dreamed of a happy ever after, even if deep down I already guessed it was either an illusion or anything but the panacea commonly advertised in countless movies, books and songs. But still it remained like a ghost at the back of my mind, nagging away.

On one hand, I was joyful that my sexuality now had meaning and focus, but on the other I still yearned for a form of intimacy that I hadn't managed to find. Yet.

Under She and Lauralynn's careful tutelage, I became even more involved at the club, no longer hovering full of curiosity and concern or practising my rope-tying skills on chair legs or my whip-cracking talents on thin air. I became actively involved as a domme, yet during the day I worked at the music store. Living a double life still came so naturally.

I hadn't heard from Liana for months and felt guilty about it. We had once been so close and maybe the knowledge I had acquired of her submissive nature was coloured by the fact that I hadn't quite reconciled myself to the way that I treated the male subs I would punish and play with in the evenings.

In my more private interactions, I played only with subs that I had some sort of personal connection with. Although it wasn't love, far from it, I gained some satisfaction from the knowledge that I was giving them pleasure and that outweighed the idea that I was being cruel. But working at the club I was required to occasionally beat slaves that I didn't know well or didn't particularly like and sometimes I despised them for their weakness and servility, and I knew that I was treating them more harshly because of it. They loved my cruelty, but I couldn't forgive myself for abusing a person out of anger or spite instead of mutual pleasure. This dark shadow inside me – wanting to forget all the logic about what was right and what was wrong and behave like an animal – persisted. I recognised the same chord in Liana, but she had accepted it within herself and I hadn't.

Over the course of a week, I tried to call Liana a few times, but she never picked up. I left a couple of messages. Remembering what we had spoken about the last time we had talked in earnest, I was worried about her.

But then life took over, and I briefly, if shamefully, put her out of my mind. Maybe she was the one who wished to steer clear of me.

It was a few weeks before she made contact.

'Hi, slut!'

I was in Denmark Street on a quiet day in the shop and had only sold a few sets of guitar strings all morning.

The sparkle in her voice told me immediately that the Liana of old had returned.

'Liana!' I was so loud that Jonno turned quizzically towards me, with an expression of disapproval that made him look like an irascible librarian.

'It's been ages, I know,' she apologised.

'No matter. You've called me back, that's the main thing.'

'There's been a lot happening,' she said.

'Talk to me.' I was so chuffed to hear her again.

'Well . . . I've moved to Amsterdam,' she announced triumphantly.

This left me speechless.

'Really?' I finally managed to say. 'Tell me all about it.'

I'd caught the train from Schiphol airport and twenty minutes later it drew up at Centraal Station. It was a grey day, a thin drizzle falling like thin mist, ripples flowing across the ever-present canals crisscrossing the city centre. It was only my second visit to the Dutch capital and my initial impression as I walked out into the open space beyond the station's vast portico, past the file of waiting cabs and a mess of noisy construction work, was of a savanna of bicycles, twisting and turning in every possible direction, skipping between tramlines, crisscrossing roads with both serenity and alacrity. I hadn't been on a bike since I was fourteen, but Liana had told me she would put a spare one at my disposal when I visited. The first time I had been here, Leonard had been waiting for me at the airport and had whisked me straight into town by cab and we hadn't ventured further east than the Dam Square where he was staying at the opulent and old-world Krasnapolsky Hotel.

I had a simple map that Liana had emailed me before I left London explaining how best I could reach the house where she was staying. It wouldn't take me more than twenty to thirty minutes to walk to her place and all I was carrying was a rucksack with some spare clothes. I pulled up my hood and unfolded the sheet of paper with Liana's directions, trying to shield it from the rain.

It was just a question of locating the right canal and then a group of parallel bridges, although I'd never been very good at reading maps at the best of times.

As I wandered along the cobbled paths by the canals, I was struck by the reassuring quietness of the city which settled all around you from the moment you moved off any of the few main roads. This was so unlike London's frantic rhythm, pedestrians ambling with no sense of urgency, windows with no curtains at eye-level everywhere I walked, as if there was no need for privacy. A city with no secrets. Yes, I thought, this was the sort of place I could find it easy to live in, and felt unsurprised that Liana, with whom I had so much in common, should have come here.

She'd mentioned that she would be working until mid-afternoon at the flower market, a temporary job but one she enjoyed, and had made arrangements for me to pick up the key to her flat from a downstairs neighbour, so I wasn't in any rush.

I stopped for a coffee in a small bar whose stone steps led partly underground to a vaulted area full of comforting warmth and a seductive blend of smells, in which sweet alcohol, cinnamon and a faint trace of tobacco lingered. I felt sleepy and fully relaxed.

The building where Liana lived was a tall three-storeyed one carved out of ancient stone, squat and imposing. From the outside, as I looked up, the windows on every floor seemed huge. Liana's flat was situated at the top, and could be reached through a steep, circular wooden staircase.

The old woman who lived on the ground floor and appeared to be the building's owner, looked and dressed like a stereotypical granny. She flashed me a twinkly smile when she opened the door and complimented me on my appearance, mentioning that I looked just like Liana's sister. Liana didn't have a sister. We were both only children. But this was not the first time such a remark had been made, despite the differences in our appearances.

Once inside, I dropped my rucksack to the parquet floor and slipped out of my lightweight coat, rivulets of rain still dripping off it as I searched for a cupboard or convenient recess where I could hang it up.

It was a large, airy room, with wide, high windows through which the outside light bathed the flat in a warm glow. I looked out and gazed at the peaceful flow of the small canal and the orderly lines of bicycles parked alongside it. Beyond the roofs of the buildings on the other side of the canal, I could see the broken crest of a line of trees where Oosterpark lay.

I found somewhere to sit, a small, narrow sofa covered by a lemon-yellow patchwork spread, and lost myself in contemplation. The silence was eerie. Normally, in any city, there would always be a distinct rumour of noises, voices, traffic in the distance, but here the afternoon was altogether cleansed of sounds. At first, it was an unsettling feeling but soon, as I relaxed, I allowed the peacefulness of the mood to flow over me until I was almost dozing. I was just content to sit there, vaguely daydreaming, staring at the room's walls or the fading light outside through the windows, purposefully keeping my mind empty of any significant thoughts. Normally, I would have been on my feet, seeking something to do, aching for a coffee or something to read or an excuse to stay active. I was shaken out of my torpor by the buzz of my mobile phone.

It was a text from Liana: she was on her way home and would be with me soon.

'So what happened?' I finally asked. We'd greeted each other affectionately and then strolled down to a neighbouring cafe where everyone seemed to know her. She was wearing a shapeless grey cardigan at least one size too large, a pair of denim shorts over her black tights and a pair of ankle-high boots.

Her pale cheeks were flushed and a healthy sense of radiance spread appealingly across her face. She genuinely appeared happy, so unlike the last time we had met when she had been so visibly torn and anguished.

'I left him.'

'Your Brighton dom?'

She had always refused point blank to reveal his name.

'Yes.'

'Good. He sounded like a dickhead. But why Amsterdam?'

'It was as good a place as any,' she replied. 'I once had a pen pal here when I was still at school and I had fond memories of the place. And it's cheap and easy to travel to London.'

'How long have you been here already?'

She considered. 'Just over four months.'

I was taken aback. I knew we had fallen out of touch while I was still preoccupied with my own discoveries and minor adventures, but it just hadn't felt that long. What sort of friend was I?

'Time flies, eh?'

'Certainly does.'

She took a sip from her cup of herbal tea. Out of habit, I'd opted for coffee. It felt uncommonly bitter and lukewarm to my tongue. Liana was looking at me intently, as if about to burst into confession. I kicked my shoes off under the table. Distant strains of music ebbed and flowed in the distance, although the coffee shop didn't have a jukebox or the radio on, and the thump of the bass fading in and out felt like the beat of my heart on standby.

'Things just kept getting worse,' Liana explained. 'With the guy in Brighton. I know I'm submissive and I like to be dominated. But there's a difference, you know, between being a sub and being a doormat. Between being a dom and being an arsehole. And this guy was an arsehole. It just took me a while to work that out. He was very charismatic and I so desperately wanted that level of intimacy that I'd shared with Alyss, before him, and so I did things that I wasn't comfortable with, thinking that if I pleased him enough I could make it work.

'But eventually I realised that he didn't really care about me. He liked a power trip and having a pretty young girl-friend and that was it. So I dumped him. But I had to leave, to make sure that I didn't get pulled into it again. Some things are intoxicating, even when you know they're bad for you.'

My mouth opened. I was curious to hear all the sordid details and to relate them to my own situation, although I also knew they would affect me badly if she disclosed them. Liana was my friend and I was angry that she'd been hurt, but the dilemma sounded all too familiar as I was still in the process of assuming my own dominant nature and under-standing the dynamic of how it affected my relationships with men.

I knew that I didn't really care about most of the subs that I beat at the club and I knew that they were aware of that and got off on it all the same. Sometimes I felt terribly guilty about hurting them, even when they begged me for it. I wondered whether I would be able to hurt someone that I truly loved, or if I would want to hurt someone that I loved even more than those I didn't care about. Push the physical extremes even further to increase the emotional extremes. I longed for the sort of bond that Liana described. The sort that She and Grayson shared, and Lauralynn and her unknown man. But I feared what would happen if I got it. What sort of person I might become.

Sometimes, when the men I was domming were so servile and ridiculous and begged for me to punish them, despite my efforts to the contrary I couldn't help the scorn

I felt as I played with them, superficially wounding their bodies and their feelings, degrading them even as they pleaded with me to push them even further. But, inside, I was waiting for the day when I would have an emotional connection with one man, when there would be life beyond the play, the scenes. These men were part of a crowd, anonymous. It was the day one of them would turn out to have a face that would prove a turning point.

'I understand,' I muttered. 'I hope I do, Liana.'

'I wanted to be used and he used me,' Liana continued. 'I now realise that's all I was for him. A conduit for his cruelty, his sadism. Some people like that sort of thing, even long term, but I'm not one of them. If he'd ever said certain words, expressed some kind of affection, showed me that deep down he cared for me as a person and not as piece of fuckmeat, I would have continued, believe me. That's the way I am. It wasn't what he did, but the lack of feeling behind it all. The lack of aftercare. I kept waiting for things to change. But I knew that day would never come.'

'And?'

'I told him I'd had enough. He didn't take it well. But I swore to myself I would never see him again, even as he kept mailing me, phoning me, assuring me I would come back to him in the end, that I needed him more than he needed me.'

'Didn't you meet him originally through your work?'

'Yes, that really made it awkward.'

'It must have.'

'That was part of the reason I left. I stayed away for weeks, even though I felt so damn empty inside. I met a couple of other men, also doms, of course, online. The first one was a dead loss, another chancer, but the second one whom I met at the Pelirocco – you know that boutique hotel on Regency Square where the barman used to prepare those crazy cocktails? – I really felt was different, even though it was brief. He was so warm, caring . . .' She drifted away, her memories floating to the surface and clouding her eyes.

'It didn't work out?'

'No.' She returned to the present. 'I liked him. A lot. But I think that, in his own way, he was as mixed up as me. Uncertain of his role. He undressed me, but sort of panicked when he saw some of my bruises . . . Nothing happened.'

'I'm sorry.'

'There was no point in crying my eyes out, I reckoned. So I took a decision. I gave in my notice at the solicitors the following day, cleared my meagre bank account and almost tossed a coin. I was thinking maybe Paris or New York. I don't speak a word of French and the big Apple was too far, so I ended up here in Amsterdam. Where everyone speaks English!'

'I think canals suit you,' I said. 'You seem happy.'

'I am,' Liana confirmed. 'It's a lovely place.'

As she lowered her gaze, I realised she had only told me half the story.

I couldn't help but grin. It had nothing to do with her submissive nature, I thought, but Liana was not the sort of girl who spent long between men.

'You've met someone else, haven't you? I can see it in your smile.'

'I have,' she confirmed, all shyness washed away from her features.

I was glad for her. But I had to ask.

'Another dom?'

Her look was impish.

'Dom,' she said firmly. 'I'd never date any other sort. But – how can I put it? – the right sort.'

'You're incorrigible.'

'I yam what I yam,' she said. It was a joke the two of us had long shared, what Popeye the Sailor Man always said.

'Oh yes you are.'

'He's coming round tonight,' Liana said. 'I'll introduce you.'

His name was Leroy, and he was an American guy who had moved from New York to Amsterdam to finish his Ph.D. in Philosophy. His mother was Dutch, so he spoke the language, and he'd always wanted to try a stint in the Netherlands.

'Everyone's got to go back to their roots at some point,' he explained. 'Otherwise I think you can't really know for sure who you are, can you?'

Leroy was just a few years older than us, but in the way that men had of maturing a little later, he seemed about the same age. He was unexpectedly short, especially for someone who was half Dutch. Liana had previously always dated tall men. But he was stocky, and fit, as most people in Amsterdam were, from all the cycling. His father was Nigerian and the combination of heritages had given Leroy a beautiful bone structure and full mouth. There was something innately sensual in his appearance and the way that he moved. Height aside, I could see why Liana fancied him.

'So you two met online?' I asked, as Leroy stirred the deep pot of aromatic meat stew. He had a nice arse, I noticed, as he bent down to swing the oven door open and check on the garlic bread.

Liana and I were sitting at one end of the long wooden trestle table in the kitchen, each sipping a glass of red wine. She followed the line of my gaze as I appreciated Leroy's pert buttocks and winked at me.

'Not bad, eh?' she mouthed at me as he was distracted keeping an eye on the food.

Leroy turned to respond to my question.

'Yep,' he said, 'online. It's the only way, really, if you're looking for someone on the scene. Trying to work out if someone is kinky otherwise is fraught with danger.'

I giggled, imagining how that conversation might go down on a first date. The wine was starting to go to my head.

'We met, we clicked,' Liana said, raising an eyebrow at me to hint heavily that the connection hadn't been purely conversational, 'and the rest is history.'

Leroy spooned the food onto dishes and brought it over to the table. He set the plates down in front of us and returned with his own a moment or two later.

'Shit!' he cried, just as he finally sat down. 'The garlic bread.' He leaped up again and pulled the oven door open in the nick of time.

Questions that I was dying to ask bloomed on my lips

and then faded away before I could summon the courage to ask them.

Why? I wanted to know. What was it that drove us to seek these extremes of human connection? I doubted that there was really an answer to that question. I'd asked the same of She and Lauralynn and both of them had said basically the same thing in reply. Some people are happy in the shallow waters of life, others like to ride the rapids. Some people like chocolate ice cream, others like rum and raisin. It's just the way people are built and nothing more to it than that.

Watching the two of them together, I couldn't deduce much more than that they got along well and were both happy. There were tiny gestures – things that might well have existed between any ordinary couple but which held an extra weight when I saw them occur between kinksters.

The way he rested his hand so heavily on the small of her back when they stood alongside each other in the kitchen. The grace with which she so naturally slipped down onto the floor in front of him and rested her head on his calves instead of taking the seat alongside him when we moved into the living room and I observed how he gently stroked her hair with such tenderness.

I was only staying for a few days, but settled into life with Liana in her Amsterdam flat as if we'd never been apart. We both agreed that if we closed our eyes we could easily be back in Brighton at university again. In some ways, we'd changed and grown so much that we were barely the same two people at all, but in other ways we were still the two girls exploring the Lanes and getting tattooed together on a whim.

Liana was still new in her job so hadn't been able to take more than a day off work during my visit so instead I came down to the flower market in the mornings and informally helped her out. The heady scent of the flowers reminded me of the night of the ball and the tropical scents that had pervaded the air and I felt an eerie sort of peace working outdoors with my hands. It was such a contrast to the dark corners of the club or even the confined and brightly lit space of the music store.

Leroy didn't visit again for the next two nights, though I knew that he and Liana texted each other often. He wanted to give her some space, he'd said, so that she could spend time with me. But her phone lit up frequently with his messages and with it her expression.

It was the day before I was due to depart when, out of the blue, Liana asked me if I would like to watch them making love.

'I know the last time was traumatic for you,' she said. 'With Nick. And I wondered if you'd like to see it for yourself, what we do. So you can understand. And know that I'm safe.'

I was standing in front of the refrigerator at the time, drinking orange juice straight from the carton and nearly choked on my mouthful. It was the first time that Liana had ever acknowledged what had happened on that night, or that I'd even seen her have sex before.

Liana patted me on the back.

'Serves you right,' she said, 'for not using a glass.'

'You want me to watch you having sex?' I asked weakly.

'Yeah,' she replied casually.

'I'm not sure what to say. How . . . ?'

I wanted to ask if she thought I'd be involved. Was Liana looking for a threesome? The last time, with Nick, had been shocking, but the situation had arisen naturally and it had been clear at the time that I was only an accidental bystander. This was different. And I'd disappeared before I'd had to speak to either of them in the morning, so I hadn't had to endure any awkward moments.

'You want me to watch?' I asked again, dumbly.

'Watch. Not get involved. We won't even notice you're there.'

I wasn't sure if that made it better or worse.

Of course, I'd seen all manner of things at the club, and the ball, and during the time that I'd spent with Laura-lynn and She. I'd seen entire roomfuls of people fucking or domming and subbing. But Liana was an old friend, and it felt so much more intimate with just the three of us.

My skin crawled at the thought. Yet I was curious. More than anything, I wanted to watch Leroy. To see how a couple behaved together and to imagine what it might be like for me if I ever met someone that I felt that way with.

'OK then,' I said.

'Great!' she replied, breezily, as if she'd just issued me a dinner invitation and not a promise to watch her and her man copulating.

It was a bad time to visit Amsterdam's disappointing Sex Museum, which was a quarter of the size of the one Leonard had taken me to see on one of our Paris weekends. When I saw the giant replica of a penis that was bigger than I was and the various representations of sex through the ages, all I could think about was Liana and Leroy and what

I was in for later. My mind in imaginative freefall, I took a few bridges too many and ended up near Leidseplein, having lost my bearings and had to carefully retrace my steps.

When the allotted hour finally arrived, I was pleased to see that Leroy looked as nervous as I felt. Or was he just excited? He'd arrived at Liana's with a duffel bag that made a dull thud when he lowered it down onto the wooden floor in the living room.

'Heya, Lil,' he said. 'How you feeling?'

'I'm good,' I replied with false cheer.

We skipped dinner. I was too nervous to eat. Leroy said that food would make him fall asleep. And Liana was worried about gagging. I winced at the thought.

It was Leroy who finally started things off. Liana suddenly went quiet and her expression took on a questioning quality as if she was waiting for something to begin, as I was.

'Come,' he said. She stood up from the table and began walking down the hall to the living room. She moved as if she were on a lead, or being operated by remote control, although she was in front of him. I trailed uneasily after them, not sure what to do with myself. Not for the first time, I wished that there had been some kind of etiquette manual for how to behave in these sorts of situations. In school science lessons I'd learned how to put a condom on a banana, which had proven no use at all. What I had really needed was a lesson on what to do when your best friend asks you to watch her fucking. Why was it the most difficult scenarios in life that always came without an instruction booklet?

'Shall I put on some music?' I asked. I was barefoot and the wooden floor was cold against my feet. I wanted to go and find some socks, but didn't. It seemed an inappropriate time to think about laundry.

'No,' Leroy replied. 'She likes the sounds.' They hadn't begun yet but immediately a pornographic soundtrack began to play in my head, bodies slapping wetly to the backdrop of an improbable 'oh, oh, oh'.

Liana had gone silent, and began to sway very gently on her feet. Her eyes were closed. Leroy circled around her like an animal stalking its prey. It was as if all the tension that had left her body had gone into his and he was coiled like a spring ready to pounce. I sat down on the couch. They'd forgotten that I was there already.

He kissed her, in just the same way that I had kissed the ballet dancer at the ball. First, he encircled her throat with his hand in a protective caress. She relaxed her head back as if she were offering herself to him. Then he raised his hand and softly stroked her cheek, before wrapping his fingers into her hair and pulling her neck back with one hard, sharp tug.

Though they were almost the same height, he seemed to tower over her by virtue of the way that he bent her to his will. Her mouth opened and she made a mewing noise like a kitten. He growled and planted his lips on hers in the sort of manner that suggested he was only moments away from tearing at her flesh. She kissed him back like a child searching for food from its mother's breast.

'Turn around,' he said softly.

She was so eager to respond to his command that she

spun too quickly and almost lost her balance. Leroy caught
her with a steadying hand.

'Pull up your skirt.'

Liana's hands shook and her movements were imprecise
and clumsy, as if she'd just had a glass of wine, but
eventually she managed to gather together the vast swathe
of flowing fabric from her long, bohemian-style skirt and
bunch it up around her hips. He stood back and watched.
Let her stand there untouched. Made sure that I had a
perfect view of her naked arse. She wasn't wearing any
knickers. I guessed that Leroy had instructed her to go bare
down there.

'Touch your toes,' Leroy said. 'As low as you can go.'

Liana stretched down until she managed to find a position where she could rest her hands on the floor a couple of
feet in front of her as if she was in the middle of an awkward
downward dog.

Her angled stance made her already long, thin legs seem
even longer. She was built like a wading bird. Bony, but
with a natural grace to her and the firm curved backside of a
dancer, although as far as I knew she had never danced.

'Lean back. Spread your arse cheeks.'

It seemed like an impossible task. The state she was in,
she would surely fall headfirst onto the floor. But Liana
managed to curve her back up and hold her body out flat as
she hitched her skirt up so that she was gripping the fabric
between her wrist and her hips and she placed one hand on
each buttock and pulled.

Leroy wasn't even close to touching her and yet I could see
from the twitching of her body and the way that she was
softly moaning that Liana was already on the edge. I forgot

my shyness and leaned forward, fascinated, watching the myriad emotions that swarmed over her face as her cheeks turned pink and her lips parted in an expression of sensuality.

I wished that I could be her, that I could feel just once what it was like to lose oneself so utterly in the moment, to be such a willing slave to pleasure. When I was domming I got carried away at times, but never as completely as this – I was always aware of the need to keep an eye on my sub's wellbeing.

Submission, I realised then, was an act of surrender. That's why she looked so relaxed. She'd given herself not just to Leroy, but to the sensation of each moment. That's why it was so intense. Without the need to focus on anything at all besides physical feeling, she must be aware of even the most infinitesimal currents of air on her skin.

Finally he reached forward and ran his fingers along her pussy. She jumped and shuddered in response to his touch, as though he'd nudged her with a cattle prod.

His fingers glistened when he removed them. He brought his hand to his mouth and licked her juices off with relish.

'You're very wet,' he observed.

Liana moaned.

'What are you?' he asked. 'Say it. I want to hear you say it.'

'I'm a slut,' she said. 'Your slut.'

'Louder.'

'I'm your slut!' she shouted.

She'd said exactly the same thing to Nick. A coincidence, I wondered, or did she get every guy to demand that of her? I wanted to ask Leroy how much of what he did was because it was what he wanted, and how much of it was what she wanted. I knew from my own experience that submissives could be very demanding. I spent hours at the club giving slaves what they begged for. Half of the time I felt as though they were the ones who were dominating me.

'You're my fucking whore,' he announced in a satisfied voice. His tone had become darker, as if something in him that he had been reining in had now snapped. His arm shot out and he grabbed a hank of her hair and wrenched her head back hard. He was driving his other hand into her with such force each thrust was more like a punch. Yet instead of reacting with fear or pain, Liana relaxed even more, spreading her legs wide and leaning against him and shuddering as though she would come at any moment. Her eyes were closed and she was smiling.

Leroy let go suddenly and she stumbled forward without making any attempt to stop her fall. She didn't even let go of her arse cheeks. Because he hadn't told her to, I realised. Even her body's natural defences had submitted to Leroy. She'd let herself go so much that she was relying on him for everything, even keeping her upright. If I tripped over, then my hands would immediately come down to break my fall without any conscious thought. But Liana's body followed Leroy's commands instinctively, even more instinctively than she protected herself. He caught her easily before she hit the floor.

He gripped her on each side of her hips and bent his head down to the pucker of her arse and slid his tongue inside and then ran it in a straight line all the way up the length of her spine to the base of her neck where he sank his teeth into her. She arched her back and pressed herself against him. It was like their own strange version of a hug and seemed oddly nurturing.

The nurturing didn't last long.

With one quick push Leroy had Liana on her knees. He yanked her up by the hair again, so firmly that I was surprised she still had any. Maybe all the tugging helped it to grow faster.

Faced with his penis, Liana took it into her mouth like a starving person who hadn't had a meal for a week. She didn't lick it playfully first or indulge in any of the techniques that she had laughed at and I had blushed over back at the Brighton flat when we were both close to relative innocents. She impaled herself on him as though she wanted to eat him alive and he held her by the sides of her face and swung her head back and forth as though he were fucking her cunt and not her face. Every minute or so she would make a noise like a cat with a fur ball and just when I thought she could take no more he would stop for long enough to let her inhale and then she would thrust herself right back onto him and continue sucking him into her throat as if he was her source of air.

Leroy started to shake and clench and I was sure that this was it, he would come in her mouth and then I would be faced with the dreadful moment of wondering what to say once they'd finished, but he stopped her before he exploded.

'Shhh,' he whispered, and that one word was like a code between them. Liana sank back onto her haunches immediately and her face softened. She released his cock from the grip of her mouth and nuzzled her face into his groin, landing soft kisses around his thighs and nibbling at his balls. His dick was still hard and she pressed it to her face as though it were the caress of his hand. Liana had turned from rabid to romantic quicker than I could blink.

He reached down and cupped her breasts. Softly at first and she purred and burrowed against his hands. Then, in another one of those momentary power exchanges that seemed to flash silently between them, he switched from cuddly to rough and, placing one hand on her breast bone and the other on her back, he flipped her over in a flailing tangle of limbs.

She fell back, totally exposed and that was when I noticed the silvery glint. She was completely smooth down below and the petals of her labia were engorged and spread open displaying the piercings that I hadn't known she sported. A steel ring glistened at the hood of her clit and two matching silver circles were threaded through each of her labia. She hadn't mentioned getting them done, although it was the kind of thing that Liana would normally take great pleasure in telling me all about. Both the plan and the execution. Yet she hadn't.

I'd seen a few men and women who had been pierced either by or for their dominants. Some wore a dog tag to denote ownership. I suspected that Liana's jewellery might have been a result of her relationship with her Brighton dom. That would explain why she hadn't mentioned it. And it would be typical of Liana to leave it in. She didn't think of the past as a type of baggage to be dropped at the earliest opportunity. She was too pragmatic for that. Liana enjoyed her demons, she didn't fight them, and she held her mistakes close to her chest in a loving embrace as a reminder of who she was.

I yam what I yam, as she always said.

'Close your eyes, and don't move until I say,' Leroy hissed.

She was now flat on her back and didn't look as though she had any intention of going anywhere.

He rooted around in his duffel bag until he found a couple of lengths of deep-red bondage rope. Liana responded to each clink that the objects inside the bag made with a soft moan or a shudder. Leroy smiled as he watched her twitch and I was certain that he was purposefully taking his time and shaking his bag of toys around to build the anticipation up more.

As the rope brushed against her skin, she broke out all over in goosebumps and made a plaintive crying sound as though the expectation of pleasure was too great to bear.

Leroy bent each of her knees and bound her thighs to her calves so that she was wide open to him, but unable to do little more than wriggle. He then pulled her arms over her head and tied her wrists together. The more roughly he pulled on the rope, the louder her moans of excitement became, but his roughness was only a show, I noticed. For all the appearance of harshness, he was careful to run his finger between her skin and the rope to check that it wasn't too tight for her circulation, and every few minutes he would glance down to make sure that she wasn't turning blue and clutch her hands to warm them.

Finally he pushed her knees apart and pulled himself on top of her body. His cock was rock hard and glistening wet. He made no move to reach for a condom and somehow the idea of him entering her bare thrilled me more than anything else. It was such a personal act.

'Tell me what you want,' he said. His voice was hoarse. The effort of holding himself back was evidently causing him so much pain that I had to stop myself from leaning forward and pushing his cock into her myself.

'Oh God,' she said. 'Fuck me. Please fuck me, please, please, fuck me . . .'

She repeated the same phrase over and over like a mad woman and Leroy growled and lifted himself up and thrust into her again and again as hard as he could. Bound and trussed, she was unable to push against him but she still tried to rock her hips and wriggled and squirmed until he took hold of her wrists and held her down.

I was on the edge of my seat now and breathing rapidly along with them. I wanted Leroy to reach over and grab my hair and pull me up hard against him, but I restrained myself, remembering the number-one rule that was repeated on signs all over the club: *Never interrupt a scene.*

Liana jerked harder and harder, grinding herself against him. The nub of her piercing seemed to be stimulating her clit and the harder she rubbed, the quicker his thrusts became until she bit her lip and begged, 'Oh fuck, let me come, please let me come, please let me come . . .'

'Come for me,' he cried, and the moment the words were out of his lips she arched her back and strained against the ropes and screamed so loud that I jumped a foot in the air and nearly screamed right along with her.

'Oh fuck,' he said, and he lifted her arse and clamped her against him and held her still as the tremors of a climax visibly ripped through her body.

'Did you like that?' he growled, with a look of extreme concentration on his face.

The poor man was going to burst, any second, and I doubted his ability to hold on any longer, but he managed to until Liana stopped shaking for long enough to murmur a fervent 'yes'.

He gripped her shoulders, pressing himself into her, and finally let go.

When his orgasm was over and his body relaxed, she curled herself towards him. He laid her flat and swiftly untied the ropes that bound her arms and legs and then he pulled her into his arms and rocked her back and forth like a child. 'Shhh,' he said again, each time that she mewed and buried herself into him. She looked as though she was trying to crawl into his skin. As if close would never be close enough.

At that point, I left them. Watching the sex was one thing, but watching them embracing afterwards was something else altogether. The obvious intimacy between them had left me with mixed emotions. On the one hand I was desperately jealous. I wanted to feel that way with someone. On the other hand, it was so all-encompassing that I was afraid that opening myself up that way would leave me too vulnerable. I was afraid of being hurt. I was afraid of letting go.

I tossed and turned for hours that night before I eventually managed to fall asleep. The sex had left me undeniably turned on, but I couldn't bring myself to masturbate over Liana. I didn't want to think of her that way. It would change things between us.

The next morning I lay under the covers and snoozed until I was sure that Leroy would have left so I would not need to face him. It was cowardly, but I didn't care. I could thank him for his generosity in allowing me such an intimate glimpse into their lives another time, when I didn't feel so embarrassed.

Liana was happy, and unusually quiet. I poured myself an orange juice, into a glass this time to appease her and sat down at the kitchen table.

'Did you get it?' she said to me at last.

'Yeah,' I replied. 'I got it.'

Neil and I met up during our respective lunch hours, the day after my return from Amsterdam. He worked such long hours these days that I rarely got to see him in the evening. By the time he finished work, I'd begun at the club, so snatched lunchtimes had become our regular way to catch up. He was wearing an anthracite-grey suit, a tight-fitting white shirt, a dark-blue tie and black brogues polished to an inch of glassy smoothness and looked every inch like a master of the universe. On every successive occasion we spent together he seemed to be morphing into a brand-new person, distancing himself from the chrysalis of his Brighton years, casting off the callow softness of youth, while every time I looked at myself in the mirror I didn't seem to be changing at all on the outside, still appearing younger than I was.

Growing up suited him.

He'd booked a table at Kettner's, a plush eaterie in Soho, where I felt out of place in my casual clothes and clumpy boots, unpolished and clumsy. I reckoned even my some-times fetish wear would have fitted in better.

Neil, on the other hand, seemed in his element, gliding along from the salon to the restaurant floor full of poise, holding my hand casually in his, as the greeter guided us to our table.

It was when the conversation turned to more personal matters that he began to lose his assurance.

How often did he have to proclaim that he was so terribly fond of me, as he put it, fumbling in dire fear of a certain four-letter word? And how he wished we could make a go of it, even if he awkwardly attempted to explain how my lifestyle scared him.

He was struggling with his inner demons, in search of some form of equilibrium, as he wrestled with his feelings and a way to fit in what he had discovered of my sexuality and the appetites I had acquired into the equation.

His heart, and the old-fashioned morality he had been brought up within, yearned to offer me the princess scenario, the good old picket fence, the semi-detached house in the suburbs and even the fat-cheeked babies he had been indoctrinated from birth to strive towards, while trying to reconcile this with the more basic instincts that had come to the surface during the photography session with Grayson and that he had been a witness to at the country house and which had disturbed him to the core.

He was mixed up.

But then so was I, and his lack of articulacy and the fact I couldn't come up with right words in a crowded restaurant to explain how I felt or what I really wanted only served to magnify my own irritation and our halting exchange quickly turned rather petty and we parted on strained terms. Jonno and the others at the music store quickly made a note of the cloud I was walking under and steered clear of me for the rest of the day.

I felt in no mood to return to my room that day. I'd eaten too much at lunch and knew I'd just pussyfoot around, munching unnecessarily on crisps and watching reruns of reality shows on TV or slob around to no purpose and feel even worse about myself.

I hadn't heard from Dagur for some time. First he had been on tour with the band and had only returned to London while I happened to be in Amsterdam and unavailable. I decided he would the best possible distraction for me tonight.

I called him up.

'Hi.'

'Hello, Teardrop, it's been a long time.'

'Busy lives, eh?'

'Feel like meeting up?'

'I'd love to. Are you free now? I could be along in half an hour.' Dagur shared a house with the band's bass player in Brixton, just a stone's throw from the tube station on a quiet road behind the Ritzy cinema. His housemate was never present, seemingly permanently shacked up with one of his string of girlfriends, so we'd always had the run of the house.

'Come on down.'

'On my way.'

I knew sex with Dagur would be unburdened. There would be no unwelcome mention of feelings or sentimental complications, and he wasn't the sort of man who harboured submissive tendencies so I would not be tempted to turn the tables. For my dominant streak to surface properly, I needed men who would respond instinctively to my taking the lead, guys who secretly craved having the tables turned on them.

I rushed down the escalator to the Northern Line at Tottenham Court Road station. There was a long-haired guitarist singing 'Wonderwall' on the busker pitch where the corridors separated and I remembered how shortly after my arrival in London, I had marvelled at the melodious sounds of a young woman who had been playing violin on the very same spot, her eyes closed and a rapt expression on her face, but whom I'd never seen there again. I swept by as the singer hit a false note.

It was dark by the time I reached Brixton. The lights in the windows of the shops on the High Street shone bright, bathing South London in what felt like a Christmas atmosphere, although the festivities were still months away.

'The door's not locked. Just turn the handle and make your way in,' Dagur's voice echoed through the intercom, the recognisable strain of the Rolling Stones 'Let's Spend the Night Together' playing in the background. 'I'm in the bedroom.'

In the initial throes of my affair with Dagur, I had once spent a whole week of nights at his house, commuting to and from Denmark Street in the early morning and evenings, so I knew the lay of the land well. His bedroom was on the top floor, a vast space that had been carved out as part of an extensive loft conversion.

I ran up the stairs and pushed the door open.

Dagur was in bed.

But he was not alone.

The first thing I unavoidably set my eyes on was the perfect circle of a woman's arse, as a blonde with unfeasibly long, straight hair falling across her flanks and porcelain-coloured buttocks busied herself sucking Dagur's penis.

She was on all fours, but even in that compromising position I could already see she was the owner of an endless pair of model-like legs.

I held my breath.

Finally Dagur acknowledged my entrance.

'Hi, Teardrop,' he murmured distractedly, still under the influence of the blonde girl's attentive ministrations.

Hearing this, she abandoned his cock for a brief instant and turned her head in my direction.

She was straight from a glamour photographer's portfolio, her breasts compact and firm, her cheekbones razor-sharp and her eyes a pale shade of seablue. She flashed me the friendliest of smiles. Then moved back to her blow-job, her full lips swallowing Dagur's length in one elegant gulp.

Dagur winked at me.

No doubt I was wide-eyed.

'Why don't you join us, Lily?'

At least he remembered my name.

I stood there rooted to the spot.

'I don't think so,' I said calmly.

I wasn't jealous. Neither was I possessive of Dagur. He was a musician and women threw themselves at the likes of him and others in the band. We'd never sworn each other any form of exclusivity. We were fuck buddies, and until now, that had proven enough for me. I'd even been involved in a threesome with him and Grayson, so the thought of a sexual variation on it even had its attractions, but I was not in any mood to compete with another girl. I would just be a third wheel. And I wanted to be in charge.

I walked out and left them to it, knowing all too well this was the last I would ever see of Dagur.

9

The Music of Bodies

I'd been asked to deliver an assortment of replacement violin strings and return a bow we'd repaired to a rehearsal studio in the bowels of the Barbican complex. It was mid-afternoon, so there was no need for me to return to the West End and the store.

I crossed the Thames on the Millennium Bridge, feeling its vibrations sway gently beneath my steps, and was soon facing the squat façade of the Tate Modern, watching the pale autumn sun briefly eclipsed as it journeyed across the museum's central tower. It was getting late in the day and there was a nip in the air. Under my green parka I had on a short denim skirt and a thin pair of tights, and I missed the warmth of the jeans I normally wore for work as well as leisure.

Grayson was previewing his new exhibition of photographs of nudes and musicians in a private show at a fashionable gallery close to the Oxo Tower in Southwark and I had been sent an invitation. A few nights ago at the club, reminding me of the date, She had hinted that some of the pics Grayson had taken of me had made the cut and were being included in the show. Which left me a trifle nervous, as I well remembered the circumstances that had given birth to the snaps in question. I also knew that he had later organised a successful session with Lauralynn, to which she had brought her cello. I was unaware of who else might also have been involved.

I hadn't seen much of Grayson since, and never without She on his arms. I didn't think he was avoiding me; he was probably just too busy seeking out extra subjects for his photos, in addition to his regular sought-after fashion work.

The walk along the South Bank between the Globe Theatre and the National Festival Hall was one of my favourite London itineraries, and I was in no hurry to reach my destination, ambling along with the lazy river to my right, along paths and short tunnels, the city skyline unfurling like a slow tapestry on the farthest side of the Thames. As a result, I arrived long after the party had begun. The exhibition space was on the top floor of a tall building and as I emerged from the lift, the main room was already a throng of sharply dressed people, the insistent beat of electronic music punctuating the rumours of swirling conversations against the backdrop of clinking glasses.

There had been a cloakroom downstairs and I'd left my parka and tote bag, but already realised that even with my skirt on, I was distinctly underdressed – most of the women present were wearing couture, outperforming each other in elegance and expensive fabrics and teetering on exquisitely high if impractical heels. With my Doc Martens I felt like the hired help, were the waiters in attendance not all male and black-and-white uniformed like butlers.

Picking up a glass of champagne or prosecco from one of the circulating trays, I planted myself in a corner of the gallery's main hall and looked around the room.

Grayson and She were in a group at the far end, he in

designer jeans, a flouncy white shirt unbuttoned at the chest, and a sand-coloured suit jacket. A broad smile played across his face, and his hair was rakishly slicked back. She stood by his side in a form-hugging fire-red latex outfit that seemed to have been poured over her opulent figure, matching her lipstick and boots. In one hand she held her glass aloft, while in the other she gripped a leash which led, as my gaze descended, to a male slave positioned on all fours like a dog on the gallery's stone floor, his head pointed downwards.

I recognised the middle-aged man from the club where I had often seen him at She's feet, begging to be punished and abused. He was naked but for a ridiculously minute posing pouch inadequately holding his genitals. It was so small one of his testicles was pouring out of the pouch, making his plight even more absurd. The string of the thin silk pouch cut sharply across his butt crack. His arse cheeks still displayed red lines from a recent whipping.

Occasionally She would shake her cigarette ash across his bare back and a thin smile would cross his satisfied lips. I had once seen him feeding from a dog bowl under She's instructions. I was just surprised that he had agreed to be displayed so humiliatingly in such a public space, unlike the club where the audience was somewhat more selective and accustomed to such activities.

I was about to cross the room to go and greet Grayson and She when I saw them being joined by a group of three. I recognised all of them.

In the centre, as if formally escorted by the two women accompanying him and hanging on to his arms, was Viggo Franck, the notorious lead singer for Dagur's band, the Holy Criminals. We'd been briefly introduced on a few occasions when I had still been an item with Dagur, but we'd never truly spoken. His reputation as a provocative ladies' man was widespread and he was fodder for the popular press with his pranks and dalliances. At least, like me, he'd not dressed specially for tonight, his long, spidery legs in the skinniest of clumsily patched-up jeans, laced-up black leather boots, studded cowboy belt and a loose washed-out T-shirt.

To his left, the tall blonde with curls falling to her shoulders was dressed all in white and even in the artificial light of the gallery it was evident she wore nothing beneath, her long limbs outlined clearly. The gown was simplicity itself, although I knew it must have cost a lot, reminding me of a tailored Roman toga, cinched by a gold belt, with all its subtleties mindfully engineered – the way it fell across her body and flared out as it married the very shape of her slim body.

The moment I saw her face, though, I knew she was also the nude dancer I had seen at the country mansion whose underwater performance and ecstatic look had just taken my breath away. Seeing her accompany Viggo Franck was not a surprise. She would, of course, be the sort of ethereal beauty he would easily attract, although my first impression was that she was so much more charismatic than him. Maybe it was his shaggy, high-brushed hair that prevented me from taking Viggo seriously and made me think of a spoilt, mischievous brat?

The other woman, however, I knew not only from the many photos I'd seen in the press, but also, I realised in a flash of recognition from that brief glimpse all those months ago busking on the underground. It was Summer Zahova, the famous classical violinist. That red hair was unmistak-able. I also remembered Grayson mentioning how much he wanted to contact her to see if she would participate in his project. Maybe she had.

She was wearing a simple green silk dress that reached down to her knees and, one of her professional trademarks, a corset as outerwear, bound tight around her thin waist almost in a parody of bondage. The expression on her face was distant, as if she had something important on her mind and was not quite physically in the gallery right now, sharing herself with another person or event.

How typical of Viggo to attend the showing with two such striking women.

I froze. No way was I going to join them.

I exchanged my empty glass for a full one and resolved to go and take a close look at the actual photographs making up Grayson's exhibition. This was, after all, what I had come here to see, as I had no truck with the superficial social niceties of the occasion.

Out of the corner of my eye, I noticed Lauralynn arriv-ing. Even later than me, but quite unconcerned. The way she manoeuvred her way past a crowd of shorter people made her appear more Amazonian than she actually was, sporty, relaxed, clad in tight black leather, predatory in the best possible way. She saw me and waved from afar, indicat-ing with a gesture of the hand that we'd meet up later in the evening.

The large prints were distributed across the long, white gallery walls with geometric precision, each image carefully brought into focus by an individual spotlight, aligned like soldiers on parade. On the floor I noted a red line, punctuated by decals of small arrows piercing a cupid-shaped set of lips, indicating how the spectator – the voyeur? – should view the exhibition, to properly appreciate the sequence of photographs and the increasing boldness of the successive images on display.

It was as if Grayson, or whoever had hung the prints, wanted to tell us a story.

I stepped forward, obediently following the scar-red road, knowing the scenario was about to become more interesting.

The first photo was of one man giving another a blow-job. A flute lay abandoned near the feet of the man on his knees. A symbolic phallus, cast aside? Perhaps I was reading too much into it. I studied the picture closely, looking for some sign of airbrushing on the model's back. Dagur had posed for some of these pictures, I was sure of it, and I knew that he had male lovers. The thought made me shiver with a brief pang of arousal. On the night of our threesome, Grayson and Dagur had both concentrated entirely on me, but at the time I had wished that I could watch them spend some time with each other.

Two women embracing in the next shot did little to banish the image of Grayson's long cock inside Dagur's mouth. I admired the beauty of the feminine form and wasn't averse to the idea of having sex with a woman, but in reality I was almost exclusively attracted to men and I had to make an effort to focus on the pictures in front of me instead of the homoerotic fantasy that had begun playing out in my mind.

Some of the images were shockingly explicit, yet no one in the crowd milling around me seemed in the least bit perturbed. Perhaps the audience had been selected from a known group who were comfortable with full-frontal nudity, which would explain why none of them had so far raised so much as an eyebrow at the sight of She's near-nude slave cowering on all fours.

A picture of a woman with a recorder inserted inside her opening caught my attention. She was sitting on a glass coffee table with her legs spread wide, using the instrument like a dildo. Her back was arched provocatively and her long, dark hair hung like silk around her shoulders. Her face was out of shot and her long neck bared, inviting the viewer to lean in and kiss her.

Grayson had taken a similar image of me. It had been one of the most explicit pictures in our photo session and one that I was particularly proud of. I was so aroused by the time that he had suggested it that I hadn't been horrified at the idea. I'd wanted something inside me so badly that I had immediately agreed when the idea came to him. And I knew it was a shot of me that he could have used, because my face hadn't been in focus.

But he hadn't used it. He'd chosen this woman instead, and he'd modelled her pose on mine. Or perhaps he'd modelled my pose on hers, and it hadn't been a burst of inspiration that had suddenly popped into his head when I was naked in front of him but a ruse that he used on every aroused woman who posed for him just for the pleasure of watching them stimulating themselves in front of his lens. Maybe he'd thought my legs were too scrawny and he preferred the shapeliness of her smooth, plump thighs.

Grayson was an artist, not a creep. I knew that instinctively but I was still pissed off. He was a selfish artist. He didn't care about his subjects; he cared only about what he captured on film. He kidnapped moments as if he owned them. I threw him an angry glance across the room, but my eyes boring into the back of his head were entirely ineffective. He was facing away from me, chatting up Luba, the blonde Russian ballet dancer, no doubt bringing all his charms to the fore in the hope that she would agree to pose for him too. With her unusual beauty and dancer's movement, even a blind fool would be able to see that she was a photographer's wet dream.

My anger dulled only slightly when I finally discovered the pictures of me and realised that he'd included my shots further down the line, closer to the end of the narrative. I still wasn't sure what that meant. I wasn't sure what any of it meant, but the order seemed to signal a significance of some kind. My pictures were in the final part of the series, mixed in with images of another woman with a violin. I suspected that the other model was Summer Zahova, but as all of them were headless, I couldn't be certain.

The initial shot in the final series of photographs was in black and white, just a woman's back framed from the curve of the neck down to the rise of her buttocks. Immaculate white skin against an ebony black background. Simple, unadorned. It could have been anyone. It was followed by another image, where just a violin stood against a similarly dark wall. The third image was of the same violin, but this time it was in glorious colour, the burnished orange and brown shades of the instrument like an explosion, every single feature of the antique wood as if under a microscope, revealing the richness of its texture. The fourth image as I walked along, jostling other spectators to get a full view, was of the same woman's back, in an identical position but this time no longer in black and white but with sharp flesh tones that made you want to touch it.

My picture was next. Despite all the build-up and expectation of what was coming next, I was taken aback when I saw myself in print. The shot was one I hadn't seen before. Grayson had gone through the images with me on his computer screen, and offered to delete any that I wasn't happy with. He hadn't specifically told me that he had shown me all the pictures he'd taken, but he had certainly given me that impression. Evidently he had kept a few aside for his own personal – now public – collection and having given my verbal permission for the shoot and never signing any paperwork, I had no course for complaint, whether I liked the finished product or not.

The shot had been taken from below. At the time I had been leaning over him with my cunt directly over his face, growling angrily, dominating him and he had been begging for more. She had walked in just a few seconds later and interrupted us.

Every muscle in my body was tensed, flexed. I looked like Leroy had when he had circled Liana in Amsterdam. As though I was about to pounce. My stance was in total contradiction to the body of the violinist in the images that surrounded mine. She was so relaxed in her repose, inviting the voyeur's gaze, displaying herself wantonly to the camera's eye. I was rebelling against the lens. With my legs up to the ceiling and my cunt lips open like a maw waiting to swallow up the nearest man and my body curved forward and limbs stretched out I looked like I was about to bite the photographer's head off, though it was impossible to tell for sure as I was only pictured from the neck down and angled in such a way that my orchid tattoo could not be seen.

So was the other model, I noted, who I was now certain was Summer. She had disappeared from the exhibition soon after it had opened so I didn't have the chance to study her for long, but I could see that the woman in the pictures had the same unusual sharp curve in her waist. And, of course, the violin was an obvious clue, and the fact that I knew how Grayson had seen her as the prize in his little project. I could see why now. She embodied everything that he had been trying to capture.

I was close to running from the room, but gulped down a deep breath and forced myself to continue. Right at that moment, out of the blue, I longed for Neil. Someone to lean on, someone who would soothe my anger and upset and fight my corner whether it was reasonable or not. Liana's presence would have helped, but she'd admire my nudity and brush off my emotion and try to get me to laugh along with her to cheer me up. Neil would defend my honour to the end, and that was what I wanted. Submissive or not, he would walk right up to Grayson and punch him in the nose if I asked him to.

The next shot of me was a variation on the first, only this one was even more aggressive. My arms and hands were reaching forward towards the camera in a violent gesture. I had been just about to wrap them around Grayson's throat, and it showed. From the angle he'd been shooting, my limbs were elongated so I looked a little like a deadly spider, all arms and legs and anger.

Summer's final shot showed her in almost the opposite stance with her body curved inwards and her violin held aloft over her pussy as though she was about to bring it down like a weapon against her own sex, not the camera or the viewer.

I took a step back and looked again.

Then I realised what Grayson had done, the story that he was telling with our bodies. Sex and music, sure, particularly with the first series. But Summer Zahova and I, we were domination and submission. Sex embodied. Without emotion, without intimacy. Faceless. Mindless. Meaningless. All the things that I didn't want to be.

The fury swept through me like a wave. It started as a small flame in my belly and then the flame became a seething cauldron as I walked right up to She and Grayson and hissed at them.

'Gray,' I said snarkily. It was She's nickname for him and the first time I'd referred to him that way. My tone made it clear that I wasn't using the sobriquet as a term of endearment.

They were both deep in conversation with Luba. Grayson turned to me and raised an eyebrow.

'Yes?' he queried.

'This is not what I expected. It's not what I wanted. Take the pictures down.'

I straightened my spine and rose to my full height. High heels or not, I refused to bow down to either of them.

She laughed at me.

'You should have thought of that, dear, before you took your clothes off in front of the camera. The lens doesn't lie, you know.' She inclined her head towards the prints. 'That's who you are, whether you like it or not. It's not as though you've been misrepresented.'

'I don't give a fuck who you think I am,' I replied. 'I don't like it.'

'Lily.' Grayson's tone was softer and he laid a hand gently on my elbow to pull me away from the crowd.

Luba was grinning from ear to ear. Her beauty took on a mischievous quality when she smiled and distracted me momentarily from my rage. Under other circumstances, I would have liked to get to know her better, and find out more about how she came to be in the underwater pool at the ball. Water suited her. She reminded me of a mermaid.

I turned my attention back to Grayson.

'Look,' he said, 'I'm sorry you're upset. But that was the risk that you took when you agreed to this project.'

'You didn't show me these photos. You showed me the others. You knew. You lied, or near enough.'

'Can you not see the beauty in them? What I was trying to achieve? That's you, Lily. The perfect domme.'

His voice took on a far-away quality and I knew that in his mind he was travelling to that mental place where his ideas came from. Already thinking of the next project, the next picture, in which the model would be another pawn in his game.

'It's not me,' I replied, in small voice.

Deep down, though, I knew that it was me. The body didn't lie. It might have been me through Grayson's eyes, manipulated by his editing and composition skills and the mood of the narrative that he had put together, but it was still me. Lily the domme. But this version of me was just the domme part without the Lily. I had lost myself in the ritual, forgotten to keep looking for the intimacy that I longed for.

The sex and everything associated with it had just become mindless.

I turned around and walked away. There was no point arguing with him. It was like asking a river not to flow. Grayson was as much a product of his desires as the rest of us were, and his selfishness and artistry were a part of him. She was right. That was the risk that I had taken by posing for his project.

The cool night air hit me in a rush. Lights from all directions glinted on the water, usually a sight that I would take pleasure in but tonight I just wanted to stamp my heavy boots on the concrete footpath as loudly as I could and I was in no mood for admiring the scenery.

It was still early in the evening. The actual exhibition itself began in a few hours. Grayson had opened the event early to provide a selection of guests with a special preview of the photographs. Some of the pictures had 'sold' tags on them already, I recalled. I wondered if anyone would buy mine. If I would be memorialised like that for eternity on a stranger's living-room wall. Or, maybe worse, if no one would want my photograph and it would be packed away at the end and stored in Grayson's studio, gathering dust like a bad memory.

A busker dressed all in black cut a lonely figure despite the milling crowds on the South Bank. He seemed a step apart from the world around him so I stopped to listen for a few moments and tossed him a couple of coins, then cursed when I reached an independent coffee shop and realised that I'd given the guitar player the last of my change. I had my credit card, enough money on my Oyster card to get home and that was it. Sometimes karma was a bitch.

I called Neil, but his phone went straight to voicemail. He was out tonight, I remembered, at some kind of fancy PR shindig. It was at the Oxo Tower nearby and he'd suggested that we might be able to meet up afterwards if I ended up being out that late. Gatecrashing his event wouldn't be possible in my denim mini skirt and Doc Martens. Luba or She or just about anyone at the exhibition dressed in all their finery would have no problem sweet-talking the bouncers, but I looked far too ordinary for that. Too ordinary for Neil. How the tables had turned.

Finally I decided to give up and head for home. A hot bath and good night's sleep would cure what ailed me. I had nearly reached the tube when I noticed the travel shop. It was the only retail store that was open and I felt a pang of sympathy for the staff working within before my eyes landed on the posters of exotic locations stuck to the windows and it occurred to me that perhaps what I needed was a change.

Liana had moved to Amsterdam and that had worked out for her. Maybe I could do the same thing. Start some-where fresh. Build a new life.

The doorbell jingled as I pushed it open. Behind the counter sat a bored-looking man in his early twenties with a mop of ginger hair and the beginnings of a thin mous-tache. His complexion clashed terribly with the store's bright-red colour scheme. Alongside him was a plump, cheerful middle-aged woman whose eyes lit up when I walked in. Perhaps it had been a slow day. Her nametag read 'Sue'. She looked altogether too eager to deal with in my current state of mind so I stood in front of the redhead and waited for him to look up.

'Can I help?' he asked, in a tone that made it obvious he would rather not.

'I'm thinking of going somewhere.'

'I guessed that much,' he retorted with a heavy hint of sarcasm. 'What sort of somewhere?'

'As far away from London as possible.'

He pepped up after that. My obvious gloom had struck a chord.

'America?' he suggested.

'Too many Americans,' I replied unthinkingly, a defensive form of wit getting the better of me.

He nodded sympathetically.

'Australia?' he asked.

The glossy gleam of the red earth on the brochure he pushed in front of me was almost the same colour as his hair.

'Too many beaches,' I replied. I wasn't sure I could cope with all those svelte bikini-clad surfers. It would be like living in a Cola commercial. I wanted something rougher.

'I want to go somewhere that other people don't,' I said.

'You should go to Darwin,' he said sagely. 'It's the arse end of the world. I went there for a training course once. It's full of people trying to get away from something. And the army barracks. Strange place. It looks a bit like this, though,' he added, stabbing a rough, bitten-down nail at the bright-blue sky on the brochure. It was a funny shade of blue. Much more vivid than any horizon I had ever seen in England. That made my mind up.

'How much is the ticket?'

'Single or return?'

'Single,' I said firmly.

'We have a sale on,' he replied. 'That's why we're open late. But there's only a short window for the cheap flights.'

'Which is?'

'You'll have to travel next week.'

I felt just like I had when I told Jonah to go ahead with the teardrop tattoo. An overwhelming sense of rightness. As though this had been preordained and I'd spent my life swimming towards this moment, travelling down the sea of life on an inexorable current from which there was never any escape. You could fight the tide, but it would find a way to pull you along anyway.

The ticket was pricey, and as I punched in my credit card details and completed all of the paperwork the realisation of what I was about to do hit me in the gut. What would my parents say? Liana? Neil?

Perhaps I could slip away without telling a soul and call them when I arrived.

My last week in England passed by without any fanfare or dramatics. I dropped into the music store and the club to hand in my resignation and took particular satisfaction in the look on She's face as I told her that I wouldn't be returning.

I saved Neil 'til last. I couldn't face telling him over the phone, so instead we arranged to have lunch. My treat this time, I said, and I chose a little place in Chinatown that did great dim sum and wouldn't eat through too much of my savings. The nest egg I'd managed to save up still looked healthy enough to get me through a couple of months if I lived frugally, but I'd need to find work shortly after I arrived in Australia.

Ten minutes had gone by since our appointed meeting time and he still hadn't arrived. I frowned. Neil was usually so punctual you could set the clock by him. My phone burst into life. I was still using the Jace Everett ring tone that Liana had saved on the handset as a joke. 'I wanna do bad things to you,' it warbled.

'Lily,' Neil said breathlessly, 'I'm so sorry, I've been called into a client meeting. No way out of it. For this new deal we're tying up . . . Can I have a rain check? I'll take you some place nice to make up for it.'

'Sure. No problem.' I tried to hide the disappointment in my voice. He was just a friend after all, I chided, and I'd be back to visit.

'What was it you wanted to tell me?'

'Oh, it's nothing. I'll tell you another time.'

'Rain check. Next week. I'm looking forward to it.'

And with that he was gone.

I sipped green tea and endured the curious glances of the waitresses for another hour as I gathered my thoughts and then I went home and packed. My flight left the next day.

I'd send Neil a postcard when I arrived.

The end of the year was fast approaching as I settled down in Darwin. I'd found a job in a local music store, which sold mostly CDs and second-hand vinyl and attracted an interesting crowd. I'd been taken on for the busy pre-Christmas period as an additional pair of hands, but another staffer had left to get married ahead of the festivities and I'd been offered the position full-time and gladly accepted. Most of the money that I'd saved had been spent on travel and subsistence since I had left England, and it was good to be able to rely on a regular, if modest, income.

Christmas Eve had been spent, of all places, on the beach

with the guys I had befriended from the store and their crowd. It felt odd celebrating in the sand, wearing only a bikini, knowing almost everyone I knew back in Europe was sheltering in the cold and crowding around log fires. A warm Christmas, albeit in the wet season, just didn't feel right to a cold-weather Northern hemisphere girl like me and this disquieting feeling unsettled me. Maybe it was the permanent smell of eucalyptus like a chemical trigger affecting my senses.

I woke up late with a bad hangover on Christmas Day and the untidy sight of my small room conjured up a deep well of depression and self-pity. I had no plans for the day, or what was left of it, and most places I reckoned would be closed, so I couldn't even avail myself of the comforting darkness of a cinema or the air-conditioned busyness of the local mall and its brightly lit windows.

I sighed theatrically, as much for the mirror facing me on the bathroom wall as for the invisible spectators of my pretend road to Calvary.

Maybe later I would phone my parents, who had both proven totally unsurprised by my sudden move to the other side of the world, although I seemed to recall them mentioning some time back that they had plans for the holiday season so might not be home, even after factoring in the time difference. I sent Liana a text message with the usual banalities for this time of year, and then, as an afterthought, sent an almost identical one to Neil, who had never even responded after I'd left the UK. I guessed he'd taken my departure as a personal affront, and I thought it best to leave him simmering.

Surprisingly he responded within the hour, even though

it must be night-time back where he was. Maybe he had forgiven me by now.

Miss you. Hope you're having a lovely time. N

Was he partying? With someone? Or was he alone like me?

I realised he was one of the few friends I still had left and I missed him too in a strange way. It would have been nice to talk, exchange gossip or news.

I had deleted the numbers of Dagur, Grayson and She from my contacts list some weeks back, so they were out of reach, but I didn't regret that particular decision. Leonard was still listed; that was one step too far for me to take. Sometimes you live with hope against hope, even though everything around you tells you just shouldn't.

Had I ever spent Christmas alone before? No, and it felt awful. And then I knew that in seven days' time, it would be New Year's Eve and I would have to confront my loneliness all over again. Memories of the riotous times we had all spent in Brighton when we had been students came swirling back to the surface of my mind, and I couldn't help but smile. The silliness, the companionship, the sense of belonging. All things I had lost.

I forced myself to get out of bed and shower, then had an improvised breakfast of milk and cereals, but still the bleak rest of the day lay ahead of me.

I plugged in my laptop, and walked over to the trunk in which I kept a messy assortment of books, old magazines and my DVDs. Half of the movies I had accumulated, mostly unwanted duplicates the store was ready to dispose of, were no longer in their cases, the discs scattered haphazardly along the bottom of the trunk. I picked up a handful at random, wondering whether I was in the right mood for a comedy or an action flick. Romances were certainly off the menu.

Carrying the DVDs and the laptop to the bed, I closed the room's curtains to cut off the daylight and tucked myself into bed. The patterns of the screensaver danced in the artificial penumbra I had created. I moved my finger over the pad and the screen came to life, its tidy line of icons like a bedrock frieze.

I was about to insert one of the DVDs when my attention was caught by the blue Skype icon. I clicked on it and scrolled through the directory. There were only half a dozen, mostly family and someone I didn't even recognize. And Leonard.

A symbol indicated he was online right now.

My heart jumped.

I called him.

The screen flickered and his face appeared.

'Hello, Lily.'

He seemed tired, his eyes imbued with sadness. Behind him, a bookshelf stood in half darkness. There was a terrible bleakness about the surroundings and his ghostlike features at their centre.

'I . . .' I swallowed hard. 'I just wanted to wish you a happy Christmas.'

'That's very kind of you, my love,' Leonard said.

'I still miss you, you know.'

'Me too, Lily, but we've discussed this before and—'

I raised my hand, sensing his irritation, forcefully interrupting his words. It had been a forlorn hope calling him the way I had. We gazed at each other silently, both deep in thoughts. It was strange seeing his familiar face on a screen, the skin I knew so well now a pale accumulation of pixels. Leonard appeared a little older now, as if the passage of time since he last touched me and my lips had surveyed the private landscape of his body, had accelerated in the absence of me. More likely it was the distancing effect that this mode of communication imposed on us. And as that thought occurred to me, I also felt a tsunami-sized sense of both relief and tenderness for him, and began to understand his renunciation of me better. He was the one who was sacrificing himself for me. Not the other way round. The storm clouds surrounding my heart lifted.

I was about to break the news that I was now in Australia when Leonard began speaking again.

'You haven't changed a single bit,' he said. 'You are so lovely.'

'Why, thank you.'

On impulse I lifted the top of the thin nightgown I was wearing and showed him my breasts.

On the other side of the world, Leonard smiled.

'They haven't changed either,' he remarked. 'As scrumptious as ever.'

'Well,' I pointed out, 'I might be young, as you so often remind me, but I'm not likely to grow into a large cup size. This is what I am.'

'You always had that mischievous streak, didn't you?'

I nodded.

I wished him a merry Christmas one more time and closed the connection.

I knew I would never see Leonard again. He had set me free. Once and for all.

*

As ever, the heavens opened at four-thirty and the heavy rain pelted down, cleansing the air and the town. By evening, the skies were clear again. I was told the wet season usually lasted all the way to May.

It was New Year's Eve. I'd tried to hook up with some of my co-workers, but all had family obligations. It would be another evening spent on my own.

As I reflected on the past year and its varied adventures and sorrows, as well as occasional joys, I found myself drawn to the sea front after an aimless walk through the Smith Street Mall where most of the stores were closing early.

There was a bar by the beach that also served as a restaurant in the evenings which I was quite fond of, simple and uncluttered and with friendly staff who were not too inquisitive. I'd grown to enjoy parking myself in small bars and observing others, trying to guess their occupations, their past, their personal stories. I had once done the same at the fetish club in London before She had got me more involved in the action, and imagined elaborate stories, some the size of novels, about the visitors to whose special tastes we catered. There was no harm in speculating and it kept me entertained.

Here the visitors to the bar were, of course, less colourful: transient hippies whose contrived appearances all seemed to originate from the same mould; older locals who gave the impression they hadn't left Australia's Northern Territory in their whole lifetime, wedded to the land and sea like burnished icons; restless youth dressing the way they thought hipsters did in the distant big cities and mostly getting it wrong and advertising their blissful ignorance.

But, for me, every single one had a story to tell. Maybe one day I would try to write about them.

Lily the writer.

It had a nice sound to it.

The nice thing about this place, the terrace with its ring of palm trees and thick white sun umbrellas looking over the vivid blue of the ocean, was that no one minded if you sat, either at the bar or in a quiet corner, sipping your beer and making it last for hours. Today, they were busier, the staff preparing the tables, juggling with large white plates, distributing glasses and cutlery and chintzy little pots in which candles were being inserted. New Year's Eve must be one of their best nights of the year for business, I guessed.

The evening's first diners were beginning to arrive and, in the small alcove where I had taken refuge, I called for another beer and asked for the snacks menu. I was in no mood for a full meal. The bar offered a mix of wraps and sandwiches.

I watched as the place filled up. Terry, the young waitress who had been looking after me, came to the end of her shift and was replaced by Stellios, an elderly waiter with a pronounced Greek accent who'd been working here for over twenty years he'd once proudly informed me with fatherly concern.

'No big plans for tonight, Miss Lily?' he asked me, frowning as I sat alone in my recess.

I nodded.

'It's a shame, a pretty thing like you. No boyfriend, no man?'

I blinked and grinned.

'Ah, a woman of secrets. I'll leave you to it.'

He moved on to take an order on the terrace, leaving me at my improvised observation post.

I sipped my beer, later switched to coffee, idly biting into the turkey and chutney sandwich and daydreamed and watched the diners, the new arrivals and latecomers as they came and went.

An older couple at a table by the terrace's entrance were savouring a huge plate of oysters. There was something old world and charming about them, I thought, yet not without a hint of danger, although I couldn't quite put my finger on it or come up with the right story for them. Like seasoned partners in crime, relaxed, suave, worldly.

Stellios hovered by, three cups of coffee balancing on his tray. He dropped mine off and continued to the old couple's table and served them the remaining cups just as the beach restaurant's sound system was switched on behind the bar by the duty manageress who ruled from afar. Unctuous strings began to swirl across the terrace, familiar melodies spilling onto the beach, gliding through the small lights hanging from the trees. It felt like a picture postcard, although a kitschy one at that. The first song was a waltz.

The bamboo dance floor at the end of the terrace extended into the sand.

I saw the older couple both turn their heads to the dance floor as some younger diners began to rise from their tables and make their way to the bamboo matting. I followed the direction of their gaze and noticed a tall blonde with short hair and her partner, a rugged athletic guy in jeans and white shirt, moving hand in hand and begin dancing. I hadn't seen them before as the table they had been sitting at was obscured from my view by the bar counter.

The older couple began whispering to each other, as if they were commenting on the handsome new arrivals.

The woman wore a modest white dress that reached down to her knees, and flat ballet pumps to attenuate her height. Amber earrings hung loose from her lobes, and I noted the deep emerald hue of her nails, a perfect combination of colours.

They began to dance.

Even though her hair was so much shorter than on the two previous occasions I had seen her, I recognised the woman instantly. It was the dancer whose very particular act I had witnessed at the country mansion and then seen later on Viggo's arm, alongside Summer Zahova, at Grayson's private view in Southwark.

It was definitely her.

It was as if, along with the cropped hair, her features had grown softer and the ice princess within had melted away. She danced with her partner as if they were the only souls on the terrace, floating above the bamboo matting, oblivious to their surroundings. I couldn't take my eyes away.

Captivated, I began to imagine their story and the travails they had both endured before coming to Darwin. My imagination was running away with me. But people often said that truth was stranger than fiction, and I smiled to myself as I imagined what the dancing couple would guess about me and my history if the tables were turned. I bet nothing they came up with could better the strangeness of the reality.

A few songs later, they returned to their table, settled their bill and departed. By then the older couple had also left, though I had not seen them go, plunged deep in my crazy thoughts, my final coffee now cold and useless.

Half the tables on the terrace were empty, I realised, as the evening dragged on. It was time to go home.

I waved at Stellios on my way out and he returned my smile.

'Happy New Year,' he cried out as I stepped into the small car park where I had left my bike. I peered at my watch. There was half an hour to midnight. I could get back to my room and watch the celebrations on TV.

When I reached the house, I noticed through the shadows a dark form slumped against the steps. Damn, a drunkard, I reckoned. I just hoped he would not prove aggressive when I asked him to move.

I approached, holding on to my bike, ready to give the sleeping refugee a nudge to wake him up, and caught sight of a suitcase standing next to him.

There was a movement in the darkness and the shape looked up at me. The nearest street lamp was a few houses away, so I had to squint to see better.

'Lily! Thank God!'

'Neil?'

'Yes, it's me,' he gasped. There was a look of sheer terror in his eyes. 'I thought maybe you'd gone away for New Year, that I'd come all the way here for nothing.'

I was dumbfounded.

I had a million questions.

'What the fuck are you doing here?' was all I managed to say in a splendid show of inarticulacy.

'I came,' Neil said calmly.

10

At the House of Bamboo Dolls

He stumbled to his feet.

'You came?' I repeated, dumbly. 'All this way, for me?'

'Yes. I came for you.'

'But—'

'Just shut up and kiss me,' he replied, and pulled me into his arms.

The line was so straight out of a Hollywood film that I began to laugh, and consequently when Neil's lips met mine my mouth was half open. His tongue slid along my bottom teeth with a flick and to my amazement sent a shudder rippling through my body.

'Oh,' I said in surprise.

'Oh, Lily,' he moaned in return and began to kiss me in earnest.

His mouth was warm and wet and our lips melded together in uncanny harmony. Our tongues danced gently, hovering on the tightrope between teasing and too much and never crossing over.

He buried his hands into the back of my hair and pulled me so tightly against him I thought that soon I would have to fight him off just so that I could draw a breath. Neil was trying to inhale me. We rocked back and forward on the front step, pushing against each other, each of us warring to devour the other.

I grabbed his wrists from where they rested at the base of my neck and flipped his arms over his head and pushed him up against the door. The deep grunt of animal pleasure that rose in the back of his throat as I did so, a heavy 'ungh' noise, got me right in the guts and I dropped my bag and forgot my plan to wrestle my keys out of it and get us both indoors and instead I slammed my body into him so that his legs were spread to make way for my hips. He lowered his head to my neck and began to suck hard on my skin and I leaned into him, enjoying the pull as my blood rushed to the surface. I hadn't had a hickey since we were at university together, I thought with a flicker of amusement, but the thought disappeared again as I noticed the hard bulge of his cock pressing against my thigh.

At that moment, more than anything else in the world, I wanted to take Neil's cock in my hands and feel the entire length of him in my mouth. A little cry of disappointment burst from his lips as I dropped the grip that I had on his wrists. That was soon followed by a questioning murmur as I took hold of his leather belt and tugged at the buckle.

'I can see I'm going to have to gag you,' I said under my breath.

He moaned again.

'I'd stuff my panties into your mouth,' I continued mischievously, 'but I'm not wearing any.' It was true. I had discovered just as I was leaving the house that all of my laundry was still damp after I'd forgotten to bring it in before that afternoon's storm.

He dug his fingers into my shoulders and banged his

head against my front door as another shudder rippled through his body. I was worried that I'd made him come before I'd even managed to get a glimpse of his erection, but I needn't have. Neil was still hard as a rock.

His trousers pooled down around his legs and I took his shaft into my right hand and prepared to take his head between my lips. He smelled fresh. A musky male backdrop against the tang of clean skin and soap with a hint of citrus.

He'd come all this way for me and I was overwhelmed by a sudden surge of affection for him. My old friend. More than a friend. I wanted to get to know him better in every possible way and I planned to begin in the most primal, basic way that I knew.

When it came to blow-jobs, I wasn't like Liana who tried to swallow her men whole in one gulp. For one thing I hadn't had much experience. Seeing She at the ball go down on the submissive with the 'Eat Me' sign was a shock to me. Dommes didn't go down on submissive men as a general rule. At least, they didn't talk about it, and besides that single occasion, I'd never seen one do it in public. Leonard had been so eager to please me orally that he rarely allowed me the chance to return the favour, and Dagur had enjoyed having his cock sucked but he had always wanted to pull me on top of him and sixty-nine, and in that position I found it impossible to concentrate and even harder to position my mouth so that I could pleasure him without accidentally catching any sensitive parts on the jagged edges of my teeth.

Whether or not oral sex was a dominant or a submissive act was one of the age-old arguments that the artisans of kink loved to debate and write about on online forums. Of course, I loved the feeling of having a man pinned between my lips and knowing that he couldn't move even if he wanted to. Going down onto my knees was neither here nor there to me. I was shorter and far slighter than most of the men I had dominated anyway and I had long ago learned that there was much more to demonstrating power and encouraging another's surrender than whatever position I happened to be in at the time.

When I took Neil into my mouth, I did it for pleasure. Both his and mine. Nothing more than that. His silky skin gliding against my mouth. The enjoyable sensation of being filled to the brim. The familiarity of finding a rhythm and holding it in a steady up then down motion. The sound of his moans as I caressed him. It was a simple act, but one that brought me a great deal of joy.

He tangled his hands in my hair but didn't grab my head as I always saw doms do to their subs in the club, or as Leroy had done to Liana. His hands stroked my locks gently as I licked up and down his sizeable shaft and circled my tongue around the furrow of his glans.

I shifted my weight into a crouch as my knees were starting to ache on the concrete step. Neil gasped as I changed position. I had inadvertently taken his cock deeper as I did so and brushed his head against the rougher skin on the roof of his mouth.

'Like that, do you?' I said in a muffled voice, my mouth half full.

'Oh God,' he replied. 'I like everything you . . .' The word trailed off as he sharply drew breath when I took his balls into my hand and ran my nails lightly over his delicate skin. He tugged my hair a little harder and pumped my face back and forth, jamming his long member further towards the back of my throat.

The ebb and tide of celebratory noises floated down the street towards us as drunks wandered down the footpath outside in search of home and a car drove by with Cold Chisel's 'Khe Sanh' blaring out of the windows. A warm breeze kissed my shoulders, easing the pressure of the constant humidity. The air felt heavy at this time of year in Darwin, always building towards an explosion of rain or a lightning storm. There wasn't much of a nightlife here, so even on New Year's Eve half the town was sitting out on deckchairs on their balconies drinking beer and listening to the perpetual croak of the frogs. My neighbours were gathering on their porch in expectation of the fireworks. They probably had a clear view of my head bobbing up and down against Neil's crotch, but I no longer cared.

New Year's Eve. Neil and I had rung in several such evenings together during our time at Sussex University, but never like this. I had always avoided him as the clock struck midnight for fear that he would try to kiss me and I wouldn't know what to do. How ironic, I thought, that I'd spent so much time at the fetish club learning techniques to beat and humiliate men but I had never quite adjusted to the sensation of having them worship me.

Shouts rang into the air as the countdown began. I pulled back lightly and gripped Neil's shaft, sliding my hand around and back in circular motion as I jiggled my head up and down and flicked at his tip with the flat of my tongue.

'Five, four, three, two . . .' cried the guests at the party next door, in unison.

At 'one' I wet my finger and slid it into his arse without changing the rhythm of my strokes.

'Fuck!' he cried, as his whole body jolted and a hot stream hit the back of my throat and the neighbours shouted, 'Happy New Year!'

I clung onto him and stroked his thighs until he had stopped trembling and then drew back and licked my lips.

'Happy New Year!' I said jovially, smiling up at him. My legs were now so stiff I wasn't sure if I could stand up.

'Lily, oh, Lily,' he breathed again. 'Come here.'

'You don't have to kiss me,' I murmured, well aware that my mouth was still full of the lingering taste of his orgasm.

'No, I want to kiss you. I want to kiss you always and for ever.'

He pressed his lips to mine.

'We should probably go inside now,' I said, 'before the people next door start pointing their video cameras at us.'

My bunch of keys seemed heavy and noisy in contrast with the lightness of the moment and I fumbled to turn the lock.

'Lily,' he said, lifting my hair and whispering into my ear. His breath was warmer than the temperature outside, but I shivered anyway. 'There's something I've always wanted to do to you. May I?'

'Well, you haven't told me what it is yet, but OK.'

I tensed in apprehension. Even if it was Neil, the kindest man I'd ever known, I wasn't used to handing the reins over.

'Relax,' he said, and then lifted me up and swung me into his arms. He batted my hand away from the key, turned it easily, kicked the door open and carried me over the threshold.

He'd hitched his trousers up, but hadn't belted them up and after two steps they dropped around his ankles again and severely hindered our progress.

'This isn't going quite how I'd imagined,' he said glumly as we shuffled forward and I burst out laughing.

'Put me down,' I said with mock outrage, 'or I'll spank you.'

'In that case,' he replied, 'I'm never letting you go. I hope you're comfortable.'

'Oh, I see. You want a funishment.'

'Funishment?'

'Don't pretend all innocent, like you haven't been all over the Internet reading up on BDSM since you saw me with a whip in my hand. Funishment. It's a punishment that's fun.'

'Aren't they all?' he joked.

I thought of She and some of the torture that I'd seen her inflict on her slaves. It certainly didn't look fun to me, but if there was anything that I had learned since my introduction to the alternative scene, it was that everyone had their own ideas about what was and wasn't likely to be an enjoyable experience. For some people the fun was all in enduring whatever torture their dominant chose to dish out so the less pleasurable the immediate sensation, ultimately the greater the reward. It was all very complicated, but it reminded me that Neil and I had never really talked about what we each liked and didn't. He'd hinted that he wanted to be dommed. But to what degree and in what way I wasn't certain.

Before I could ask him, he pressed his hands lightly against my breasts through my T-shirt and began to move his thumbs in a slow circular motion, stimulating my nipples. They were hard in seconds. I loved having my breasts played with, and because they were small, had often been disappointed when previous boyfriends had not paid them as much attention as I would have liked. Learning to ask for what I wanted had been a slow process and my self-awareness didn't always keep up with my desires.

'Isn't your suitcase still outside?' I asked, breathlessly. Darts of arousal were taking root in my spine and I was having trouble holding onto any kind of rational thought.

'I don't give a fuck if a dingo runs away with it,' he replied forcefully. He tugged my T-shirt out from the waistband of my cotton skirt and reached inside, taking one of my breasts into each hand and kneading. With every few strokes he would twist my nipples lightly between his fingers.

It was as if my breasts were in complete accord with my cunt. I leaned into him and relaxed. Neil was making me wetter and wetter with every touch.

'There isn't anything I don't want to do to you,' he said, 'to you, with you, for you. Where is your bed?'

I righted myself for just long enough to indicate the way towards the bedroom and he pulled his shirt over his head and kicked off his shoes and trousers and picked me up again and carried me there, laying me down gently onto the bed as if I were the most delicate of tropical flowers with petals that needed preserving.

'May I undress you?' he asked tentatively.

I looked up at him. He was standing at the foot of the

bed looking down at me with an expression on his face that suggested that he was already seeing me completely naked and perhaps spread out in a ceremonial bathtub filled with rosewater with a crown on my head. It felt strange to be idolised so, but also unusually wonderful. I could certainly get used to it.

Neil was now completely naked. I pushed myself up and spun around onto my knees so I could get a better look at him. He had definitely been working out, but he was still the sweet, slender, boyish-figured Neil that I'd always known. I doubted he would turn completely buff if he lifted dumb bells every day for the rest of his life. He just wasn't built that way. He had a smattering of hair and a few copper-coloured freckles on his breast bone. His nipples were a rosy pink, and completely erect. His cock was even harder. It slapped against his thigh as he shifted uncomfortably from one foot to the other.

'No,' I said. 'You may not undress me.'

His face fell.

'I'm going to ride you first.'

I took his hand and pulled him towards me until he clambered uncertainly onto the bed over the top of me. As soon as he began to lower his body weight, I flipped him over onto his back.

'Wow,' he said in shock. 'You're stronger than you look.'

I grinned. 'Close your eyes,' I instructed him. 'Until I say so.'

He complied and I leaped up and raced to the wardrobe. Right at the back I had hidden the bag of toys and other paraphernalia that I'd collected during my last few months in London and half-heartedly brought along here. The restraints were one of my favourite bits of kit, as I was still unsure of my rope-tying prowess and I found it hard to appear dominant when my fingers were fumbling and I had to refer to a bondage guidebook every few minutes to get the knots right.

Neil hissed in anticipation as I wrapped a padded-leather cuff around each of his wrists and ankles and spread him out over the bed, spread-eagled, attaching the other ends firmly to the bed posts and tightening the slack so that he could squirm and wriggle a little bit, but was otherwise trapped exactly where I wanted him.

His cock was dead straight and pointed into the air like an arrow seeking a target. I fished a condom out of my bed-side drawer and then crawled towards him across the covers, cat-like, with the wrapper between my teeth, although he still had his eyes closed. My domme character was taking over. It was like slipping into another skin, putting on another mask, but not as a way of hiding. Just an easy transition into another version of me. Like taking the lid off a Russian doll and finding another replica underneath, virtually identical yet different in some infinitesimal, vitally important way.

I bent my head and blew softly onto the head of his cock, without allowing my lips close enough to touch it.

'Hmm,' he murmured. His eyelids flickered.

'Keep them closed,' I barked.

His skin broke out into goose bumps in response to the harsh tone of my voice.

I tore the wrapper open on the condom and Neil shivered.

'What do you want?' I asked him. 'Tell me.'

'Anything,' he said. 'I want anything, Lily. I want everything. I want you so bad.'

'That's good,' I replied, 'but can you be more specific? What do you want right now?'

I balanced the condom on the head of his cock so he could feel it.

'Shhhiiiit, fuck me. Ride me, I want you to ride me!'

'Please,' I reprimanded him.

'Please. Please, Lily, ride me, ride my cock. I want you to ride my cock.'

'OK then,' I said breezily and smiled as he arched his back and lifted his hips in invitation.

I rolled the condom down with my lips even though I hated the taste of latex. It was a trick that Liana had taught me in the kitchen of our Brighton flat using a banana as an ersatz penis and the idea had always appealed, although I checked over it with my hand to make doubly sure that it was secure.

He slid into me easily, like a knife slides through honey.

'Fuck, you're so wet.'

'Open,' I commanded, and immediately I was looking straight into Neil's eyes. Right into his depths. His expression was so full of longing and wonder and something else – love? – that on any other occasion I might have been unnerved by the overwhelming intensity of it all but then and there, with his cock filling me so fully, the look on his face just made me more aroused.

I resolutely met his gaze and ground into him harder and harder and harder. He strained against the bedposts so hard that I thought he was going to tear them straight off the frame and injure us both, but the bedhead held, along with the cuffs, as I pumped back and forth and back and forth and Neil screamed in desire and frustration and I screamed along with him.

Damn the neighbours.

'Tell me what you want.'

He didn't reply. His eyes rolled back in his head. He was lost in a whirlpool of sensation.

I brought my hand up and down on his face with a slap.

'Oh fuck, yes!' he cried. 'Do that again. Do that again.'

I slapped his other cheek and he bucked harder against the bed as I bounced up and down on his length, riding him, dominating him, pleasing myself. I ground down harder, rubbing my clit against his stomach.

'I want to see you. I want to feel your tits,' he moaned, hypnotised by the sway and fall of my breasts beneath my T-shirt as I moved. He pulled uselessly against the cuffs again and then relented and put all of his struggle into moving his hips up to meet mine.

'You're not getting free until I let you,' I advised him.

'I don't ever want you to let me free,' he said. 'I want to be yours. Your pet. Your toy. Your anything.'

His eyes were great depths of green and brown swirls with an endless well of emotion and affection in them. That was when I knew for sure that no matter what I did to him, Neil would love me unconditionally. For ever.

I stopped suddenly and kissed him.

'I want to be yours too, my darling,' I whispered.

He shuddered and came inside me.

'Fuck. Sorry,' he said. 'I was trying to hold on, but you just . . . pushed me over the edge.'

'It's OK,' I laughed, leaning over to undo his cuffs. 'We've got all night. And all day.'

We barely left my flat for a week other than to pick up food and drink. I spent most of the time reclining in bed as Neil brought me plates of cut-up fresh mango and papaya and fed me slices with his fingers.

'You're only here for such a short time,' I said to him, 'I should at least show you around Darwin, even if you won't see the rest of the city.'

'Fuck Darwin,' Neil replied. 'Fuck everything. All I want to do is fuck you, Lily.'

I'd never heard him swear so much in all the time I'd known him, but he was true to his word. We made love in every possible variation under the sun and more besides. I tried all of the kit that I had on him. The rope, the flogger, the paddle, my fur mitt, even an electro stim kit that Lauralynn had given me, which scared me even to look at. Neil was open to just about everything, but what gave us both the most pleasure was skin-to-skin contact. He loved it when I spanked his arse or wrestled him under me and then climbed on top of his cock as though he didn't have a choice. He liked to be taken.

'Just imagine that you're a highwayman,' he said, as he tried to explain what it was about being overpowered that turned him on so much.

'And you're a fine young lady with her bodice ripped?' I asked. I couldn't keep a straight face after that and ended up falling on top of him in fits of giggles.

'Why do we do this?' I asked him one night after I'd

whipped his back until my arm was sore and then we'd made love like animals on the hardwood kitchen floor.

He held me tight in his arms like he always did and stroked my hair.

'Because there's more to sex than fucking,' he said sagely. 'As much as I do love fucking you. There's more to it than that.'

Neil then convinced me to come back to London with him. He was still employed by the PR agency and had just taken a short leave of absence to come to Australia.

'I would have quit in a heartbeat if you wouldn't come back though, Lily. Nothing matters if I don't have you.'

I felt exactly the same way about him, and was only surprised that I hadn't known it before. Australia had been nice for a change, but I was made for the cold, not the hot weather. I was too melancholy to live by the beach, even if it was so full of dangerous creatures that it was impossible to swim in.

We managed to arrange a one-way ticket for me to match up with Neil's return flight, with a stopover in San Francisco. I had never been there before and it was a city that had always held a spell on my imagination. The inhabitants were made out to be so wild and carefree, and any place like that I was sure to feel at home, I felt, and if not at home then at least we could be assured of a good time. We planned a stopover for forty-eight hours so we could explore the city.

I'd emailed Lauralynn that I was on my way back to England and shared my excitement about the few days we had managed to fit between the long flights involved. She was American and had once lived in San Francisco, so I asked her to recommend some places to visit, besides the normal tourist traps of Golden Gate Bridge and Haight Ashbury.

The hotel the travel agent had found us was downtown, in the shadow of the Coit Tower, one of the more boring, business-orientated parts of town. One of our first destinations was the Bay, where parades of stores guaranteed we would find a pearl inside the oysters they allowed us to pick and chose. As the oyster I'd ceremoniously picked was opened in front of me, I was as excited as a little girl on Christmas morning, holding Neil's hand in a tight, nervous grip, and yes indeed there was a pearl, albeit a miserable and minuscule black one with no shine or spark whatsoever. The pearls in Darwin had been so much prettier. Next came Chinatown, and it was yet another disappointment, nowhere near as large or colourful as London's and even the meal we had in a busy emporium of a restaurant, lacked the flavours and diversity of Gerrard Street.

By the time evening came, I felt jaded and unenthusiastic at the prospect of roaming further afield.

'Come on,' Neil insisted. 'We have to make the best of it.'

I growled, my mood growing more brattish by the minute.

'I don't know.'

'Let's check out some of the places you told me Laura-lynn had recommended,' he suggested.

I'd printed out her response shortly before we'd left Darwin. It wasn't a long list. Two items and addresses

Vina Jackson

caught our attention, both, it appeared, within a reasonable walking distance of where we were staying, as we had no energy to travel to the other side of town. One appeared, judging by the map I'd called up on my mobile phone, to be close to the famed City Lights bookstore we had visited that very morning, a stepping stone on San Francisco's traditional places to go and see. I'd even found an interesting second-hand book there which I was hoping to begin reading on the flight to London.

All Lauralynn had provided us was a name, the House of Bamboo Dolls, and an address. The other place recommended was an Italian restaurant called Bucca di Beppo, where she insisted we should dine in either the Pope or the Madonna room. Neither Neil or I felt hungry, so our choice was made.

'So what is it?' Neil asked.

'I haven't a clue, but knowing Lauralynn it can't help being *interesting*.'

He gave me a dubious look. For reasons unknown, Lauralynn was not his favourite person.

The House of Bamboo Dolls was an anonymous red-brick building just a block away from Chinatown, on a steep hill not served by any cable cars.

There was just a number on the stark wooden door: 19. No name or sign to indicate what lay inside.

I rang the bell.

There was a shadow of movement as the light shifted on the other side of the peephole.

'Yes?' a hushed voice behind the door queried our presence.

270

'Is this the House of Bamboo Dolls?' I asked, self-consciously turning to look at the street behind me in case anyone was listening. It all felt ridiculously melodramatic.

I couldn't determine whether the confidential tones of the voice belonged to a man or a woman. 'Invitation only,' it replied.

Neil gave me a nudge, suggesting we move on and give up.

'Lauralynn Wilmington recommended we come,' I said. 'We are friends of hers.'

There was a moment's silence, and then the door finally opened and we were allowed in. It was a woman, tall and long, wearing a man's black tuxedo, dress shirt and a raffish Homburg hat, standing in a long, badly lit corridor.

'It's OK,' she said, and with a wave of her impossibly long arm she gestured for us to walk down the corridor to a set of stairs where the lighting was more helpful.

There was another door at the top of the stairs. I could hear music on the other side. I pushed it open, and we walked in.

It was a medium-sized room and it looked just like a private club, with a long bar at one end, and an assortment of bottles and all types of glasses aligned on shelves on the wall behind.

The barmaid wore a French beret, an impeccably white T-shirt, and she even looked a little like me, pale-skinned, short, looking younger than she probably was. Because of the bar counter and my distance from it, I couldn't see whether she was wearing a skirt, trousers or anything for that matter. She did not have a teardrop tattoo, but her resemblance to me was uncanny. So much so that as she turned her head towards another customer, I didn't immediately notice the colourful spiral that ran from her right ear all the way down to her shoulders before snaking into the white material of her T-shirt. I could only imagine how far this reptilian tattoo went, and I guessed from her manner that she was the type of person who would have one all the way down her flank to her feet. I was almost jealous. Talk about a manifesto of rebelliousness.

Tearing my eyes away, and oblivious to Neil tugging my hand, I surveyed the rest of the room. An assortment of low-slung tables and, along the walls, a set of red alcoves, occupied by silent drinkers, most of whom were now examining us.

It was only then I realised they were all women.

A voice greeted us.

'Welcome to the House of Bamboo Dolls.' It was an older woman in her forties, I guessed. She was dressed in a tight-fitting kimono, black with thin filigreed streaks of gold, through a slit of which a dark-stockinged, taut and shapely leg emerged. She wore Christian Louboutin high heels. I'd know those red soles from anywhere, not that I could ever afford any. 'Your first time, I gather?'

I nodded.

She gave Neil a dismissive glance.

'The young man is yours?' she asked me, indicating him, as he stood nervously, visibly feeling out of place.

I acquiesced, although I was curious as to why she had used the possessive as opposed to ascertaining that he was with me, which was obvious anyway.

'It's allowed,' she said.

'Allowed?'

'There are rules,' she added, a faint smile spreading fast across her lips. She looked Neil up and down as if he was cattle. He fidgeted uncomfortably in place.

I must have appeared quizzical, so she continued. 'Is your sub for general or personal use?'

It then dawned on me that Lauralynn was playing a mischievous joke on me, having heard that I would be travelling with Neil. I had confided in her about the ambiguous situation the two of us were navigating. This was all a game for her.

Neil shot me a despairing look, as he also began to size up the situation. His eyes pleaded with me.

'Personal,' I quickly said. 'Is that OK?'

If she was disappointed, the woman in the kimono didn't show it. 'Of course.' She paused. 'In that case, may I have your assurance the young man is properly marked?'

My eyes opened wide.

'The Network insists that personal property should be marked,' she reiterated.

'Marked?'

'I take it he isn't, then?'

'Hmm . . . no.'

'Otherwise, he may be used freely for our entertainment and pleasure. Did Lauralynn not advise you?'

'No, she didn't.'

'Very naughty of her, but then she was always was. It has always been an obligation for anyone who attends the House of Bamboo Dolls to bear a tattoo, as a sign of recognition.'

Neil and I looked around the room. Indeed, all the women here displayed one as our gaze travelled freely.

Facial ones, shoulders, arms, elbows, some fully visible, others just peering out from material and clothing.

Neil swallowed hard. Whispered in my ear that there was no way he could be tattooed across his face.

The woman overheard him.

'A sub's mark must be on the body, so only his or her owner is aware of his condition,' she indicated.

Neil looked at me, and then back at her.

'I'll do it,' he said firmly.

'What?' I replied. 'No, we'll leave. This isn't the right way to get something so permanent.'

He glanced pointedly at my teardrop tattoo and raised his eyebrow. Neil was right. On this count, I could hardly protest or offer advice.

'I'm yours, Lily. I want to always be yours. I want to be marked.'

'We have an excellent inker on the premises,' the woman said. 'Follow me.' She didn't seem in the least surprised by Neil's response.

We were led to a backroom.

'This is Nibbles,' the woman said, introducing us to a short, gamine, razor-cut-fringed young woman with a nose ring sitting there at the computer. She had pale-blue eyes and tattoos of flowers running all the way down the side of both her legs. She looked up at us, mildly curious.

'The boy,' the woman in the kimono declared.

Nibbles' expression didn't change, remote, businesslike. She rose from her chair and walked out of the room to fetch her equipment and was back within a minute, during which time neither of us had said an additional word.

'How rude I've been,' the older woman said to me,

breaking the ice. 'I didn't introduce myself. I'm Madame Violet.' She didn't even look at Neil, as if he was barely worth addressing.

'I'm Lily.' I didn't introduce Neil, as I knew she did not expect me to. Some of the rules of the House of Bamboo Dolls were becoming clear to me.

Nibbles returned from the side room, carrying a medium-sized metal-framed flat Samsonite case. Her equipment.

She followed the direction of Madame Violet's gaze and turned to Neil, sizing him up. There was a deep streak of cruelty shining through her translucent eyes.

'So?' she asked, speaking directly to me.

Madame Violet helped me out. 'Where do you want him marked, and how?' It was to be my decision.

I deliberated hard and fast, ignoring Neil's panicked expression.

'His butt,' I said.

Madame Violet, Nibbles and Neil were all hanging on my next words.

'My initial. L for Lily.'

I noted a faint tremor of disappointment running across Nibbles' scarlet-drawn lips, as if she had been hoping for both something more profoundly humiliating and a more degrading location. But it passed quickly and she puffed her cheeks up and opened the large flat leather case and laid out her instruments on a low-slung table. Some I recognised; others appeared as if they had sprung from a medical horror movie or the brain of David Cronenberg. Neil swallowed hard and held his breath.

Madame Violet and Nibbles looked expectantly at Neil.

He was rooted to the spot, his face paler than I had ever seen it.

'It won't be bad,' I said quietly to him. 'And it won't hurt that much. I've been through this too, you know, and on my face.'

'Come on, boy,' Nibbles said sharply.

Neil failed to understand.

'Get your boy to undress, Lily.'

It dawned on Neil that the point of no return was irreversibly long gone. He slipped out of his beige tailored cotton jacket and draped it across the back of a chair. He was about to unbutton the front of his silk blue shirt when Madame Violet peremptorily shouted out, 'No! Just your trousers. We have no wish to see your puny chest.'

I stifled a murmur of protest; Neil was no buffed body-builder, but neither was he an eight-stone weakling.

Now increasingly self-conscious under the voyeuristic gaze of three women, Neil's hands tentatively moved down to his leather belt, which he unfastened. Then he pulled his zip down and stepped out of his trousers. Down to his jockey shorts, he had no hesitation – as if he had now grown resigned to his fate – and swiftly took them off.

Yet again I couldn't help admiring the tense harmony of his butt cheeks as he was bending over. He straightened and his long, thin cock came into view. He was semi-hard, involuntarily aroused by the turn of events. But he still had his black socks and shoes on and I couldn't bear to see him look ridiculous. 'Take those shoes and socks off, Neil. They make you look like silly.' This time it was me giving the orders. He meekly obeyed and ended up standing there bottomless in our presence and totally helpless.

Madame Violet circled him, and briefly took a hold of his dangling cock, as if weighing it before she let it drop.

'His ass? You're really certain, Lily? Last time we marked a sub, we were much more imaginative . . .' Her grin was truly wicked and a parade of obscene visions flashed in front of my eyes. But I fought the impulse.

'His arse. An L,' I confirmed.

'So be it,' Madame Violet concluded. She gripped Neil by the hair and led him a few steps to a tall stool, and forced him to bend over it so that his butt was fully displayed, almost as if he was being disposed for a spanking or a flogging. Neil offered no resistance.

Instruments in hand, Nibbles approached and dabbed some disinfectant across his arse cheeks, lingering maliciously as she did so. She took a step back and kicked his legs further apart to compound the humiliation. Standing behind him, with an obscene view of Neil's arsehole, I could only imagine the look of horror taking hold of his features.

'I think Gothic lettering sounds right,' Madame Violet proclaimed. Nibbles nodded her agreement and bent over Neil's backside, her instrument purring monotonously and began tracing the letter across his skin. When I saw how large it was, I had an impulse to stop her, but I held back in silence, remembering the indelible impression the number 1, just a few inches from her smooth pubis, had made on me when I had seen Thomas leading his slave at the ball, and also recalled in a flood of warmth the way I had seen marks and words denoted in all their various forms on both men and women by way of collars, paddles with letters set into flesh that marked the word 'Slut' in fierce bruises, Liana's genital piercings, even once a barcode.

Now, Neil would be forever associated with me, whether I liked it or not. I hadn't planned it. But the thought excited me more than I would have imagined before our visit to the House of Bamboo Dolls.

'You could have just said 'no' and I'd have willingly left the place,' I said to Neil. 'Not gone through with it.'

We were in London in his new flat near Maida Vale. From the bay window on a clear day we could see the low walls of Lord's cricket ground and below a faint, distant strip of green from the pitch. We'd been back two days already and were still fighting jet lag. The initial ardour of our frenzied week in Darwin had cooled and a sense of unease had fallen over us both since our return to England and the events in San Francisco.

Neil was sitting on a kitchen stool and appeared uncomfortable as he shifted from side to side, seeking some form of balance.

'Does it still hurt?' I asked him.

'Not really. But I feel like scratching it all the time and have to hold back.'

I hadn't seen the mark on his arse cheek, my mark, since the House of the Bamboo Dolls after he'd quickly scrambled back into his pants and we had fled the establishment after a few coffees and some desultory form of conversation with Madame Violet and some of the other dommes present who were curious about our story and backgrounds. Freshly inked and dark black, it dominated the pale surface of his arse like a scarlet letter, a heavy gothic font. I wondered how often, when I was not present, Neil would take a peek at it in his bathroom mirror and what it made him think of. And in what manner he now associated it with me.

'We could have left the place, not gone through with it,' I remarked again.

'No, Lily, it was my choice,' he declared. 'My way of accepting the dynamic of our relationship.'

In the heat of the tropical sun on the other side of the world, his exuberance had seemed so natural and I had enjoyed being waited on hand and foot, worshipped. But my behaviour at the House of Dolls had shocked me, and now that we were back to normal day-to-day life, I feared what we might become.

I felt bad about it all. As if I had deliberately lead him on and not given him anything in return, treated him like a pet, played with him and taken his emotions for granted. Whatever I felt about it now, he would wear my mark forever.

Tomorrow his holiday break would be over and he had to return to work. Should I keep on crashing in his flat or should I somehow begin to look for somewhere of my own to live? And a job? I couldn't sponge off him eternally, even if he got off on the way I treated him and never complained.

'Why me, Neil?' I asked him, just as we were about to slot a DVD into the player. We had spent ages arguing about the choice of movie to watch and reached a halfway compromise which neither of us was enthusiastic about. 'With your job, your looks, you could have any girl, surely?'

I observed him choosing his words ever so carefully before gazing up at me, looking me straight in the eyes.

'I've always wanted you, Lily. From the first day we met. It's not a question of looks. Though, for the record, I've always thought you beautiful. When you know, you just know. You attract me, you annoy me, you sometimes make me angry and at other times I feel like shouting at you, but it makes no difference. I've never felt this way about a woman before.

'Initially, I wanted to be with you, to fuck you, sweet or rough, in all ways possible and obscene. I was even ashamed of all those terrible fantasies you evoked in me, the things I wanted to do with you, that sometimes made me feel ashamed of my own thoughts. Don't laugh, but for months on end I would fantasise of dominating you, taming you, using you like a whore, exposing you in public with a rage I didn't know I was even capable of, ordering you to do the most degrading, disgusting things, offering you to other men and watching. See how sick I was . . .'

I opened my mouth but he resolutely continued.

'So imagine my surprise, my terror, when I found out that I was the submissive one when I was with you, that I had to silence all those thoughts and the only way to be with you was for me to be your pet. At first, I was taken aback by this streak you have inside you, but then I realised that pleasure works in such different ways, and reconciled myself to the fact that accepting your nature was the way to keep you, to be with you.

'And now I find I am addicted. I need you. More than ever. And I'm scared that you don't truly understand this and that, eventually, you will tire of me, drop me for another pet, abandon me, empty and unfulfilled. It's not just the physicality of it, it's the emotional involvement. When you use me, you take me to places I never knew existed, and I, melodramatically, think I'd die if I were to be denied access to that space again.'

'I think I understand, Neil, but I'm not the only domme around, you know. Others are so much more experienced, I'm still learning.'

'I realise that, but I don't have that personal connection with them that I have with you.'

'I just don't want you to depend on me, Neil,' I protested. 'I don't know if I'm capable of being all the things that you want. That you need.' His shoulders stooped as if I had delivered a mortal blow.

'I agreed to be marked for you, Lily.' He was pleading now, and all it did was stoke my anger. I hadn't asked for this level of dependency. I didn't want to own him. He was a friend. A close friend. A lover. I didn't want him to be just a toy. It was a responsibility too far.

I knew what I didn't want.

But did I know what I wanted?

II

Eighty Days

The woman wore only black boots that reached above her knees and a thin gold chain around her waist. She was not in the prime of youth any longer, probably in her forties, but with gym assistance and a suspicious all-over tan, she could easily have been mistaken for someone ten years younger. Only the lines in her neck betrayed her.

Both men were bald or, at any rate, shaven-headed and similarly tanned, as if they'd just stepped off the plane from a nude beach in the Caribbean. They were stocky and, from a distance, could even have been taken for twins. The woman had been laid out on a thick grey rubber mat and lay slightly on her side so that one man thrust into her from the rear while she raised her head an inch or two to accommodate the other hairless man's cock in her mouth, sucking it greedily, her moans orchestrated by the bobbing movement of her head as he held her hair and pulled her towards his hard shaft with machine-like regularity. The men were relentless, pounding her metronomically, like synchronised athletes in training, never missing a beat or a thrust inside her.

I stood there with my mouth gaping.

It was animalistic, but it was also beautiful, a ballet of flesh in motion, a hedonistic dance of the senses.

I'd arrived at the club around mid-evening hoping to find She and to convince her to let me have my original coat-checking and general dogsbody job back. My anger at the way the photo shoot had panned out had long since faded and I wanted to extend the olive branch. I hadn't recognised the bouncer at the door, but he was relaxed about letting me in after I'd advised him that I used to work there.

In my absence, the main room had been totally reconfigured and the atmosphere had radically changed. The stone-clad walls that used to house all the paraphernalia of BDSM – rows of instruments and toys, hooks, chains and pulleys and a dazzling assortment of hardware whose use had not always been clear or demonstrated to me – were now concealed by heavy velvet curtains, which made me think of a suburban Indian restaurant. The lighting, once muted and elegant, creating areas of light and darkness in clever harmony allowing for both discretion and exhibitionism depending on the evening's mood, was now harsh and unforgiving, isolating the protagonists in an explosion of white light, while the rest of the room was not just in dark shadow but murky and uninviting, a haven for voyeurs and hangers-on. The club had lost all its joy.

But, nonetheless, the spectacle of the copulating trio was gripping, if only because of the expression on the woman's face as she was being fucked. It was beatific, not far off the look I had often witnessed on subs' features when they reached that special space. This was the happiest woman in the whole wide world and she was totally oblivious of anything happening around her, the spectators, the other couples sitting in alcoves in varied states of undress, a few lone women on the dance floor staggering on awkward heels to the beat of some terrible electro-rock, drunk like refugees from the storm.

The club had changed beyond recognition and had now become a sex joint. I tore my eyes away from the rutting trio as the sounds from the woman's throat took on a despairing note as she rode the waves of her orgasm and the untiring duo carried on her orchestrated destruction.

There were a dozen or so people in the room, and I noted their attire was different, vulgar, shoddy, devoid of all the ritualistic gleam of BDSM nights, like bikers crashing a wedding, loud and cheap.

I looked towards the bar and again didn't recognise any of the staff.

My attention was drawn to the stairs that led down to the dungeon. A curtain was spread across the vaulted entrance, and access to the club's lower levels was blocked.

I stepped back into the hallway just as the two men swapped places inside the woman and, out of the corner of my eye, I noticed the one who had been face-fucking her slipping on a condom. The new bouncer was standing there.

'The club's different,' I queried. 'New people, new . . . activities.'

He gave me an odd look. Then smiled. He was almost two heads taller than me, built like a distaff wrestler, his biceps straining the material of his black T-shirt.

'Oh yes, love, there are new owners. It's now a swingers' joint, no more of that leather and kink stuff any more . . . You didn't know? They begin work in a couple of weeks downstairs to change the space into a sauna, so we'll be properly up and running.'

Noting my disappointment as I stepped out past him

onto the street, he called out to me, laughing, 'Sorry to disappoint you, girlie, but come back any time and I'll let you have a good spanking in private. Won't even charge.'

I gave him the V-sign.

What had happened to all the regulars? To She and Richard? Had they found a new place, or were they now orphans in the storm, cut off from their pleasure fix?

I assumed She was still with Grayson and I could find either of them in Shadwell. Or should I take this as an omen, a sign that part of my old life had now come to an end? I knew one thing, though: with or without Neil, I was not about to begin attending swinger parties.

As I made my way back to Neil's place to consider my options, I couldn't help recalling that transcendent look on the woman's face as the two men fucked her, as if she was visiting a place I'd never managed to approach. Even with Leonard, when the lovemaking had been alternately tender and rough and my insides melted alongside the rational part of my brain, I knew I could never quite let go in such a manner. Likewise when I was domming men. It was a different kind of pleasure altogether.

I wryly recalled Leonard once saying one evening in Barcelona, 'The problem with folk like us, Lily, is that we think too much. Sometimes we can't avoid holding back. Simpler people are so much less complicated when it comes to their pleasure. They assume it unconditionally.'

My sweet and sad philosopher and soft-hearted philanderer.

Where was he now? Out of my life was my only certainty.

*

The club I had known and where, in a way, I had perfected the latter part of my sexual education was gone. Replaced by a cheap, vulgar joint where people unemotionally swapped partners or just prostituted themselves on the altar of no-strings sex. It made me feel unclean, but also conflicted. Who was I to judge the people who now went there and seemed satisfied with their lot? Surely, had they known, they would see me as the freak, the girl with the teardrop tattoo who got off on dominating men, cruelly playing with them, all in the service of my anger and frustration and an illusory sense of superiority over the common masses. They couldn't understand me, or the ecstatic deliverance I offered the subs who kneeled down to me, figuratively speaking. We were on opposite sides of the mirror and it dawned on me that no one knew what the right side of the mirror happened to be. We were all right and we were all wrong. And I was caught in the middle, Lily in wonderland, Snow White wielding a whip.

Neil arrived back from his office around seven. He'd left a message earlier asking me not to cook as he wanted to go out and eat Chinese tonight.

'The fetish club has been turned into a sex joint,' I mentioned to Neil. 'It looked so . . . sordid. Did you know about it?'

'It happened just a few weeks after you left for Australia,' he replied.

'Why didn't you tell me?'

'I thought you would have known.'

'I didn't. How did you find out?' Apart from his visits there with me, I didn't think that Neil had visited the place on his own.

'From She,' he said.

'You're still in touch with her?'

Neil looked up at me, blushed.

'What is it?'

'Yes.'

'Yes what?'

'I did see her again a few times. Following your departure.'

His tone was hesitant.

'Tell me about it.'

'The property company they had been leasing the premises from wanted to redevelop the block, so notice was served. At one stage She was hoping to convince Grayson to pitch in and make an offer for the club instead, but something went wrong, and after planning permission was declined by the council, it passed into the hands of some sauna and swing club group. I haven't been since.' He averted his eyes.

'But you went on your own before it closed down?'

Again there was something shifty about his attitude.

'Er . . . Yes.'

'Just you?' I was curious. It just didn't sound like the Neil I knew.

'I went with She, Ms Haggard.'

'Oh?'

'She contacted me, wanted to find out where you'd disappeared to. At the time I didn't have a clue where you'd gone as you hadn't yet been in touch. I just informed her. She didn't appear particularly concerned. Became all friendly. Well, you know her. She was fishing, of course, but I had nothing to hide. Then the subject moved on to the things you got up to with me. I was aware she'd been your mentor, had trained you. She dropped heavy hints she could provide me with . . . more. Show me—'

'Neil!'

'You weren't here, Lily. And you'd given me a taste for it. I was craving those feelings, those emotions, the play had awakened in me.'

'You went with She?' I'd seen her at work on unsuspecting if consensual victims. I was a child in comparison, still a junior domme in training. She was cruel and rough, unbending.

For a brief moment, I felt a terrible arrow of jealousy run through me like a flash of lightning across a night sky at the idea that She, of all people, had 'owned' Neil. Surely, she knew he was mine.

My eyes betrayed me. I felt an irrational tear break the dam of my indifference. Neil looked at me, pleading silently for my forgiveness. But was he the one who needed to be forgiven? Or was it me?

I had to know.

'Tell me,' I asked.

'Do you really want to know?'

I braced myself.

'I do.'

He sighed deeply.

'I went to the club a number of times. And also to her home. It wasn't like what we have . . . but I won't lie to you, being with her was electric. Like walking on the tightrope of a nightmare and all the time I felt simultaneously held and as though I would surely fall. It was like dangling in mid-air hundreds of metres from the ground and not being able to see or feel the rope.'

I nodded encouragement for him to continue. He reminded me of Liana. That same desire to go right to the edge. But the philosophy of it I already knew and understood. I wanted to know what she had actually done to him. Already I could feel the hair on the back of my neck standing up like an animal ready to defend its young.

'She flogged me so hard that I couldn't sit down for a fortnight. And used misery sticks . . . on my cock.'

I winced. Misery sticks looked tiny and harmless compared with a riding crop or whip but, depending on how they were wielded, the pain could be immense and, unlike other types of impact that eased very quickly after the initial strike, the throb from the misery stick endured. I couldn't imagine the pain that might be caused from wielding it on a sub's penis. And I had seen She use them on her slaves before. She wasn't gentle.

'And more. Humiliation. I cleaned her boots with my tongue. Was only ever allowed to approach her on my knees. I wore sissy outfits. A frilly pink and white skirt and high heels. And a pink studded collar and leash.'

'How did it make you feel?' I asked, more curious now than anything.

'The outfits weren't really my thing. I've never had any desire to wear women's clothing. But I suppose that's what made it humiliating. It would have just been a bit of fun otherwise. All the other things . . . they made me feel whole. As if I was finally admitting that I wasn't worth anything more than a piece of shit on the bottom of her shoe. And coming to terms with it made me complete. Peaceful.'

I began to protest.

'No, don't. It's hard enough to talk about as it is. Please just let me continue.'

The words stuck in my throat like a craw.

'And I let her fuck me. With a strap-on. I imagined she was you. You use your finger, but I've always yearned for more.'

I nodded, mutely.

As Neil related his story, the expressions on his face travelled through a whole landscape of emotions. From apologetic to lustful, from craving to shame, and back again through a tortuous, complicated road littered by his senses in disarray.

When he reached the end, and described how She had impaled him and ridden him with a cohort of her other playthings dutifully in attendance, watching with intent, either yearning for similar treatment or fearful their most private openings would soon be breached in turn by the hard instrument of her wrath, his face displayed a feverish blend of pain and ecstasy.

'Did it hurt?' I asked. I had used many things on him but never had penetrated him in this way, just the random finger to stimulate his prostate in an attempt to edge him, that would have felt like a blessing or a caress in comparison with She's ferocious ivory length. I had witnessed grown men crying as she had savagely penetrated them with it.

My stomach churned. I knew from my own experience that when my partner took the right care, anal sex was wonderful, but before that, when I had lacked any knowledge about the process and had been with someone as inexperienced as I was, then there had been an agonising initial burst of pain along with the rise of pleasure as they had entered me from the rear, but I knew that none of their cocks had been the size or the rigid hardness of She's Japanese ceremonial strap-on. And I doubted that She would have been careful.

'Yes,' Neil said. 'A lot.'

I blinked in sympathy.

'The thing is, she pushed me hard, but none of it was anything I didn't want. Parts of it were a release and nothing more. A way to accept myself. But other things she did turned me on so much. The pain. The misery stick on my cock makes me come, Lily. Just from that.'

'Why did you stop?'

His eyes shied away from mine and he whispered, 'I wanted it to be you, Lily. I submitted to her because I wanted to be punished for sending you away, it was my stupid way to seek forgiveness, but in the end I had to admit that all I wanted was you. So I followed you to Australia . . .'

'You're a fool, Neil,' was all I could find in myself to say, but even as I did so I regretted my words.

I was reaping what I had sown.

My heart leaped, spinning out of orbit.

'Come here,' I said.

He stepped towards me, timid, expectant, vulnerable. And for a moment, I wanted to be him. To know what it felt like to love someone so unconditionally. For better or worse.

I took him into my arms and we kissed.

The softness of his lips came as a shock and it dawned on me that we had never truly kissed before, with innocence and feeling. Even when we first reunited in Darwin, it had been a step along a complicated road of pain and anger and longing. But now it felt so simple, as our tongues tentatively teased each other, our breaths melded and my hands began roaming inside his shirt, tiptoeing along the hard muscles of his firm abs.

I undressed him.

Licked, teased and playfully bit and pulled on his nipples. My eyes travelled lazily across the almost smooth avenue of his chest as I mentally bade a final farewell to Leonard and his forest of dark curls and banished him for ever from my mind.

Neil sighed. As if he knew already the next steps of our dance, the way I might take clumps of his hair and mercilessly pull on them until it brought tears to his eyes, the manic grip of my hands across his vulnerable balls and the razor shave of my teeth against the ridge of his cock, anticipating the flat of my hands raining against the soft flesh of his arsecheeks, predicting the neutral mind space he would allow himself to drop into as I added to my arsenal, flogger, paddle, leather, cat-o'-nine-tails or whatever I might have secreted away from She's defunct dungeon. His whole soul trembled on the threshold of the unknown, yearning for the pain, the submission, accepting my will, my desires. Trembling because he had no way of knowing what would happen next and that very ignorance was part of the process, rendering him helpless so that when the next blow or the next command would come it would actually be a relief, a blessing I was granting him.

We disentangled.

I rose. Stepped out of my clothes.

Silently, Neil kneeled at my feet, looking up at my eyes like a supplicant at a church altar.

'No,' I said and extended my hand towards him. 'Today you're fucking me. And you will be on top.'

I opened my arms.

Through the darkened window pane the light of a lamp on the street outside the block of flats shone against his face and his eyes had the brightness of fireflies glinting in the night sky.

He got to his feet.

I lowered myself and took the comforting heat of his cock into my mouth until it reached the back of my throat. Neil was holding his breath.

Tonight all I wanted was to be fucked. And I harboured the faint hope that when I came, my face would be half as beautiful as the older woman's being ploughed by the two men in the pitiful surroundings of the sex club. It wasn't much to ask, was it? And if Neil felt it wasn't enough, I could still spank him or rake my nails across his back later, couldn't I?

I'd decided that the girl with the teardrop tattoo, the mixed-up Snow White of the uncertain, bifurcated path, would see life, live life, from both sides now.

I wanted it all.

Epilogue

The gloom of London's winter was finally making room for the premature seeds of spring, although mornings were cold, and frost on car windscreens lasted in the shadows until at least nine against a sky of uniform blue.

Lily had returned to work at the music store in Denmark Street and was welcomed back with open arms by her erstwhile co-workers, as if she had never left. She knew it was a dead-end job and was determined not to spend her lifetime there and had enrolled in an external journalism course, which she studied at home. She had already triumphantly succeeded in her first two modules.

She was unsure whether she actually wanted to become a journalist, but was intrigued by the possibility of freelance work in publishing. The famous violinist Summer Zahova had, one recent afternoon, come to the shop seeking accessories for her instruments and they had engaged in conversation. Lily had approached her and quizzed her about the novel by Dominik that Lily had come across during her travels and that she seemed to have inspired, seeking confirmation about the actual author. Summer, with a wry smile, had indeed admitted it was by her boyfriend. The revelation was a liberation for Lily, as if the many pieces of a puzzle were finally coming together.

To reward herself for the high marks she had managed on her course, Lily had made a detour through Covent Garden on the way home to Neil's flat and treated herself to a present in a classy store off Seven Dials. A present to herself, but also to Neil.

'Unwrap it,' she had demanded, mischievously clearing the table top in the kitchen and replacing the plates with a medium-sized box, wrapped in gold foil.

'For me?'

'No,' she said, 'it's for both of us.'

He leaned forward to pick up the box, weighing it, noting how light it was and then cautiously pulled the wrapping material away, careful not to tear it. Lily couldn't help giggling. If it had been her opening the present, she would have been hasty and merciless, tearing the paper into a thousand shreds.

A frown crossed his face when the first glimpse of a sleek black leather handle came into view. He gripped the base of the rod firmly and eased it out of the tissue paper. Soft lengths of suede slithered from the box, snake-like, and made a faint 'thwack' sound as Neil theatrically swung the length of the flogger off the table.

'Both of us, eh?' he said. 'You mean it's a present for you to torture me with?' He grinned from ear to ear.

'Even if that were true,' Lily replied, 'don't act like you won't love it.'

'I can't argue with you there.'

'Go on then, have a closer look.'

Lily fidgeted in her chair impatiently. Christmas with Neil would be a nightmare, she thought, if this were how slowly he approached every gift.

His hands fiddled with the tissue for what felt like an eternity until, finally, he pulled another flogger from the box.

'Two?' he asked quizzically. 'Are you going to swing them both together like poi?'

She groaned and grabbed the two floggers by the whipping ends and turned the two handles to face him.

His face lit up like Christmas morning.

The words 'His' and 'Hers' were engraved in gold gothic font on each handle. The same font as the letter L that was engraved on his arse.

'You'll let me use one on you?' he asked.

'Yes,' she replied. 'If it feels right, and you want to.'

Lauralynn, with whom Lily had remained on friendly terms and had become something of an accomplice in crime, invited her for afternoon tea at the Ritz on Lily's day off, warning her to dress conservatively for the occasion. Lily had, provocatively, worn a short Burberry schoolgirl skirt that only reached halfway down to her knees, which even had Neil blushing whenever she wore it for play. With it she had a tight, white starched shirt and a tie she had borrowed from Neil's drawer, which she thought was actually his prep school one.

Lauralynn was wearing a man's business suit, all straight lines and rigour. She felt they looked like Laurel and Hardy when the hotel doorman bowed and doffed his hat as they passed through the revolving door and emerged into the Ritz's teeming lobby. Heads turned, but no one ran up to them to suggest they leave. The hotel had a dress code, but they had managed to cleverly circumvent it.

Lauralynn loved to gossip and was never short of startling

news about the crowds she was involved in. Much of it was deliciously scurrilous and funny, indiscreet and witty. Lily enjoyed being with her as they exchanged confidences. Lauralynn was a trifle disappointed at the way Lily's relationship with Neil had evolved into a game of two halves, where of common accord both took it in turns to dominate the other, switching with their mood and their inclinations.

She even revealed that once there had been a man in her life with whom she could have reached a similar compromise, but his connection to another woman of their acquaintance had prevented all his inner submissive elements from coming to the surface.

'Who?' Lily interrogated her thoroughly, but Lauralynn would not say.

'Do I know him?' Lily was intrigued, another shadow moving behind the curtain of her life.

'You do,' Lauralynn confirmed. 'But I'll never tell.'

'You spoilsport,' Lily protested.

Lauralynn took the last cake to her mouth while balancing the perfectly shaped porcelain teacup in her other hand, the very image of a lady. She put the cup down, looking intently at Lily, as if the news she was about to impart might not be appropriate.

'What?' Lily finally said.

'She is reopening the club,' Lauralynn said.

'Really?'

'In the same premises. The developers decided to get rid of the property as no planning permission was likely to be granted and the esteemed Ms Haggard convinced her pet photographer, the great Grayson, to finance a buy-out of the building.'

'Wow.'

So many memories came rushing back, as Lily considered the news.

'You still haven't made contact with her again,' Lauralynn asked.

'No.'

'Nor Grayson?'

'Him neither.'

'They speak of you kindly, you know,' Lauralynn declared.

Lily hesitated. 'I'm not sure if I fit into their world any longer,' she confessed.

'Rubbish, Lily, it's in your blood. I can already see that twinkle in your eye. It's part of you now.'

As the words sank in, Lily knew that Lauralynn was right. She sighed, vowing that this time, though, it would be different. For her and for Neil.

'They're opening on Valentine's Day,' Lauralynn said. 'I'll get you both an invitation.'

She had something altogether different planned for the club. It had come to her while she had been viewing the premises along with the official from the council's planning department. Stupid man, she thought to herself as he coughed nervously. She imagined that she had him on all fours on a leash crawling uncomfortably along the stone floor and that each time he spoke he would feel the relentless pull of her leash on his collar. The fantasy improved her mood considerably. Perhaps she would make him wear one that was studded on the inside. She watched his Adam's apple bobble as he spoke and imagined the press of sharp studs against his soft turkey neck.

His words brought her back to the present. 'I really don't think it will be possible to—'

'Don't be ridiculous,' she replied. 'Everything is possible.'

Before the old swingers who had temporarily taken over the club had given up the ghost on their project, they had begun rebuilding the series of old underground tunnels that swarmed out like so many threads of a spider's web around the original dungeon area. A long time ago, before the advent of health and safety regulations, the tunnels and the small caverns that lay at the end of each one had been used as a cool place to store goods that were being sold at the nearby Smithfield Market. The swingers had planned to create a downstairs grotto of baths and pools that they hoped would add a false modesty to the place, as punters could pretend that they were attending a health spa rather than going to some seedy sex joint to get their rocks off.

She had a poor opinion of both swingers and health spas, and an even poorer opinion of the two combined. But when she discovered the tunnels, in a very rare moment of totally unabashed joy, she had dropped her fearsome Ms Haggard persona, gripped Grayson's arm and squealed like a child in a candy store.

'Look!' she had cried, clapping her hands together. He'd smiled back and each time a bill arrived for the latest renovations he remembered the expression on the face of his beloved mistress and mentally confirmed that it was worth every penny to see the happiness spread over her features.

The various official permissions that had stymied the

swingers' plans were no problem for She. One of her slaves worked in a senior position in the local authority and it had been a matter of pulling some strings, or rather chains, she reminded herself with no small sense of satisfaction.

When She was finally satisfied with each last detail of the renovations, she set to work planning the opening night and organising the invitations. Her list of chosen ones was exclusive, and entrance for those who were not included would be granted under no circumstances whatsoever, but she did not make her selection based on looks, wealth or age. Patrons were appointed according to a strict criterion that boiled down to She's own value system.

'Only those who truly understand what we're about,' She informed Grayson. 'The real players. No tourists, no matter how long their latex-clad legs or how deep their pockets might be.'

The invitations came on thick white card embossed with lightly gold-flecked deep-red lettering that glinted in the light and simply stated the date, 14 February, and the address.

'Are we going to another wedding?' Summer Zahova, the flame-haired violinist asked Dominik when she spotted the notice pinned to the fridge alongside the menu to their local Chinese takeaway that made the best roast duck she had ever tasted.

'No,' he replied. 'That club by Smithfield, reopening, I think. Not a wedding.'

'Thank fuck for that,' she said, breathing a sigh of relief. 'I don't think I could bear to sit through another one. Shall we go, then? It's been a while.'

'So it has,' he said, resting his hands on her hips and pulling her back against him. 'I'm surprised She hasn't asked you to come and play for the event.'

'Now that you mention it,' she replied, 'my agent has been calling. Something about an opening night that I'm not allowed to be seen dead at under any circumstances, let alone performing.'

Dominik laughed. 'And you've been practising ever since, I bet?'

Across the wide open space of Hampstead Heath, Viggo Franck was wordlessly protesting about his latest task under the watchful eye of Lauralynn. He'd just been finishing his weekly house-cleaning session when the doorbell rang. It was the postman waiting on the door's threshold with some letters and a parcel that wouldn't fit through the slot.

'I don't care if you're the Queen of England,' the post-man said when Viggo offered through the intercom to give him the alarm code so that he could open the door and deposit the mail on the floor just inside. 'It's not good enough, mate, I need your signature. More than my job's worth if I don't play by the book.' He was implacable.

'Go on, then,' Lauralynn said. 'Off you go.' An expression of merriment lit up her face and her eyes twinkled.

Viggo paused and looked down at himself. He was wearing a cheap and tacky PVC maid's costume. Not even a black and white one. Worse than that. This one was a pink and white short-skirted monstrosity with a baggy frill that didn't even swing as it ought to around his hips, but hung low on his bum, giving him a slovenly, lopsided appearance that he hated. In his right hand he gripped a matching feather duster with a nasty plastic handle.

'And don't act like the paparazzi are going to snap you. No one gives a damn. They already know you're a pervert.'

Yes, he wanted to say, but there are perverts and then there are *perverts*, and no one really knew what kind he was. That was half the fun of it.

But where Lauralynn was concerned, he was powerless to stop himself from following her orders so he blithely opened the house's front door with all the dignity that he could muster while tottering on a pair of hot-pink high-heeled shoes and returned a few moments later with a pile of mail and the box that, unbeknownst to him, contained a new toy that Lauralynn had purchased as soon as she had got wind that She had begun to distribute the invitations.

'Here's your parcel,' Viggo said to her without a hint of irritation. 'I think, from now on, we'll find the postman more agreeable. Either that or we'll never see him again.'

Luba's invitation had even further to travel, all the way to Darwin. She had just locked her bicycle to the rail outside the jewellery shop when she noticed the corner of the white envelope poking out from the crack under the door. Chey was already inside, but so wrapped up in studying the precious shipment of amber that he had finally managed to get his hands on that he hadn't noticed the post.

He rose to greet her when she entered and brushed away the stray locks of blonde hair that the helmet had displaced. Luba still wore her hair short. Each time he looked at her, he was overwhelmed by the memory of cutting her long blonde locks to disguise her feminine features after they had managed to escape from Dublin and the Russian mobsters who had tried to kill him. They had now made a new life for themselves in Australia.

Luba placed the assortment of takeaway fliers and bills down on the desk and turned the thick white paper over in her hands. 'There's no stamp,' she said, 'or address.' She tore it open swiftly, fearful that Chey's enemies had finally tracked them down, although she knew that Viggo Franck, who had helped them elude capture on that fateful night, along with Lauralynn, Summer and Dominik, had created a long stream of diversions to keep their pursuers from ever discovering their real location.

She relaxed when she saw the red lettering and read the short note that had been included, along with the date and address. 'Something to do with the Network people. They want me to dance again, and say that everything will be taken care of.'

'Is it safe?' Chey asked.

'I know them well. They're practically magicians. And it would mean that we could visit Europe and I could dance one last time.'

He bent forward and laid a gentle kiss on her forehead.

Neil had just worked up the courage to bring the 'His' branded flogger down onto Lily's bare back when the flat's buzzer rang.

'Dammit,' he said, 'stay there.'

'It's not like I'm going anywhere,' Lily replied drily.

Neil had received a substantial bonus for winning a big client and he'd used the proceeds to kit his entire apartment out like something from a Kink.com film set. Lily was standing spread-eagled in the living room against a St Andrew's cross, totally naked, with her hands and wrists cuffed in black leather restraints, waiting for Neil to return and continue his beating.

'Anyone important?' she asked when she heard his footsteps padding back to the room.

'Nothing as important as what I'm about to do to you,' he replied, tossing the white card on the counter top unopened.

The night was perfect, when it finally arrived. The air was still and icy. A light frost had settled over footpaths and windowpanes and Lily's breath hung in the air like a cloud when she exited the taxi.

Neil held the door open for her and helped her with the train on her oyster-coloured gown. He was wearing a sleek black tuxedo, crisp white shirt and bow tie, but only for the journey there and back. In his arms he held a large carry-all that contained, amongst other things, a pair of tiny rubber shorts with 'Property of Lady Lily' emblazoned on the back in silver letters.

Lily wrapped her white faux-fur coat around her tightly. The dress beneath, the same one that she had worn at the ball, was beautiful but did little to protect her from the elements. Her Doc Marten boots crunched on the ground as she stepped up to the club's door. She would change into the matching silk slippers when she got inside. Though if Neil was naughty, he might yet feel the soles of the boots trampling his back.

'What's under there, do you think?' she asked Neil,

pointing up at a black velvet curtain that had been erected outside to cover up the club's new name.

'I haven't a clue,' he replied, 'but I'm sure we'll find out soon enough.'

Inside, a line of greeters stood side by side, ready to take their coats and show them around.

'Would you prefer an Alice or a rabbit?' asked the head greeter, a short, voluptuous, dark-haired woman with a sumptuous and totally sheer frilled frock on that left nothing to the imagination. Her skin was painted all over with stars and moons in a blend of silver, blue and black like the night sky.

Lily looked down the line. 'A rabbit, please,' she replied.

The Alices, she noticed, were the swan-like ballet dancers from the ball. They were all wearing bright-blue dresses with lace pinafores over the top and matching white gloves and bobby socks. The rabbits all appeared to be women, but instead of the typical Playboy bunny style costume they were dressed in white latex tuxedos and black top hats with a red trim. Each of them wore red handkerchiefs folded into breast pockets, and large silver pocket watches. Bright-red lipsticked mouths sported tiny curled fake moustaches.

A rabbit bounced out from the queue and beckoned Lily and Neil to follow.

'This way,' she cried. 'I'll show you around.'

They raced to catch up with her as she disappeared down corridors that Lily had never seen before, even though she'd been into the building dozens of times. They hadn't even had time to remove their coats yet or to change. 'The coat room is on the way,' the rabbit yelled as if she'd read Lily's mind.

The first room was painted in a lustrous glowing white, like the landscape of the moon. Lily held out her hand. Something appeared to be falling from the ceiling. Snowflakes, or some kind of crystal rain. But it was neither, just a stage trick that made it appear as though everything was being bathed in light.

A long bar ran all the way around the room. The surface glittered with tiny crystals that were set into the countertop. The bevy of bartenders bustling behind were all wearing Mad Hatter costumes and serving cocktails in a mixture of tall thin glasses and old china teacups.

Lily grabbed a tall drink from a passing tray and pressed it to her lips. Pomegranate, she decided, as she swirled the mixture around in her mouth. And vodka.

'Your mouth is covered in glitter,' Neil pointed out as she brought the glass away from her lips. 'It's all around the rim.'

'It'll be all over everything and everyone by the end of the night!'

'I imagine that's the point,' he replied.

The next room was in total contrast to the first. The walls were pitch black and lit with burning candelabras. A heady musk incense perfumed the room.

'For your inner goth,' Neil marvelled, staring around at the heavy silver restraint systems that lined the walls.

At the front of the room, on a ceremonial dais, sat a middle-aged couple dressed in matching Victorian-style costumes, like a couple of vampires waiting for willing victims to wander in. They were each holding a purple saucer and drinking from matching teacups. The glitter had migrated onto their teeth so that when they smiled at the two young people who had just entered the room, their mouths glittered.

'She looks familiar,' said the woman to the man she sat alongside. 'Have we seen her somewhere before?'

'Hmm,' he reflected, casting back. 'Probably.'

'It's that teardrop tattoo, Ed. Just looks so familiar.'

But before Clarissa could isolate the memory, the young couple were gone again, dragged along by the hostess who was showing them around. Most likely they would bump into them again later, possibly in a much more intimate manner.

'Wow,' Neil said. 'I wonder if we'll be like that in twenty years?'

She really was going to have to gag him, thought Lily, who had barely said a word since they got inside. She just wanted to soak it all in. The wonder of it all. It was as if she'd woken up and found herself landed in the middle of the happiest of daydreams and discovered that she didn't need to leave.

A wall of humidity hit them when they entered the next corridor. They were in a glass house full of tropical plants and flowers. Birds tweeted and a soft breeze brushed against their shoulders.

Right in the centre of the room stood a beautiful blonde woman. She was completely naked with her arms held over her head and painted like the petals of a Lily. Neil's eyes immediately dropped downwards. He blushed internally. He tried not to be too obvious about his voyeuristic tendencies, but sometimes he just couldn't help himself.

'Is that a gun?' he whispered to Lily. The tiny picture was etched just next to her pussy. Neil had long since discovered that he was by no means the only one with a tattoo in a private place. The thought pleased him. He belonged somewhere at last.

'Yes.' Lily smiled. 'We must stay here and watch her dance. She's wonderful. The other rooms can wait.'

Luba unfurled her arms and began to sway. After a few soundless beats, the clear notes of a violin echoed through the room.

Vivaldi's *Four Seasons* again. Lily looked up, trying to locate the origin of the music. It didn't sound as though it were coming from speakers.

Summer Zahova was suspended in a glass platform near the ceiling. Lily could just make out a flash of her red hair, and the familiar curves of her body. And she would recognise that music anywhere. The platform was right in the middle of the room, and Summer wasn't wearing a costume. She was completely naked so that anyone who looked up would have a perfect vision of the musician's long, slim legs and if she shifted her stance so her feet were slightly apart, the viewer might be gifted with a brief flash that would confirm their suspicions that she was indeed a natural red head.

In the background, Richard the circus master was posturing in full regalia like the uncontested master of his domain.

Lily then noted the two men who sat at the back of the room, nearly hidden by the undergrowth. One of them was dark-haired and the other blonde, and they were dressed in tight latex trousers and mesh tops. They made an undeniably handsome pair, but both looked slightly sheepish. Ruled by their women, exactly as they should be, Lily thought smugly.

She looked again, and recognised that one of them was the man that she had hired the violin to in the Denmark street store, those few years ago.

Dominik.

'Heya, beautiful,' called a brash voice from behind them, carelessly interrupting the show.

It was Lauralynn, poured into her favourite catsuit and high-heeled boots, with Viggo trailing after her on his hands and knees, totally nude. At least she had done him the kindness of allowing him to wear pads on his hands and knees to protect his bony joints from the flooring. He moved closer into view and Lily nearly burst out laughing when she noticed the butt plug that he wore in his arse. It was a long, black, curling pig's tail.

'Don't you *dare* ever put one of those in me,' Neil hissed at her. 'It's a hard limit.'

Lily patted him on the knee reassuringly.

'Hey!' cried another voice from a fern behind them.

Liana and Leroy stepped out of the bushes.

'We got started early,' she said, wiping her mouth without a hint of embarrassment. Leroy's leather trousers hung loose at his thighs and as he tucked himself in, Lily noticed a flash of glitter decorating his bare cock.

'The whole gang is here for the show,' Lily said.

'I know,' Liana replied, 'isn't it great?'

At the stroke of midnight, all the guests were ushered out onto the pavement outside, champagne overflowing from their tall crystal glasses, some drunk, some merely merry, some dressed and others in manifold states of ceremonial undress, spilling into the narrow street, an effervescent cocktail of leather, silk, latex, the flimsiest of cottons and every material under the sun.

'This is it,' She cried out. She was wearing a skin-tight outfit of impossibly sheer latex that revealed more than it covered, and vertiginous diamond-encrusted heels. Pulling firmly on a pink length of bondage rope, she unveiled the club's new sign. For half a second it remained dark and everyone held their breath. Then the neon began flickering and exploded into letters of light.

EIGHTY DAYS

'The club is now baptised,' She proclaimed loudly to the cheering crowd.

As the guests began to walk back in single file into the club to continue the festivities, Lily was jostled and for a moment found herself side by side with an exultant She. The supreme dominatrix flashed her a toothy smile.

'Why Eighty Days?' Lily ventured to ask as they stood close together. 'What does it mean?'

She laughed out loud.

'Nothing, Lily. It's just something we came up with out of the blue. It really means nothing, but now we can all live happily ever after.'

Acknowledgements

Writing and publishing the Eighty Days series has been an exhilarating adventure from the moment the two authors who make up Vina Jackson met by total coincidence on a train heading west.

Many people must be thanked for their contribution, assistance, support and trust along the road. These of course include our redoubtable agent Sarah Such at the Sarah Such Literary Agency; our publishers at Orion, Jon Wood and Jemima Forrester; our foreign rights representative Rosie Buckman; and the various overseas publishers who took us on. They all paved our way onto the bestseller lists and our success would not have happened without any of them.

A large number of personal friends, partners, ex-partners, close and remote family have also been instrumental in the inspiration behind Eighty Days but cannot be named as the dominant publishing powers feel that, at this stage, both our identities should remain cloaked in mystery. But let it be known that their importance was paramount. You all know who you are!

One half of Vina Jackson also owes a major debt to their kind employer who made the journey easier, along with Gideon K of Black Hay for creative and musical encouragement; Kaurna Cronin, a busker who doesn't even know Vina walked by on one sunny Berlin morning while researching *Red* and stopped to listen to his amazing rendition of Springsteen's 'I'm on Fire'; Scarlett French for Florence and riding boots; Garth Knight for his inspirational 'Enchanted Forest' images; Matt Christie for photography; Sacred Pleasures for support and technical advice; Ella Vakkasova for verifying geography in Kreuzberg and recommending Café Matilda; and Verde & Co in Spitalfields for providing a cosy stool and the best flat whites in London.

The other half of Vina Jackson wishes to thank Kristina Lloyd for verifying our knowledge of the geography of Brighton, and Richard Kadrey, author of the splendid Sandman Slim series and also a great fetish photographer in his own right, for inadvertently providing us with the House of Bamboo Dolls, which behind his back we moved from Los Angeles to San Francisco and turned into a somewhat different place altogether in the process.

The Eighty Days series currently comprises five novels and one short story, and it's at this stage that we leave Summer, Dominik, Lauralynn, Luba, Chey, Lily, Liana, Leroy, She, Grayson, Viggo, Dagur, Neil and many others who have become close to our hearts. But Eighty Days will return soon with a whole new raft of characters, bigger and better than ever.

Watch those bookshelves!

Vina Jackson, December 2012

Want to know more about Vina Jackson and
Eighty Days?

Connect with Vina on Facebook/Vina Jackson, or
follow her on Twitter @VinaJackson1.

www.vinajackson.com

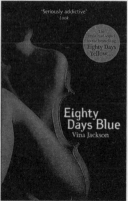